Zoe

THE WOODCUTTER OPERATION

By the same author:

THE XYY MAN
THE CONCRETE BOOT
THE MINIATURES FRAME
SPIDER UNDERGROUND
TRAP SPIDER

THE WOODCUTTER OPERATION

KENNETH ROYCE

HODDER AND STOUGHTON
LONDON SYDNEY AUCKLAND TORONTO

All the characters in this book are fictitious and bear no relation to any living person. Copyright © 1975 by Kenneth Royce. First printed 1975. ISBN 0 340 19385 9. All rights reserved. No part of this publication may be reproduced or transmitted in any form or by any means, electronic or mechanical, including photocopy, recording, or any information storage and retrieval system, without permission in writing from the publisher. Printed in Great Britain for Hodder and Stoughton Limited, St. Paul's House, Warwick Lane, London EC4P 4AH by Richard Clay (The Chaucer Press) Ltd, Bungay, Suffolk.

For Stella

I

THE FIVE MEN re-grouped at the corner of the square. No word passed between them and they were never to be seen so completely together again. They stared silently about, as if unsure of where they were. In fact, without exception, they knew the layout of the square intimately. It was really a rectangle; four quiet streets with a railinged green in the middle of the inevitable inner cog of parked cars.

It was mid-morning and October, the plane trees still largely green but fringed by dying leaves like a halo of rust. There were few people about. The movement of ambulances suggested the proximity of a hospital; actually there were several close by. Ancient squares are common enough in London and had never been short in the older part of Bloomsbury. The only noticeable break in the grey monotony of the buildings was the beige Italian hospital at one corner of the square; but at least there was no uniformity in shape and size. There was age and character and respect here in the general quietness.

It did not reach the five men. A second look might have revealed a grimness beneath their apparent indifference. One of them wore dungarees and carried a sling tool grip. The other four wore cheap suits and had hold-alls about the size one might use if collecting a discharged patient and his effects. They all wore toupés but the fair-haired one's was detectable under close scrutiny. His carefully questing blue eyes would discourage any derogatory comment; he was not the sort of person to poke fun at, nor to a lesser degree, were any of them. The fair one was chewing gum, his slow jaw-movement part control, part tension. He was a British army deserter. While they stood there, quietly surveying, further along the square young nurses entered and left buildings, their variety of neat caps implying different hospitals.

When the five men were satisfied, four of them turned to

the shortest, dark-haired, stocky and firm-faced. He gazed at them each in turn, probing for last-minute weaknesses, faults, but if there were any they were well hidden; there was no hint of reluctance and he was left with the impression that they were more concerned about him than he was with them; he was, after all, the only amateur. Yet without him there was nothing. They need not have worried; his sense of injustice was too deeply rooted, his resolve too strong. They detected it under their own scrutiny of him and when he gave one brief nod, stood aside for him to precede them. The tallest of the group joined him, matching his stride; there was not enough difference in their heights for them to appear odd. Both were solidly built men. They did not hurry; there was no sign of haste in the square. Above them clouds hovered like grey waste but there was no rain. The few leaves in the gutters curled and died silently.

John "Ginger" Shaw kept his gaze straight ahead, barely aware of Allbright by his side; he could hear him, sense his presence, but could not see him even on the periphery of his vision. No word passed between them. It was as if neither wanted to be reminded of the other's presence, yet they needed each other; their bond of desperation and individual expertise had welded them soundly and they trusted each other to do what had to be done. That was it, reflected Shaw; trust, not friendship; respect, not warmth. They appreciated what the other had to offer for the job in hand. That was all there was to it. It was unlikely, whatever the outcome of what they were about to do, that they could ever be friends. And yet as they walked side by side towards their destiny, Shaw, with sudden insight, realised that he had deliberately denied them that possibility when he had turned off all emotion. Emotion was a two-faced enemy, had caused him nothing but grief; he had promised himself he would never become emotionally involved again. With the gnawing hate in him he had found it surprisingly easy, refusing to recognise bitterness as emotion. Not far to go now. His pulse rate quickened.

The professional in Bob Allbright encouraged no introspection. Fifteen years in prison had eroded most expression from his toughened face. But not only prison had done that.

He was thinking coolly, logically. He liked Shaw, saw him as a tough little bugger, even if he was an amateur. Shaw had never talked about it and Allbright was too much a pro to probe. But it was the wrong reason for turning to crime. There could only be two reasons worthwhile; bread and enjoyment. Even so he had confidence in Shaw, the man had guts. About two of the other three, now thirty feet behind them, he had reservations. As an ex-army man he didn't like deserters and that cold-eyed bastard Beatty was one. But they needed him too and he had a lot to lose if he was caught. He had the qualifications. Allbright was a realist. He had worked before with others he hadn't cared for. In this game you chose men for their professional capability and for no other reason; if you got on with them it was a convenient bonus.

The round-shouldered McQueen, Allbright didn't rate at all. He may have been the zombie of the party but he was essential ballast; his lack of imagination and general intelligence at least reduced his fears; he was strong and he'd do what he was told and that was all they required of him. With his toupé and beard he looked like an ape. Barret, the last member of the team, he considered to be adequate. Allbright permitted himself an inward smile; it didn't reach his craggy face nor the brown eyes that had hardened over the years. In his mid-forties he accepted that the clock couldn't go back now. It was too late; at his age he couldn't start learning. He no longer dwelled on the laughing, adventurous kid he had once been. And anyway, where had that got him? They were nearly there. He stole a sideways, downward glance at Shaw, saw the rigid jawline and spoke for the first time.

"Relax, for Christ's sake, or you'll give the bloody game away."

Shaw hesitated in his stride and slowed his pace as Allbright had deliberately done. He knew he was tense, he had a lot to be tense about. He tried to relax, difficult for him, much as he needed to. "My mind was on the job," he explained, side-mouthed. "I just want to get on with it."

"Don't we all? But we don't have to advertise it."

Shaw nodded and even that small action he knew to be too severe. They reached an intersection not far from their destination. They stopped, looked at each other and noticed that the three behind them had started to idle. "We might as well," said Shaw. "Just in case."

The two men turned down the intersection until they came to another much narrower one running parallel to the street they had to return to; it terminated in an untidy dead end of tall buildings, its width depleted by the ragged line of parked cars. At the bottom end was a brick and concrete outhouse, a seemingly odd structure in such a position. Shaw and Allbright stared for a few seconds. Nothing had changed. No one was in sight in this short narrow street leading to nowhere. They returned to the square and continued on.

They stopped outside the Queen Mary Hospital, hesitated fractionally, then mounted the washed stone steps without glancing back at the others. They entered the bright hall, attracting no particular attention from the uniformed porters behind the reception desk. Two boards listed names of some thirty consultants, showing it to be a hospital of specialist importance. Shaw and Allbright crossed the wide hall to one of the corridors. There were people about; doctors, nurses, visitors. They passed the pharmacy, a hole in a wall where out-patients collected prescriptions, and a refreshment dispenser where three visitors sat down to a makeshift meal. When they reached the basement steps, Allbright was relieved; he hated hospitals. There was no smell of disinfectant and ether here but it was too reminiscent of prison.

The steps led to a rabbit warren of cellars whose paths they had rehearsed too often to lose themselves in now. The cellars, more than anything else, betrayed the age of the building. The smell of the kitchens reached them. The engineering offices were down here, too. But in the main the maze of corridors and cellars was empty. It would make no difference if the two of them were seen; it would be assumed that anyone down here belonged to the staff.

They passed the coffin lift and Allbright moistened his lips; a normally brave man, he would never conquer *that* fear. The door they wanted was curiously recessed into one of the cave-like cellars and reasonably hidden from view. Shaw stood guard while Allbright applied the hard experience of years to the lock. He had brought with him half a dozen likely skeleton keys and the fourth one had worked; it was better than forcing the door.

Inside they closed the door behind them without locking it and switched on the light. It was a smallish, low-ceilinged room of white-washed brick walls. This was the main switch room, the electrical heart of the whole hospital. It was unmanned and unimpressive. Allbright found it difficult to grasp the enormous power within their reach. But Shaw knew. He gazed round at the equipment, reaping the benefit of the long struggling hours into the nights he had so repeatedly made after a full day's work in order to qualify. For Ruth; to please her; to succeed; to put clothes on her back; to give her pride.

Immediately to their left was a short row of tall converters, like filing cupboards inset with dials. These converted the main A.C. current to D.C. usually for use on the E.E.G. machines. They weren't what Shaw wanted. Facing him was the battery of main fuses, metal boxes on a steel trellis standing upright like a grotesque flower display. He moved forward. Each box was labelled, its function clearly stated. The bank of switch boxes were of different sizes and roughly in three rows. Into the heart of them, curling from the far wall, were three multi-wired cables, the centre one as thick as Shaw's sturdy forearm, the flanking pair thicker than his wrists.

Allbright stood aside while Shaw examined them. The electrical engineer took his time; he had to be right. His square, grim face was sweating slightly but not enough to make his darkened eyebrows run. Under the electric light the shadowing of his features did not disguise their openness, nor the crevices around the tightened lips where he used to laugh. A determined man; everything about him proclaimed it. And in his searching grey eyes was blatant honesty. Allbright, watching him, was very aware of Shaw's presence at that time; it was impossible to escape the forceful personality of the man; he'd never done anyone down in his life. So what had gone wrong?

"You'll have to be damned careful." Shaw stood back. "The alternator feeds back through this bottom box, the big one."

"The alternator?"

"Generator; if that's put out of action we'll be out of business."

"Can't we just switch off and jam the switches?"

Shaw shook his head, still eyeing the battery.

"We want it out of action for twenty-four hours to be safe. I want it blown here, here and here." He indicated the areas on the three cables. Then, in further detail, "Can you blow this much out on each cable? Accurately?"

Allbright examined the cables carefully. "I can't guarantee the exact amount. It's been a long time." He was making excuses. He had practised, they all had in one form or another. Shaw said nothing, surprised at Allbright's sudden show of nerves and equally so at his own coolness. It should be the other way round. Then Allbright grinned sheepishly and ran a coarsened hand over his flattened nose; when he did that he was almost boyish. "How much room for error?"

"As long as you don't damage this particular box."

"Okay. No problem."

"You sure?"

"I'm sure. In the old days I'd have done it on my head." He was thinking of the many years ago when he'd been on bomb disposal. Handling explosive devices had been second nature to him then. It had been dangerous and different, and it had kept him straight. The army had been the only phase of his life when he had been completely straight. His mistake had been in leaving it.

Allbright took plastic explosive, detonators and fuse wire from his bag and started doing his mental sums. Mostly he worked from instinct and judgment. He might be rusty but he'd always have a rapport with certain things, he'd never forget how to do them. His big spatulate fingers worked deftly, his uncertainty gone with action. Shaw watched him with detached interest; Bob Allbright; the world knew him as one of the great bullion raiders let out on parole after fifteen years. He had little to lose now. Shaw had some idea of what he'd already lost and here, at least, they had a common denominator. Allbright was filled with a sense of injustice, too, but of a different kind. The explosive was carefully taped to the cables at the points Shaw had indicated. Allbright inserted the fuse wire into the detonators, then crimped their ends with his teeth, a method he would never have used when a sergeant, at least not in front of the men. He held his breath as he did it to keep hot air from the sensitive explosive. He then inserted the detonators into the main charges and ran the wire back to a box he had placed at the foot of the fuses. He knelt down and connected, looking up at Shaw. "Half an hour?"

Shaw nodded confirmation. Allbright set the timing mechanism and stood up. Two pairs of footsteps approached the door and Shaw visibly stiffened. To Allbright it was old hat; they were either caught or they got away with it; he was used to both. They stood still until the footsteps passed and then Shaw carefully opened the door. They stepped out, closed the door and Allbright locked it. Still with their tool kits they retraced their steps part way along the hive of short corridors until they reached a door in the outer wall. Opening it they went through, up some metal steps to street level. Beatty, McQueen and Barret were squatting on their grips waiting for them.

A woman came to collect her car and Shaw and Allbright remained on the basement steps until she had driven off. Hospital walls and windows reared about them on three sides; through the glass they could see nurses and sometimes patients. But the five men attracted no particular attention. They were now in the short dead end that Shaw and Allbright had briefly inspected on the way to the hospital entrance. While the rest hung back Allbright moved to the low, concrete-roofed building and did his trick with the door. When it was open he stepped back for Shaw and Beatty to enter. The door was closed behind them.

Inside it was gloomy, light filtering thinly through the slatted wooden door and part of the front wall which was also slatted. There were no windows; the small building was solely utilitarian. The slats were for ventilation, the remaining walls brick. At the back was a single straight row of switches: half a dozen boxes on stalks, each one declaring its function as had those in the main switch room. Facing the front wall like three huge, bloated cannon were the generators.

Shaw noticed that the end two were fairly old-fashioned, the bigger middle one more modern. It was going to be uncomfortable in here.

Beatty was opening his grip. He took from it a Sterling ·9 mm sub-machinegun, two 34-shot curved magazines, a Browning automatic pistol, a two-way radio similar to those used by the police, a gas mask, a Thermos flask filled with tea and a plastic container with sandwiches. He was still slowly chewing and it was difficult to gauge his thoughts. Shaw watched him carefully. Beatty took the Sterling, folded back the stock so that it extended to its full twenty-eight inches, inserted a magazine in the left-hand side and cocked the gun. He placed it carefully on the floor, treating it with respect and knowledge. He thrust the Browning into his hip pocket and then turned to the patiently waiting Shaw.

"Okay. I'm ready."

Shaw took him along the switches, explaining, telling him what to do when instructed. Beatty came to life, suddenly aware of the power he wielded. "You mean if those monkeys in there are operating on some guy's brain I can cut it off, just like that? Leave him with a hole in his head?" He spoke with a mixture of accents and rhetoric picked up from the various places he'd lived, like nylon picks up static.

Shaw gazed slowly at him but failed to make him lower his gaze. There was no time for a contest of wills. Instead he said, "It'll take anything from four to fifteen seconds for the generators to wind up. When they start you'll know that the main switches have blown even if you don't hear the explosion. You know what to do from then on. You're on your own."

Beatty gave a thumbs up sign. He sensed his power. He had weighed the odds, knew what he was up against and knew that he could handle it; this part of it better than any of them. He slowly pushed the gum to the other side of his mouth. Shaw wondered whether if he wasn't chewing gum he'd be biting his nails. He was young, in his late twenties, but he knew what action was all about.

"Any questions?"

Beatty shook his head. He was already at the wall slats, breaking two of them away with the stock of the Sterling.

"I've got to see out," he explained. "No, it's okay, boss. Leave it all to me."

Shaw had no alternative, there was little time. But he was satisfied. In many ways, although isolated, Beatty had the easiest task. Shaw joined the others at the head of the basement steps.

They went down the steps and back into the hospital. Shaw led the way followed by McQueen, with Allbright and Barret bringing up the rear. They passed the main switch room again almost without a glance. Time was running a little against them. In another recessed area they passed the lift switches; another small battery protected by a strong wire cage with a mesh door fastened by a small padlock. They had held many discussions about this. When the power was off the lifts would stop but could be restarted under separate power by using the caged switches. Two considerations had stopped them from blowing these; the area was too exposed, not a private room like the main switch room, and there were stairs. Lifts out of action were an inconvenience, no more, and anyway there was another method of dealing with the lifts that mattered. So they continued until they reached the stairs, then separated; going up them one at a time at about ten-second intervals. Their target had four entrances; they would take one each.

Ginger Shaw was the last to leave. He went to a lift on the ground floor and turned into a corridor at the side of it when he saw two young nurses waiting. He made sure he was alone before he produced a two-way radio similar to the one Beatty had and pulled up the short aerial. "You set?"

"Just hanging on. Not too busy here." It was Allbright.

By pre-arrangement both men left their sets on receive with the volume low. They didn't have long to wait. Within half a minute Barret's voice whispered over the air. "Ready." Shaw acknowledged, quickly switching back to receive. It was another few seconds before McQueen came on. "Ready."

Shaw had to wait while someone passed him, then he spoke urgently into the receiver. "Right. You two on the stairs go in as soon as the first lift doors open. We're coming now." He switched off, put away the radio, went round the corner to the lift and pushed the button to call it. It was impossible to ensure that Allbright and he arrived at the same time. They had agreed to go up only in an empty lift which could mean that one or both might have to wait. So there could be a time lag, but it would make no difference to the operation.

The lift doors opened and Shaw stepped in alone. As the doors closed he pressed the button for the sixth floor. He pulled some thin rubber gloves from his grip, raced to get them on and produced an automatic Colt ·45. Finally he pulled out a short block of wood. He left the grip on the floor. The lift was old and slow and he had a second or two in hand before it rocked to a stop and the doors began to glide back. From that precise moment he stepped into a vivid nightmare. Yet in spite of the speed with which it all happened he was later amazed at the amount of detail that registered in his vision in the space of a second, perhaps two.

When he thought about it later he was able to slow the whole motion down like an action replay on television. Ahead of him was the single wide corridor of the private wing. At the further end, exactly opposite him was the lift from which Allbright should emerge. The double swing doors at right angles to each lift were already opening with McQueen and Barret appearing, each half crouched and holding a Sterling sub-machinegun. The opening of his lift doors and the appearance of the other two men was almost simultaneous. But it was the middle distance that hypnotised him.

A nurse carrying a tray and syringe was crossing the corridor towards the row of private rooms on Shaw's right. Beyond her, nearer to the other end, two white-coated men he took to be doctors stood talking by one of the private room doorways. Shaw stepped forward at the same time, bending swiftly to insert the piece of wood between the lift doors to prevent them from closing. The unexpected action undoubtedly saved his life. The pistol explosions came fractionally later than the terrifying whine of bullets just missing his head and crashing into the metal rear of the lift. He threw himself flat in a reflex action; the block of wood slipped across the floor away from him. He was half in, half out of the lift. The nurse screamed as the tray crashed to the floor and she stood rooted directly in the line of fire. It was a miracle she had not been hit. The two white-coated men had now increased to three and were suddenly armed, fanning out quickly to spread their target. All had pistols. At the precise moment this registered with Shaw from his prone position McQueen opened up with the Sterling and one of the men did a grotesque dance with arms outflung, his legs gyrating as if he was trying to run on marbles.

Shaw rolled a split second before another shot came his way. The nurse was still standing with clenched hands to her mouth, screaming repeatedly. Shaw struggled to get up, and Barret let off a burst to cover him, racing towards the lift to get a better shot at one of the men who was hidden by the nurse. It was an uncharacteristically considerate act for him; normally he would have shot the girl to get at the man. It was the last decent act he ever performed. Two bullets took him cleanly and he arched back, falling where Shaw had just lain, his head and shoulders inside the lift, his Sterling clattering to the ground too far away for Shaw to reach.

Perhaps half a second prior to that the other lift doors opened and Allbright, who had heard the firing, came out at a controlled rush to contribute to it. For the two remaining gunmen the firepower was too much. They had killed one man and Shaw had been saved by sheer chance. But for this their fantastic expertise might well have saved them; they might even have won against the odds. As it was, and as Shaw at last added his contribution, they took a glut of bullets that flung them ruthlessly in opposite directions and they died ingloriously on a bloodied corridor floor; a trio of heroes scattered and mangled in postures of eternal pain and protest.

Shaw's men were shattered and bewildered. They had expected no resistance and they were at a complete loss to understand what had happened. The nurse had stopped screaming and was now sobbing, trembling on the spot she had occupied throughout. Incredibly, she had survived without a scratch. A white-clad Sister emerged from her office opposite the private rooms and tried to comfort her, putting her arm round the terrified girl's shoulders. The whole, bloody action had taken no time at all.

Shaw tried to break the paralysis that gripped him. He was stunned, shocked to the core, they all were. He turned to McQueen. "Get the doors fixed, quick." It was not until then that he realised McQueen was holding his Sterling with one hand, his other arm pressed across his body; the padding in his shoulder was hanging out like entrails with blood oozing through it. Christ, the three gunmen had come nearer to success than Shaw had realised. Who the hell were they? How had they known?

McQueen, seeing Shaw's doubt, grinned crookedly. "I can cope." He went through the swing doors to reappear almost immediately with his grip, and started to work.

Shaw looked around at the devastation, the holes in plaster, the blood, the dead. By now Barret should have ripped out every telephone wire from the patients' rooms. God, it had all gone wrong. But they were here and they had better be quick. The brief, vicious gun battle must have been heard elsewhere.

Allbright came to life, dashed back to retrieve his grip from the lift and rammed a block of wood between the doors. As he turned back again he shouted at Shaw, "The bloody doors are closing behind you."

Shaw swung round. Someone had summoned the lift. The doors glided across before he could move and rammed against Barret's narrow shoulders stopping there; Barret, who had probably saved the nurse and even dead was still doing more for people than he'd ever done before. There was no time to move him, so Shaw left him effectively jamming the lift doors. He signalled Allbright to take over, collected Barret's Sterling, then picked up the three revolvers the white-coated men had been using and stuffed them in his grip, leaving it near the handicapped but hard-working McQueen. Allbright was warning the others.

"The first one to move gets shot. So stay just where you are."

The warning was necessary. Two more white-coated men had appeared, one elderly, short and florid; the other taller and dark-haired.

"Get your hands up. Right up on your heads." Allbright was taking no chances; was only too ready to squeeze the trigger. These early moments were difficult with one man short. Shaw ran from room to room tearing out telephone wires. He was aware that he might be falling into a trap but things had started so disastrously that his only other option was to call it all off; the price paid was already far too high even to consider doing that. As he hurried along he had little impression of the patients; for all he knew some may well have died from shock. When he had finished with the telephones he hurried back into the wide corridor to see a strange tableau still suspended by inaction. The elder of the white-coated men was glaring around like an angry bull, his head down, jowls quivering. The younger one was pale and strained. The Sister was still comforting the nurse, and he could see another nurse, too terrified to move, in the Sister's office. The office telephone started pealing out.

The elder man hunched his shoulders and strode towards the office.

"Stop or I'll blow your head off." Shaw was surprised at his calm. Death was new to him.

It was touch and go. The old boy was so furious that Shaw thought he was going to stride on towards the ringing telephone. Shaw took aim. But he did not think his action stopped the man from moving; it was probably the twisted body he would have to step over in order to continue. As he gazed down a trace of compassion erased some of his anger but that was all. Shaw guessed that the man was a senior consultant. Everything about him, his age, demeanour, attitude, proclaimed it. He was God up here and his heaven had been ravaged. Still Shaw was in no mood to trust anybody wearing a white surgical coat. "Don't do it, doc."

Then the lights went out and there was a faint rumble from the bowels of the building.

2

FRANK NESBIT HEARD the three almost simultaneous blasts, as they all did, down in the cellars. He shot from his desk, listening, wondering, thinking the worst as the lights went out. He grabbed a bunch of keys from a board near his door and raced round the warren towards the main switch room. Staff had emerged from everywhere, getting in his way, startled and jabbering.

The switch-room door was loose on its hinges but Nesbit still had to use the key to open it. Smoke was filtering through the gaps. He didn't stop to think that there might be further explosions but swung the door back awkwardly and went inside. A haze floated round the equipment like a sandstorm slowly settling. His mouth filled with grit and dirt and he tasted abrasive particles of brick and mortar, enough to make him hold a handkerchief over nose and mouth. Hospital staff crowded in behind him and he shouted at them to get back.

The place was a shambles. The battery of switch boxes hung on the ends of twisted metal like a surrealist nightmare. He almost tripped over the timing device, gave it a quick inspection and realised the worst. Big, ugly chunks had been torn from the three main cables. What was left of them reared like snakes with multiple, jagged fangs. Oh, Christ! He took quick stock, made a snap assessment of the time it would take to rectify them, and fought his way out of the room.

As he raced through the cellars towards the stairs leading to the dead end he was cursing his luck. The chief engineer was away on a much overdue holiday and Nesbit had been called in from another hospital group temporarily. Damn it. Who'd want to blow up the main switch room? A crank? Another barmy movement bringing attention to itself?

He raced up the metal stairs, reached street level and ran the few steps to the generator building. Before he reached the door a voice snapped, "Stop there, daddio, or I'll put a bullet through your head."

Nesbit saw the gun barrel and came to a panting halt.

What the hell was happening? Some of the slats in the door had been broken and the gun and a pair of eyes were all too clear.

"We've taken over the generators, dad. So push off before you stop one."

Nesbit felt he was going mad. He stood, panting, still with the foul taste of grit in his mouth. He wasn't paid to get his head blown off and he did not, for one moment, think the man was anything but deadly serious.

"Is it working? Everything operating?" It was the least he could find out.

"Don't fret, dad. It's okay for now. You toddle off like a good lad and you'll live to tell 'em about it in your pub."

Nesbit was undecided. There was no point in staying here, nothing that he could do about an armed man. The gun rattled warningly in the slats. The whole world was sick. He went down the steps and located the reserve lift switches in their cage. He unlocked the small padlock, went in, reached up and switched on the reserve power for the lifts. He hurried to the ground floor where the word had already got round that the switch room had been blown.

The Secretary was on the telephone in his office off the main hall, already a worried man. Nesbit went in and told him what had happened, finding it difficult to believe his own story even as he related it. With the nightmare shared he then rang the London Electricity Emergency Service. It would take at least twenty-four hours to fix new cables and only God knew what damage had been done to some of the switch boxes. He left the Secretary to contact the police and then found an office window on the ground floor from which he could watch the generator outhouse.

* * *

The telephone stopped ringing as if it had been affected by the same breakdown of current. The coincidence created a sudden strange aura. The consultant remained still, and the nurse stared up at the ceiling as if the Almighty was indulging His terrible wrath. The only sound was from McQueen using a compressed air drill on the swing doors.

There was no access to direct daylight in the corridor but all the patients' rooms faced the square and had big, modern windows. Light escaped through the glass-panelled doors into the corridor; the effect was like a cloud covering the sun. But it also had a sobering effect, as if everything had moved into a new stage.

Shaw turned to the Sister, only a few feet from him. "Telephone the hospital Secretary and tell him we've taken over this ward. Tell him that anyone who tries to enter will be killed. Do not tell him how many there are of us. And don't answer any of his questions."

The Sister gently released the nurse; she was now much calmer but she would live for ever with the sound of bullets screaming close to her young body. Clear eyes met Shaw's.

"Why don't you do it yourself?"

A haughty, cool bitch, reflected Shaw. But good-looking; no more than late twenties. There was no tremor of fear in her voice but he noticed how she clutched the nurse's hand.

"Ma'am, there's no time to argue. Just do it." His respect was unconscious. The Sister walked straight-backed to her office, an open wall with a counter and a door at the side. She went in, and moved behind the desk that backed on to the counter. The second nurse was still sitting there, pale and afraid to speak.

Jean Sandingham picked up the telephone and could feel herself trembling. The Secretary came on the line and it was immediately clear from his distress that he already had problems his end. She identified herself and in a flat, calm voice told him that gunmen were holding her ward. She held the phone out to Shaw. "He wants to speak to one of you."

Shaw shook his head. "Tell him I'll speak to him when I'm ready with our demands. But tell him we've blown the main switches and taken over the generator." Jean Sandingham repeated the message and put down the phone, now very white. Shaw told her to stay where she was. He turned round to take stock. The place looked like a battlefield. McQueen had finished the first pair of doors and was busy on the second. He was fixing steel bars to prevent them being opened. As he drilled the screw holes he kept each door from moving by holding it with a strong wire device which he inserted between the doors and twisted, so that its hooked end gripped the wood and held the door steady. McQueen might look like a third-rate boxer, which he had been, but he was solid and reliable, he'd got mashed up simply because he had never known when to stop. And his reflexes could be amazingly sharp. He was working away as if he was oblivious of his injured arm.

"Just what is it you guys really want?"

Shaw looked across the corridor in surprise. The tall dark man was still standing where Allbright had told him to stay. An American? What other surprises were there?

"Who're you?"

"I'm Ed Grann. I'd like to look at these people." He indicated the scattered bodies.

"Why? No one can help them. You a doctor?"

Grann nodded. "I should check that they're dead."

"They're dead all right. Who were they?" Shaw was still puzzled. How had the men known they were coming?

Grann did not reply.

Shaw said, "I'll ask you again later. And you'd better reply. Where can we put them?"

"There's an empty room behind me."

Shaw looked at Allbright to make sure he had things under control and then moved to the nearest body He searched the pockets and found an identity card. American. He looked suspiciously across at Grann, then read the identity again, stiffening and bewildered.

"Keep your hands on your head." Shaw moved across to Grann. "Face the wall." When Grann complied Shaw searched him. No weapon. He was puzzled and strangely afraid. There was something crazy about the whole scene. He searched the pockets of the remaining two bodies. All had spring clip holsters; one right hip, one left and one shoulder. All three carried pocket sender/receiver radios, more up to date than their own. Two of the men were Americans, the other a British Special Branch man. He took a chance and called Allbright across and kept his voice low.

"If I read it right these two jokers are American Secret Service men; the other one is Special Branch. They couldn't have been waiting for us." He knew that in America, Secret Service was a misnomer, that it provided bodyguards. Who were they guarding?

Allbright checked the bodies himself and came up with a different emphasis. "Did you take a good look at their radios?"

"Not really." Shaw was surprised by Allbright's worried frown.

"You should've. They've all got bleepers. One of them is down."

"The grapevine has it," continued Allbright when they were kneeling down by one of the Americans, "that these characters are supposed to sound off their bleeper at the first sign of trouble. Now this bloke did but did it sound and if it did, how long? The bloody thing's been smashed by a bullet so we can't tell."

Shaw examined the radio more carefully. Did a red alert sound off? Then common sense nudged him and he took Allbright over to the second American. He picked up the radio and switched to receive. "Come in Woodcutter Two. Do you read me?" An English voice. The message kept repeating over and over again with pauses for a talkback. Shaw switched off and looked at Allbright.

"It doesn't matter whether the alert went off or not. They're checking in and getting no reply."

The two men stared at each other uneasily. Shaw said, "Get back to the doors and I'll try to sort it out." He collected the three radios and put them in his grip with the guns, which he now examined. Two Colt Detective Specials, snub nosed, two-inch barrels, ·38 as used by the F.B.I. Not surprisingly the third was a ·38 breakback Webley; a British weapon. He moved to the middle of the corridor. "I want everyone in the office."

When the elderly man reached the door Shaw stopped and searched him. He hadn't expected to find anything but he was unwilling to take further chances. It should have been done already, amongst other things; but for Barret's death, it would have been. When they were all behind the counter he allowed them to sit down and spoke to them across it.

"Now let's get it straight. Those three men weren't here

waiting for us. They were bodyguards. Who's going to tell me who they were guarding?"

There was guilt written on all their faces but no one spoke.

"All I have to do is go round all the rooms, which one of us will do anyway once these doors are fixed. So who?"

Ed Grann spoke carefully; "It's something none of us wanted. We don't like armed men in hospitals. They arrived only an hour or so before you did. But the patient hasn't come yet. He was due in shortly."

"So these jokers were making sure the place was safe first?"

"Yes."

"Who's the V.I.P. that merits three armed bodyguards in England?"

"We have not been told." The old boy was gruff in taking up the reply.

Shaw said, "What's your name?"

"Professor Bowyer. Now you have the advantage. All we know is that the man is a visiting American V.I.P."

"What's wrong with him?"

"How can we say when we haven't examined him? He's had a collapse of some kind. That's all we've been told and that his personal physician is being flown over."

"Where were you going to put him?"

"Room three. It was being prepared."

Shaw quickly crossed the floor and peered through the glass inset of room three. It was empty; the bed stripped. He had half noticed before. Whoever the V.I.P. was, he had to be very high-ranking to warrant this treatment. Three men had died for him and a fourth because of him. He'd have a look round as soon as McQueen had finished. He went back to the counter.

"I thought V.I.P.s all went to the London Clinic?"

The professor replied wearily; "That entirely depends on what's the matter with them. This is a highly specialised hospital." And then, as an afterthought, "The finest of its kind."

So they'd been caught up in something they could do without. It was better that the V.I.P. wasn't here; it would only complicate matters.

McQueen finished bolting the doors then sprayed the windows in them with a thick, opaque fluid from an aerosol, scooping a hole with his thumb to provide a spyhole before the liquid dried. Nobody could now look in unless they were right against the door and they were unlikely to do that. He put his tools back in his grip, picked up his Sterling and took up a position at the opposite end of the ward to Allbright. Now that both entrances were sealed and covered Shaw felt a little easier.

"Let's clear up." Shaw pointed to Grann and the Sister, "You two get the bodies into the spare room. Your V.I.P. won't be coming."

"We'll need a stretcher. From the storeroom."

Shaw eyed the American suspiciously. From now on he would suspect everything. He pointed to the nurse who had been sitting throughout. "What's your name?"

"Nurse O'Connor." A soft Dublin brogue.

"You come with me."

All the facilities lay opposite the private patients' rooms. Toilets, bathrooms, a small kitchen for preparing drinks, and the storeroom which seemed innocuous enough; medical utensils, bottles, tins, disinfectants, blankets, bed linen, buckets and mops. Shaw helped the nurse out with the stretcher, aware that she was terrified of him. He didn't want her fear, only her obedience, but he accepted that the one might depend on the other. They dumped the stretcher near one of the bodies and Shaw allowed her to help the Sister lift her end, with Dr. Grann taking the head and shoulders. One by one they carried the bodies into the empty room. Shaw told the other nurse to get a bucket and mop and clean up.

While this was going on Shaw pulled out his radio and flipped up the aerial. "You all right?"

Beatty answered, "No fuzz yet. The machines are buzzing and it's getting warm. One character pitched up; I got rid of him."

"You'll have more company than that soon enough." Shaw refrained from telling Beatty what had happened; it meant going into too much detail on the air. "I'll keep one of the radios on receive; with three we can spare the batteries. Give a yell if there's trouble."

Beatty chuckled, sure of himself. "I can hold an army off from here."

"You may have to." Shaw switched off, irritated by Beatty's cockiness; but he was the only one of them who could do that particular job. Perhaps anyone as good a shot as Beatty was entitled to be cocky. He called to McQueen, "Leave your radio on receive," then realised with shock that nothing had been done about McQueen's wound. The man was so bloody uncomplaining. Angry at himself Shaw turned to the professor and demanded that he and the nurse treat McQueen's shoulder.

Barret was still blocking the lift doors, he'd be the last to be moved as he was the farthest away, so Shaw recovered the block of wood, pulled Barret clear and inserted it between the doors. Another item tidied. He looked down dispassionately at Barret's dead face, momentarily disturbed by being so unmoved. Barret had never really made an impression on him, had been just a functionary unit without a noticeable personality, unlike the experienced Allbright, or the sharp, confident Beatty or even the stolid, phlegmatic McQueen. Barret had been a man devoid of apparent emotion. Like himself. He stirred briefly. Once he had been too full of emotion. And then the trauma had begun. There could be no compromise. His life was still traumatic and perhaps it would always be. But at least he would get his satisfaction; that at any cost.

* * *

Ed Grann laid the bodies against the wall under the window. The bed could not take them all and, in any event, it was pointless. He was in turmoil and hoped to God he didn't show it. He had delivered a quick-witted lie that would probably emerge, but he'd been unable to stop himself. The professor backing him up had at least condoned it, so he must have approved. A tough old buzzard, a brilliant diagnostician, one of the finest in the world. Grann prayed that he was sitting on his feelings effectively. If only he could emulate Jean Sandingham. Her profession called for a cool head but he had discovered that her toughness was largely self-administered. A few days ago he had unwittingly touched on her vulnerability and he'd wondered if she sometimes inwardly cried out for some of the affection and love she so ably administered to patients. Like many people surrounded by others, he suspected she was lonely. While he moved the bodies he watched her, not fooled by her apparent detachment.

Somehow the English term, Sister, had formed a flimsy psychological barrier; it wasn't used in American hospitals nor anywhere he knew outside of convents and nunneries. He preferred to think of her as Jean, and called her that when the consultant wasn't around.

Ed Grann deftly searched each body they brought in. Unsure why he did it, he was aware it provoked a worried frown from Jean Sandingham, curiosity from Nurse O'Connor. It was something he felt he had to do. Two of them were Americans, compatriots, even if, like the professor and his colleagues, he had violently disagreed with their being there at all. It had been a tragic mistake and it could yet turn out to be a far worse one.

While he quietly worked away, Ed Grann tried to summon sense from the madness that had burst upon them. The stocky guy intrigued him. He couldn't slot him in at all, but the other two were more easily identifiable. Recidivists, it was written all over them.

When he had been working at the Medical Centre on First Avenue at East 31st and 32nd Streets, Ed Grann had been called out many times on emergencies to downtown Tombs, the huge police detention centre. He had seen the same noncommittal expression again and again. It seemed to him that there was always a similar mixture; a hint of resentment, an underlying hopelessness. Men with nowhere to go except back to jail.

As they eased Barret, the last body, on to the stretcher, Grann closed the eyes and folded the arms to prevent them drooping over the side. What an incredible toll: four dead in half that number of seconds. A little to one side Professor Bowyer was treating the wounded man. It was a nasty gash but probably less serious than it looked; it had taken the fleshy part of the shoulder, and the bullet had probably passed straight through, leaving torn tissues.

As Jean Sandingham could manage her end of the stretcher adequately, she sent Nurse O'Connor back to the office. The stocky man was standing beside the professor making sure he was up to no tricks. They carried the stretcher into room three and laid it on the floor. Gently they lifted the body to join the others. In death there was no discrimination.

Ed Grann ran his hands over the body and stopped. Jean Sandingham watched him anxiously; he looked composed, a fact that gave her strength. Suddenly there was a gun in his hand. She recoiled instantly, shaking her head. "No. No."

It lay in the palm of his hand; a Beretta though neither knew it then. "It was tucked in at the small of his back."

"No. For God's sake. Put it back." Jean Sandingham was unaccountably afraid. "You're a doctor, not one of them." She gestured helplessly towards the dead bodyguards.

"I can't." Grann looked helplessly at the gun. "I can't pretend it isn't here. And I can't leave it."

"They'll know it was there. They'll remember."

"They wouldn't have forgotten a thing like this. Maybe it was his personal toy; something he had to have with him."

"It doesn't matter. These men are killers."

"Isn't that a reason for keeping it?"

They were crouched near the gruesome, blood-spattered bodies. Both knew that there was no time for argument, that the stocky man would get suspicious if they were too long.

"You wouldn't stand a chance with them." The plea was quiet but urgent. "You're not a gunman."

Ed Grann gazed at the gun, unfamiliar to his touch. He'd never fired a pistol in his life. And yet he was reluctant to let it go.

"It's a possible advantage. I can't put it back."

"Doctor, *please*."

Grann smiled wistfully. "What a time to stand on ceremony. Jean, let's get out of here." He helped her to her feet at the same time slipping the automatic under his surgical coat and into a trouser pocket. "If they find out how I've misled them I might need it." He had intended to be flippant but it fell flat, merely emphasing the dangers.

By the time they'd returned to the office Professor Bowyer had finished with McQueen who now had his jacket off, one shirt sleeve cut away and his left arm in a sling. When all the staff were behind the counter Ginger Shaw began to breathe again. They had just reached the stage they should have reached at the outset. But they had lost time. His relief was premature. The double doors near Allbright were being pushed.

Allbright swung round with the Sterling, glancing at Shaw for instruction, ready to put a burst through the door. Shaw shouted to Jean Sandingham. "Get up there quick and get rid of him." He knew it wasn't the police, they wouldn't be so brash and it was too soon. If it was hospital staff they'd recognise the Sister's voice.

Jean Sandingham ran up the ward, her flat shoes making little noise. Allbright stood back for her but kept his gun levelled. The doors were still being rattled against the retaining bars and a man was cursing on the other side.

"This is Sister Sandingham." At last there was desperation in her voice. "The ward's closed. See Mr. Harris, he'll explain."

The rattling stopped, then, "Closed! What the devil are you talking about? I must see a patient."

"Please go." She recognised the voice of one of the consultants.

"Open up at once. Have you gone mad, Sister?" It was typical of the man to expect her to know his name.

Allbright felt sorry for the girl; it didn't affect the issue but she had tried and was now floundering. He shouted "Push off you silly bugger or I'll shoot you *and* your bloody patient." He fired a short burst above the glass and the woodwork splintered as the doors strained against the impact. Afterwards, the silence was complete, everyone rooted, even Allbright who was ready to fire again.

For some seconds there was no sound from the other side of the doors and then came a startled, "Good God," and again, "Good God." Footsteps went away from the doors and Allbright rushed to the spyhole to see the retreating, hunched figure.

The noise of the shots so close to her head had made Jean Sandingham bend forward with her ears cupped. Ed Grann ran up to her despite Allbright's warning and, with his arm round her shoulders, helped her back to the office, aware that she was trembling and that acting as their go-between was forcing too much strain and responsibility on her. He made her sit down behind the desk and glared at Shaw.

But Shaw was satisfied. He was not offended by the American's anger. It would have taken time for the word to go round from the hospital Secretary; this way it would spread like wildfire. Apart from the police there should be no further interruption. And they could handle the police. He surveyed the captive group and noticed their apprehension, conveyed in different ways with varying amounts of control. The professor was still glowering, staring directly at him, but he was worried just the same. "Right," said Shaw directly to him. "Which room is Lord Driver in?"

They were all taken completely by surprise. His demand had undoubtedly startled them. No one replied but an involuntary glance from one of the young nurses confirmed what Shaw already suspected. He cradled Barret's Sterling, walked slowly across to room four and opened the door, pushing it right back.

The man lying in bed was deathly pale, his face prematurely aged and sunken, his flesh almost translucent. Shaw already knew that he was in a coma. He went farther into the room so that his back was not facing the door. The two doctors followed him in, the Sister standing behind them in the doorway. Shaw stared down at the figure in bed and experienced some strange emotions. Strong among them was hate. The others watched him curiously.

A respirator was fixed to keep the lungs operating; without it, he could not live. A drip feed popped slowly, the needle disappearing into a pitifully thin arm. The steady whir of the machine informed Shaw that the generator had taken over the essential services. So far so good. He must have been looking down at the man with great intensity, his feelings showing, for the hoarse, whispered question from the professor was full of concern. "What do you intend to do?"

Shaw looked up listlessly, suddenly feeling old, memories strong. "I'm going to kill him," he said flatly.

3

As he said it, it sounded right. He gazed reflectively at the near dead face, the lids like eggshell china and lips tinged the same colour, and all he could feel was a resentment so intense that tears pricked the back of his eyes. Lord Driver and his kind were responsible for his being here at all. It would be easy to switch off the machine. The man was a cabbage anyway. Aware that he was being studied Shaw snapped off the emotion he'd thought he no longer possessed.

"Are you sure you want to go through with this?"

The American was eyeing him speculatively. Shaw realised that he had revealed too much, but the American had miscalculated. Shaw produced his radio and pulled up the aerial. He checked again with Beatty and said to the others, "Nothing will happen to you provided you cooperate. Let's get back to the office." Before he left the room he gazed again at the symbol he had learned to hate. The man was so far gone that nothing had penetrated his mind; not even the gun battle. He glanced at his watch. It was almost impossible to believe that barely an hour had passed since first entering the hospital; little more than twenty minutes since the power had been cut.

* * *

The hospital Secretary's call reached the switchboard of E Divisional H.Q. at an uncommonly awkward time. The operator tried the extensions of four senior officers in succession, then tried C.I.D., and would have been satisfied to pass on the message to the Detective Sergeant on duty there but for the sharpness of the police constable typing a report near to her. With practised hearing he had picked up the gist of what was being reported and immediately realised its seriousness.

"I saw Inspector Erskin come in. Try him."

The subdued monotones from the monitor floated into

the room, the steady indifference of voices giving a completely false impression of the amount of action taking place. P.C. Rhodes was a good policeman. Anticipating what was happening he did a quick check on locations with the policewoman on car control and segregated those already out on serious jobs while the operator raised the inspector.

As Inspector Erskin answered the call in his office he was taking a cup of coffee from the Secretary who had just brought it in. It was his bad luck that he took it from her instead of letting her put it down. As the message came over he spilled most of the coffee over the desk. The girl took one look at his face and started to mop up without a word, gently easing his fingers away from the acutely tilted saucer. The inspector hardly noticed.

He knew exactly what to do but he lacked the means to do it properly. He quickly checked on the disposition of men and cars and issued instructions. He was quick to grasp the situation and act upon it, but he couldn't make up a shortage of numbers or get men off the sick list by telling them they were fit. For a few seconds after setting the ball rolling he leaned back in his chair and rubbed his eyes. God, he felt tired. If he went on like this he'd get an ulcer, he probably already had one judging by the pain.

Erskin was a tall, thin man, balding, with sunken cheeks and heavy bags under his eyes that exaggerated his age. The hours, the overwork, the sad acceptance that he had gone as far as he could go in rank and was too old to attract attention for further promotion, all this he could take; he enjoyed the work and it had been enough for him. That was before his unmarried daughter had run off with an out-of-work slob who had put her in the family way. He might even have tolerated that but for the blame that came his way from his wife for the neglect of their children. The constant haranguing, night after night, when his mind screamed for nothing but rest; it was becoming too much for him. If it continued it would affect his judgment, might already be doing so.

As he rose and reached for his uniform cap he reflected morosely on his luck. The Law Courts had claimed a Chief Superintendent and a Superintendent that morning. A Detective Chief Inspector and a Detective Sergeant were out on a particularly nasty case. God knew where the others were. What the inspector did know was that he'd been landed with an emergency. Bloody nutters. Maybe his was the right kind of experience to deal with this particular problem? Maybe this could bring him in line for promotion before it was finally too late.

He hesitated by the door. Armed men in a hospital? He should really call in Scotland Yard. But that would mean involving the Serious Crime Squad, who in turn would get a senior officer to form a firearm squad. If that happened, almost certainly an Assistant Commissioner would arrive with a watching brief just to keep an eye on things. The place would be alive with big brass.

Inspector Erskin left his office. He'd take a look first, size things up. Then he'd decide. With luck he'd sort it out himself.

By the time he reached the street the calls to the squad cars had already gone out. The action was in an area he knew inside out, where he'd pounded the streets around in all weathers. He didn't need a map, he knew far more about the nooks and crannies than a map could ever show. A difficult area because it was impossible to surround the place. He left the police station after giving details of his future whereabouts and went out to the car he had summoned.

* * *

The two-man crew of Able Twelve were cruising along the eastern end of High Holborn; the street was thick with traffic and early lunchers were beginning to snarl up the pavements. They had been listening to the sudden activity on the car radio and were not surprised when their own car was one of the first to be called:

"Proceed at once to the first junction on the left down Powis Place off Queen Square. An armed man has taken over the generator room of the Queen Mary Hospital at the foot of the intersection. Do not approach. Take up position at junction. Do not get in line of fire. Normal procedure to apply against armed men. Inspector Erskin will contact you on location. Message timed at eleven thirty-five."

After the message was acknowledged the two men looked at each other without comment. The younger one in the passenger seat flicked on the siren and the flasher while the driver tied knots in the traffic. He cursed loudly. "No sodding lunch. That's what it means. If it's a nutter we'll be there all sodding day and go hungry. I'd like to kill the bastard."

They arrived at the junction just a few minutes later, parked one side of it and got out. The main entrance to the hospital was out of sight round the corner but they'd recognised the car already pulled up outside before they'd turned off.

* * *

When the staff were herded into the office again Shaw reached for the telephone through the hole-in-the-wall. He flashed several times without getting a reply. He could imagine that the lines would be fairly buzzing but the switchboard girl should get her priorities right. He put down the receiver in annoyance and almost immediately it rang out. He picked it up again and growled, "Hello," and a voice demanded, "Who're you?"

"I'm the joker who's taken over this ward, so who're you?"

There was a measured silence then the voice again, more controlled: "I'm Inspector Erskin from E Division, Metropolitan Police. Why don't you give up this caper before it really gets out of hand?"

Shaw was disappointed. It meant that the hospital Secretary had rung the nearest police headquarters in Theobalds Road, and it seemed they had turned out at not very high level. This business had to go to *the top*, and the sooner the better if they were to get anywhere. Still, the bloke was a copper.

"It's already out of hand, Inspector. There are four stiffs up here. Has nobody told you?" He said it to shock, to get action.

The pause was too long for Shaw; he didn't think the inspector believed him. Was it likely the local police would know about the bodyguards? "Look, Inspector, you'd better listen and you'd better act quickly. Contact Lady Driver at Cleats Hall, Panbury, and tell her that we want one million pounds in out of sequence twenties evenly divided in four suitcases by five this evening. And don't try anything stupid like bugging the cases. If we don't get them by then we turn off the machine that's keeping her husband alive. And tell the operator to keep this extension connected with the Secretary's office. Keep your end off the hook; I'll flash when I want you."

"You'll never get away with it, you *bastard*—you . . ." While the Inspector blustered to cover his horror Shaw cut in; "I want all the corridors on this floor clear. Tell your superiors that if they don't do exactly as we say we'll switch off the generator. The first sign of anyone on the landings outside these doors and we switch off. We're in radio touch; you can tune in. And if we get a cry for help from the generator room we start knocking off the patients up here." Shaw hung up, slightly breathless.

The atmosphere in the office was heavy, as if they had all been sedated into silence. Ed Grann had placed his hand on Jean Sandingham's arm and was unconsciously squeezing it. Neither noticed. The two nurses were looking uneasily at each other. Professor Bowyer's jowls quivered but his voice was even, if weary, when he spoke; "You realise that cutting off the generator will kill several patients elsewhere in the hospital?"

"Empty threats will get us nowhere."

"But that will be murder, cutting off their life support like that."

Shaw shrugged. "It won't be murder, it'll be reprisal. It's up to the police; they lay off and nobody is harmed."

"Four people are already dead."

"We didn't start it and you know that bloody well."

"What sort of person could threaten to kill a near dead and utterly helpless man for money?"

"Careful, prof, or you'll find out the hard way."

"Why should you be offended? You must have justified your action to yourself many times. You must be satisfied. I'm merely interested in how you see yourself."

Shaw swallowed, concentrated. "I'd just as soon switch off

the machine without money. But there are other considerations."

"Some kind of revenge then?" asked the professor.

Shaw's eyes flickered, softened with reflection then hardened again. "Don't probe, prof. It would take a long time to fill you in and you're the wrong side of the fence to understand."

"I'm merely trying to pass some of the considerable time it seems we must spend together amicably."

There was another awkward silence before Ed Grann voiced what they had all been thinking. "Supposing they don't pay up?"

"They'll pay."

"You understand that Lord Driver has a terminal disease? He might die at any moment."

"They'll cough up, don't worry."

Professor Bowyer was disturbed, as they all were. He did not believe in euthanasia, he was not so far from retirement himself, but those who did could not have selected a better case to prove their point than that of Lord Driver. Even if by some freak chance he regained consciousness he would immediately die; his brain was flooded. Bowyer forced his mind from the medicine where it was so invariably anchored and, with difficulty, probed the background to the case. How could a threat to kill a dying man influence anybody? Then he recalled rumours.

He looked with new interest at Shaw; a strange, intense little man with a huge chip on his shoulder. He had the strong conviction that in spite of Shaw's indifference to suffering he was a man one could trust, even now; he would not go back on his word.

There were moments when he still couldn't believe any of this was happening. It could not happen. Not this, not here. He was sorry the others were involved but he was glad of young Grann's guile, although there could be dreadful repercussions over that. Well, Grann had done his best and he had supported him, hadn't he?

If it hadn't been for the damned bodyguards there would have been no deaths. He was furious about that. Not only the Americans but the Special Branch had absolutely insisted. But the fact remained that had the V.I.P. been brought in under another name, secretly, until public exposure was inevitable if ever it was, the bodyguards would not have been necessary and would still be alive. The chances were that the V.I.P. had nothing wrong with him. Overdoing it. The way these fellows travelled the world it was not surprising at all. Time differences, ethnic differences, climatic changes, almost insurmountable problems. It was surprising that more of them did not collapse, of the few that really did the work. Anyway, he and Grann had a problem. When he surveyed the three gunmen once more he knew just how big it was.

*   *   *

When Inspector Erskin finished his brief telephone conversation with Ginger Shaw he was visibly shaken. He hadn't grasped the extreme deadliness of the situation. It had taken a very nasty turn. Four dead. Christ! Who were they? Or were they bluffing? No. There were too many witnesses to the sound of firing. How many gunmen were up there? Keeping the police in ignorance of numbers was a strong weapon; he had to assume the worst; half a dozen, then.

When his reinforcements arrived Inspector Erskin put two men at each end of the fifth-floor landings below the swing doors of the private ward. At this stage it was as many as he could spare. He had also put men on the front entrance. All were uniformed policemen but what was available of the C.I.D. were on the way, together with two armed men. His idea was to follow classic police procedure and to contain the situation. In his heart he knew that he needed an army of armed men, but he was reluctant to call them in too soon. He was an old-fashioned copper, he hated the use of firearms. This refusal to update himself, to acknowledge a changing emphasis in social violence was one of the reasons he had stood still for so long.

The hospital was full of sick and innocent people who needed a gun battle like they needed an overdose. Inspector Erskin reasoned it out, his prejudice quietly working, his mental fatigue and his domestic worries subtly undermining his judgment. He wasn't a fool; he simply wanted something instigated by himself to go right. He asked the hospital Secretary to contact Lady Driver.

He went back to his car, picked up the microphone and requested more men, more cars. He had no sooner finished than his own H.Q. came back on the air.

"Scotland Yard have been on, sir. They monitored our calls to the squad cars. They're sending a mobile H.Q. down to Queen Square and asked if you could relay any worthwhile, on-the-spot information."

Bugger it, they'd been quicker than he'd expected. He didn't want them yet, he might still manage without them. He swallowed the profanities that almost choked him and steadied himself against the car.

"Does Mr. Saunders know about this?"

"The Chief Superintendent is still in court, sir. We can't reach him until twelve thirty."

That in itself was unusual. The Guv'nor was never in court; it must have been one of those strange, complicated cases which had involved him in evidence.

"He'll never stand for it."

The girl didn't reply, feeling a certain sympathy towards his need to keep it in the family.

"Give me a link up with the Yard. Who contacted us?"

"Assistant Commissioner, Crime, sir. Mr. Roberts."

Sonny Roberts! Christ, they had once been on the beat together. A long time ago. When he got his radio link it was with Commander Gifford. He'd heard of Jack Gifford of the Serious Crime Squad. He had to be careful.

"I'm down at the Queen Mary Hospital now, sir. I understand you're taking over?"

"A mobile's on its way."

'Does my guv'nor know about this, sir? I mean shouldn't we wait for him to return? As a matter of courtesy?"

"Inspector, as I understand it there's an armed man holding the generator and an undisclosed number of armed men who have taken over the private wing. Would you mind popping up and asking them to hang on until your guv'nor gets back?"

The sarcasm was cutting, and bang on the nail. Inspector

Erskin had to admit it to himself. But it was unnecessary. The inspector's face was burning.

"I have men on the two landings, men at the front entrance, a car blocking the intersection to the generator outhouse, another on its way and other cars and men deployed in adjoining streets. I think it's under control, sir."

"Balls. What are you going to do when they blast their way out? Organise a truncheon charge? With respect, inspector, it's best discussed when we're down there. Have they made their demands yet?" When Erskin told him there was a prolonged silence, then: "All right. We're on our way."

The biggest blow was to his pride, to have matters arbitrarily taken out of his hands by someone outside the division. The procedure on crime had been streamlined along with the rest; niceties and invitations were archaic but they didn't have to trample over him in order to get their way.

Inspector Erskin hooked up the microphone and walked to the intersection. From the corner he could see the two police cars with two-men crews on each corner of the dead end. He walked briskly down to the nearest pair.

"Any trouble?"

"No, sir."

"Any sign of him?"

"Not that we've seen. You can see where he's broken the slats to peer out."

"I'll have a word with him."

The two policemen looked at him as if he'd gone mad. But Inspector Erskin did not notice; his gaze was focused on the brick building at the end of the dead end.

The senior man made an effort to stop him. "He's a killer, sir."

The inspector eyed him icily. "How do you know?"

"Well, he's armed, sir." They did not even know that the man had already threatened the hospital engineer and Erskin had no intention of telling them. "Has he seen you?" asked the inspector.

"We've shown ourselves and he can't miss the cars."

Erskin nodded. He started to walk towards the outhouse. The senior policeman looked uncomfortably at his younger comrade and called softly after the inspector: "There's no need to do that, sir. We're not supposed to engage armed men if we're unarmed." As if Erskin didn't know.

Erskin didn't turn round but he called back loudly enough for the others to hear: "Let's see what we can do with this one. Then we'll decide on the others." He could see the gap in the slats quite clearly. After a few paces he thought he could see a gun barrel poking through. Fatigue suddenly swept him and he realised that what he was doing was bloody foolish; yet it might work if he handled it carefully. Fear was creeping up but he could control fear, postpone it. Anyway, he'd gone too far to turn back. The time to hesitate was before he started. Four constables were watching his progress; he couldn't lose face now. Suddenly, inexplicably, he no longer cared what happened, he even began to hope for the worst. At that moment he realised just how near to a breakdown he had come.

* * *

Stan Beatty loosened his tie and undid the top button of his shirt. With the generators running it was getting hot and musty, an oily smell slowly filling the low-roofed building. Well, it was better than being frozen stiff. He peered out through the broken slats, carefully scrutinising the two rows of cars lining the short street.

Waiting was the worst. He had to keep on his toes and he couldn't know what was happening. Once they were out there he'd know how he stood, he'd be keyed up, he'd develop what he called high-crisis vision. And strangely he would enjoy it, particularly with such a high prize. Unaware that Barret was dead he still thought of his share as being two hundred thousands pounds. Nearly half a million bucks. For that was where he would head: the United States. He would get back in the game he started in Belfast.

Beatty knew Allbright was an old army man and he'd sometimes sensed his contempt. What Allbright didn't know and was not going to be told was *why* Beatty had deserted the army. He was no coward; his presence here confirmed it. Allbright couldn't cope down here as he would. It was just that he believed in being paid the money for the job; the return should be commensurate with the risk, like now. It was an attitude of mind that had been slowly festering from his youth and had burst in one stark second when a colleague had been shot through the throat as he stood talking to him in a Belfast street. The soldier, all of eighteen, died in a gurgling whimper at his feet as Beatty had whipped round with his automatic rifle to find nothing but blank faces and empty windows.

He gained no moral lesson from the incident, but he decided there and then that there had to be more in it for him. It could have been *his* throat. He had no feelings for the issues involved. For a while he stayed in the army and began to deal in the burgeoning drug traffic. He deserted when he sniffed the first whiff of the Special Intelligence Service.

He went to Sweden to join American deserters from Vietnam. He had taken money with him and after a few confusing weeks felt his way around and made the necessary contacts to start from where he'd left off in Belfast. And he began to make money again, quite a lot of it. He did well for three months before the Swedish Police almost took him by surprise. But not quite. He fled to his native London. Of the many villains he met there, not all connected with drug trafficking, one was Allbright.

They did not get on together from the outset, but their paths crossed from time to time in pubs and clubs frequented by their own kind. Beatty doubted Allbright's capacity to make real money in spite of his international reputation as one of the great bullion raiders; that had been a long time ago. And Allbright had been caught and *he* was still free. Moreover, from what he'd heard Allbright had damn all to come back to when he'd been released on parole. So what had he done with it? There had been no likelihood of them ever doing a job together. Their styles were different: Allbright was old-fashioned, guile would never be his metier.

And yet here they were, relying on each other because they had to and because each had something complementary to offer on this particular caper. Among other things Beatty had to contribute was his marksmanship. As a private soldier he had never carried a pistol but he could outshoot any officer who did. It was one of those things, a talent he was born with.

He could make a four-inch group at fifty yards with a pistol. And that was shooting by any standards.

A police car drew across the opening and Beatty stiffened. Two coppers climbed out and looked down towards him. He noticed that they stood on the far side of the car. Even so he could have taken them. They moved cautiously and disappeared behind the building line. He waited, the Browning in his hand. Occasionally one of them peeped round the corner and he waggled the gun, but he wasn't sure if they'd seen it.

The Browning pistol was heavy, forty ounces, but it held thirteen rounds and it had a high penetration. And he liked it, he'd never cared for lighter weapons. He let it hang loose on his lowered hand. He reported the police arrival to Shaw and continued to wait, keyed up and ready. Five minutes later a second police car arrived with a further two men. He watched the four coppers get together and was strongly tempted to take a shot. Then they played musical chairs with the two cars until they finished up nose to nose across the mouth of the dead end. The vehicles very effectively closed the road to any car trying to get in or out. It didn't worry him; any bloody fool could block a road. But what sort of a man was it who could get out regardless?

The next time he saw the two policemen on his right they had been joined by another, a taller man. Beatty could judge that the new arrival was of higher rank by the way the others approached him. Then, incredibly, the tall one was walking slowly towards him. He couldn't believe his eyes. He positioned himself and raised the pistol, coldly debating where to hit him.

4

DET. CHIEF SUPERINTENDENT ALLUN EVANS of Special Branch was worried sick. He recognised the creeping cold in the pit of his guts only too well. The first flash of the red alert and the subsequent failure to raise the bodyguards had started the agony. With his dark hair and brows, almost chubby face and lively brown eyes, his physical appearance obscured the pessimist inside.

Life in Special Branch was difficult enough. There were some who called them the Political Police, others the Secret Police. The fact remained that the bodyguards had been placed there jointly by Special Branch and the U.S. Secret Service.

While Evans worried he worked frantically. He was slowly going mad because the switchboard girl couldn't raise the bloody hospital; the lines were jammed. He had already despatched two cars, of course, and had advised the Guv'nor. But he ought to warn the Americans. He'd like to know more first, though. Panic wasn't the answer. He didn't want egg smeared all over his face. A few minutes should do it. He'd wait, just a little. Meanwhile he harangued the telephone operator to pull her bloody finger out and keep dialling until she got through. When he'd reduced her to tears he was immediately sorry, pouring out a soothing balm of words that were still influenced by traces of native lilt. He then asked to be connected with Commander Jack Gifford, Head of the Serious Crime Squad.

* * *

The first two Special Branch men to arrive were Naylor and Smith and they sensibly decided to wait for the others. Meanwhile they saw the uniformed police stationed at the entrance and approached one of them. The senior plain-clothed man flashed his warrant card.

"What's on?"

"Some armed idiots upstairs."

"Where upstairs?"

"Private wing, I believe. You'll have to ask the inspector."

"Where's he?"

"I think he went round the corner. I believe they're holding the generator as well."

"He in charge? An inspector?"

"They caught us with our pants down, but it'll be under control. What's it with Special Branch?"

The constable didn't get a reply. Naylor flashed his radio and relayed the position back to H.Q. He was instructed to assess the position, no more. It was some minutes before the second car arrived and immediately the four men had a brief conference in the hospital hall where movement was still ostensibly normal. They split up into their original pairs and went to the lifts that McQueen and Barret had taken earlier, unaware that they were only just back in operation.

When the first pair stepped on to the landing the double swing doors to the private wing were above them at the head of a short flight of stone stairs. Both men were experienced officers and were armed. They had been quickly briefed before leaving the Yard and were now able to make their own assessment of where to take up positions. Of equal rank, they looked at each other quizzically. Naylor, the livelier of the two, grinned. He pulled out his gun and backed to the wall while Smith did the same opposite.

After a mute instruction to Smith, Naylor went silently up the stairs crabwise. When he reached the small landing outside the doors he stopped. The windows had been sprayed but he located the customary thumb hole. If he looked through he would have to go right up to the doors. His head might throw a shadow on the glass. He would have to move like a ghost. Very carefully he put his gun away; it would hamper his movements. He glanced down the stairs where Smith was watching him closely.

Naylor waited, wondering what he should do. He could hear faint voices and some movement. It would be easy to believe there were no armed men there at all. Very slowly he prostrated himself on the cold floor and slid forward until his face was close to the wood. When he tried to peer through the gap between the doors he could see nothing. The doors were too thick, the gap too narrow. What he did notice was the black strip of the retaining bar higher up.

The risk had to be taken. Naylor climbed to his knees, feeling the dull pain where his pistol had pressed against his ribs. He crawled over to the wall and rose with extreme care. The spyhole was only a couple of feet from his head but it might have been on the moon for all its remoteness. He licked his lips and edged forward. Keeping his body back and craning his neck he placed an eye near to the hole.

At once he saw a bearded man sitting on a chair with a Sterling machinegun across his knees. His left arm was in a sling; new bandages. So he had been wounded up here. He no longer had to worry about what had happened to his colleagues; part of one of their radios protruded from a grip and he guessed that their pistols would also be in there. The man had hair covering his head and face; a bruiser's nose; a bruiser's posture, hunched, wary, eyes peering out under heavy brows; they swept up to the spyhole as Naylor watched.

Naylor fought the instinctive urge to draw back. The man was still peering up at him but he couldn't be sure if he'd been seen. Then the Sterling swept round with bewildering speed and Naylor flung himself back propelled by fear and his reflexes. The burst of gunfire shattered the door where he had been standing, splinters flying out. Even as he fell he was hypnotised by the deadly viciousness of it. He knew he was hit; his side was suddenly burning. The bullet increased his impetus as he crashed down the stairs head first, the sound of firing still filling his head. When he hit the landing he almost blacked out. Then Smith grabbed his collar and unceremoniously pulled him round the corner until he was squatting on the lower flight of stairs.

Now half-unconscious Naylor wasn't sure he wanted to make the effort to find out the worst. Pain pumped through his body and there was an iron fist in his side. He could only move one arm, the other was agonising.

"Come on, you stupid bugger, make an effort for Christ's sake."

Vast sympathy from Smithy who was slapping his face

both sides; if he didn't stop he'd land one on Smithy. But he realised they might still be in danger and made an effort to rise. He nearly passed out again with the pain in his arm. Suddenly Smithy was more considerate. "Put your left arm round my shoulder. Come on, Jim. We must move." Smith helped Naylor down to the next landing and rang for the lift as two policemen rushed up the stairs to help. Naylor leaned back against the wall, felt his legs going but managed to hold on with Smith's help. Unaccountably, he suddenly wanted to laugh; the pain was making him light-headed. "What's the damage, Smithy?"

Smith took stock, unable to miss the big red patch spreading under Naylor's jacket and the awkwardly dangling arm. "You've stopped one in the ribs and you've broken your arm falling down the stairs."

"That all?" God, it hurt to talk.

The lift arrived and they helped Naylor in. Smith told the police to stay on observation and turned to Naylor. "You jam-strangling bugger; you always were lucky. Hold on. That's it." The door closed.

"Lucky? Christ!" Naylor let his head loll back against the side of the lift. Smith was smiling at him.

"The only thing that's better than being wounded in a hospital is being shot dead in a morgue. And you've already had your sick leave."

Naylor groaned with pain, and then grinned. Smithy was pulling out his radio with his free hand and checking in. Then Naylor felt sick again as he remembered.

"I think the others are dead." He caught a glimpse of Smithy's changing expression just before he passed out.

* * *

At the second set of doors the other two officers had immediately spotted the bullet holes above the glass and guessed the worst. Their approach was wisely circumspect. When the shots rang out they discreetly retreated without loss of nerve or face. There would have to be another way.

* * *

When McQueen fired without warning even Shaw and Allbright were startled. Shaw's reaction was immediately to grab the phone, and Allbright's to check his own doors. He went to the spyhole and was just in time to see a figure disappear down the stairs.

Shaw was livid. "Where's the inspector? *You mean there's no policeman there?* Then *get* the bloody sergeant from the hall."

When the sergeant came on Shaw said, "I warned you not to have anyone on these landings. We've probably killed one of them. Once more, just once more, and we knock off the first patient." He should already have done it. He had said to the professor; never issue an empty threat.

The sergeant, nonplussed, was annoyed that the inspector wasn't there. "Look," he snarled, "I know the orders that went out. They couldn't've been our men."

Shaw was suddenly cautious, aware of the ring of truth in the sergeant's tone.

"Just get the word around, that's all." Shaw hung up and went to speak to Allbright. The exchange let him off the hook so far as the threat was concerned. If they were caught they'd get life, whether they killed any patients or not. But he wasn't a cold killer. None of them were, apart from Beatty, yet everything would collapse if they showed weakness. And he already had. It mustn't happen again. Fortunately McQueen hadn't hesitated.

* * *

The little group in the Sister's office was becoming increasingly shaken by the sudden outbursts of gunfire. It reminded them of the danger to the patients and themselves. But this wasn't all that worried them. There was a much graver issue that must surely emerge, unless they had luck; lots of it.

Jean Sandingham was still worrying about the gun Dr. Grann had taken. Her immediate fear had been for *his* safety, a fact she now quietly considered as she sat there. After a few moments she remembered her first job, and reached for the file of charts. The stocky man wheeled round to see what she was doing. She tried to smile. "Work does have to go on." Her voice was a shade unsteady.

Ginger Shaw said, "Get some chairs for us."

Jean Sandingham despatched the nurses and sifted through the temperature and pulse charts. She pulled out a blank, filled it in, aware that both Professor Bowyer and Dr. Grann were watching her but much more concerned by the stocky man who was not. She carefully copied the graphs from one of the other charts and slipped it in with the rest, removing the one she had copied and dropping it on to her lap. The process of tearing it up was a slow one and had to be done noiselessly. While she was doing it the stocky man joined the taller one at the end of the ward. She slipped the torn pieces into the waste bin.

Ginger Shaw watched the group obliquely as he spoke to Allbright. He was certain there was something afoot, particularly with the two doctors. He didn't know what, but something in their faces, a suspicion of occasional uneasiness perhaps, flitted from one to the other almost as a method of communication. It was natural for them to be nervous, afraid—who wouldn't be, with four dead in the empty V.I.P.'s room and three Sterlings pointing at them? But in some indefinable way it wasn't the sort of fear he expected; it was as if something else was on their minds that erased fear they felt for themselves. It was obvious to him that the American was worried about the Sister. She was cool and a cracker but he was a fool.

Allbright said, "You reckon it'll settle down now?"

Shaw looked through the spyhole. "I should think so. They won't try that again too soon."

"It's going to work, boy. I can feel it. It's turned right for us."

Shaw had the same feeling. The unexpected earlier difficulties were tailing off. It had quietened enough for them to make their last security check. He took over Allbright's position and Allbright, allowing his Sterling to hang loose in his hand, moved towards the room with the three male patients.

Behind the desk in the Sister's office Ed Grann and Professor Bowyer exchanged worried glances. The worst was happening; perhaps the inevitable. An examination of the patients' rooms may not have seemed top priority to the men, but sooner or later it would have been necessary, they all knew it. Their only consolation was that Shaw had moved to the end of the ward and could not easily see how tense they were. Ed Grann placed his hand on Jean Sandingham's shoulder and neither he nor the girl seemed aware of the pressure of his fingers. They could only wait. It all depended on Allbright.

* * *

Det. Chief Superintendent Allun Evans had to hold on the line. Apparently Commander Gifford had just left his office and someone had chased off to stop him. The Superintendent, resigned to a day of blocked telephone calls, waited impatiently. A sergeant came back on the line and told him that something big had blown up, and his guv'nor was already in his car.

"Then bloody well stop him." Evans jumped up behind his desk and stood towering over it. "This is of the utmost urgency. It'll take no more than a minute. Tell him I'm on my way down." He slammed down the phone and left his office. He took the lift down two floors, and walked the long corridor to the offices of the Serious Crime Squad. He preferred the old Scotland Yard; it had been tight on space and rambling but it had character. Anyway, they were already tight on space in this gin palace. He waited in Gifford's empty office wondering if the sergeant had missed him. Dammit, they had only to get on the radio to stop him.

Commander Gifford came in breathlessly and annoyed. "It had better be good, Taff, something big's blown up. Assistant Commissioner Roberts is waiting in the car."

"Whatever it is I can cap it, boyo. But I hope to God I'm wrong. Have you had anything through about the Queen Mary Hospital in Queen Square?"

Gifford was surprised. "We're going there now. A mobile's on its way. How did you know?"

The telephone rang before Evans could reply. Gifford strode over, lifted it and spoke curtly. "Put all calls through to Chief Inspector . . . Oh . . ." He held out the receiver to Evans. "For you."

Evans took it, listened and lost colour. He put it down slowly. "One of my men has reported in. E Division are down there and the private wing is being held by armed men."

"I know that. Why do you think the Senior Crime Squad are involved?" Gifford was irritated, aware of the loss of valuable time. At the same time Evans wasn't a man to panic, but he was shaken and that took one hell of a lot of doing. "What is it, Taff? Are Special Branch involved too?"

Evans ran thick fingers through his hair. "We are. I'll need clearance to tell you but it's worse than you think. You'll need more than a bloody mobile, boyo. Fill me in."

"Let's do it down at the car. The A.C.'ll do his nut if he waits any longer."

"The A.C. *is* doing his nut. Hello, Taff. What are Special Branch doing here?" The tall soldierly figure of Assistant Commissioner Roberts slipped quietly into the rom. Piercing grey eyes fastened on Evans.

"Hello, sir. Trouble. There's a V.I.P. in the private wing of the Queen Mary."

"Christ! I thought it was bad enough. Are we allowed to know who he is?"

"Not at the moment, it's very top level. I'll see if I can get clearance. Right now it's probably better if the information is restricted. This raid will be what it's all about so the name will come out anyway."

"I think you're wrong." Gifford, still itchy for action, held up his hand and went to his phone. "Extension seven three. Ted? The mobile should be there by now. The firearms squad is being formed by Superintendent McDonald. Initially I want two armed men at each lift and stairs on the ground and fifth floors. And don't forget the fire-escapes. We'll send out the rest when we arrive." He put down the phone and turned to Evans. "Is your V.I.P. Lord Driver?"

"Lord Driver? The multi-millionaire? Mine's a much bigger fish."

"The demand is for one million pounds in twenties to be delivered by five this evening or they'll kill Lord Driver. How does that fit in with your problem?"

Evans' first reaction was relief at his good fortune. But it couldn't last, he had to assume the worst. His feelings crossed his face.

"So they don't know?" suggested A.C. Roberts quietly.

"They can't do, sir. Not yet."

"Is it inevitable that they find out?"

"I must take that view."

Gifford said evenly, "Your V.I.P. must be foreign Royalty or a top politician or you and Special Branch wouldn't be involved. The inspector first on the scene told me on the phone that the chief villain had told him there were four dead up there. It might be bluff, although plenty of people had heard shots, or, I suppose they could have fired into the ceiling to frighten people. If *there are* four dead, Taff, you might have some ideas."

If Evans had been pale before he now lost all colour. He stood hunched in front of the others, one hand unconsciously searching for the desk to steady himself. Whatever his years in the force, however experienced he might be, the sudden prospect of what had happened rocked him. "Three of those men were probably mine." Stunned as he was, he still covered the fact that two of them were Americans.

"Good God!" A.C. Roberts realised at once just how top level the V.I.P. must be to warrant three armed guards, in a hospital of all places. Coupled with this revelation was the terrible seriousness of the deaths of three policemen, whatever their branch of the force.

"It's difficult to believe they don't know," said Evans. "They must have wondered about the reception committee."

Gifford turned to Evans as he headed for the door. "This will have to come under the Serious Crime Squad, Taff, whoever your man is. You coming with us?"

Evans shook his head. "No, sir. I'll join you down there. Right now I've got to tell certain people and they'll want my head for a football. I don't suppose one of you would like to make those calls for me?"

They smiled in sympathy. They reached the door as the

telephone rang again. Gifford shouted, "Leave it, they know where to put it through." But as Evans was nearest he reached out instinctively, unable to resist the possibility of bad news. Was it ever good? And he was right. He shrugged grimly. "For what it's worth I can confirm your report. Young Naylor, one of my boys, has just been shot. Fortunately not fatally, but bad enough. They've got the place sewn up tight; the windows are sprayed and it's virtually impossible to see in. As a short-term measure you can use the remaining three armed men I still have down there."

"I'm sorry about your men, Taff. Really sorry. We'll get the bastards, don't worry." Jack Gifford gave a sombre nod of assurance and then raced towards the lift with the Assistant Commissioner. Evans left the room more slowly, reluctant to do what he must do but knowing there was no escape. Morosely he went back to his office and sat behind his desk, glad of the privacy. Three dead men and another seriously wounded. It was all right for Gifford to promise him justice, and it couldn't be in more capable hands, but at the moment that was neither here nor there. He had to postpone the terrible pains of revenge over his men, young men, much younger than he; two of them married with kids. He would have to face their wives. These were issues he had to postpone and it made him feel a bastard, but his superiors wouldn't be interested in his feelings. They would have only one thing in mind; there would be absolute hell to pay if anything happened to the V.I.P., the repercussions would be world wide. He was sitting on a keg with a quick fuse.

Disconsolately he picked up the phone. Part of the job was facing the kicks, though he could recall nothing so serious as this; nothing touching it. "Get me the American Embassy." And when they were on, softly, "Extension one, two, double three. Evans." When the extension was answered he said sadly, "Code name Woodcutter Emergency."

*   *   *

Art Caplan still clutched the receiver after he'd put it down. His hand trembled, his face was white and he was slowly chewing his lower lip. His years in the United States

Secret Service had produced almost every kind of emergency, but never one like this. He ran nervous fingers over a brown, almost bald head and stared into space with troubled eyes. He flicked the intercom switch. "Tell the Ambassador I must see him immediately. Operation Woodcutter's blown a fuse."

Russell Vance was already agitated when Art Caplan entered his office. The lanky security man wasted no time in coming to the point. "Evans of Special Branch has just been on, there's trouble at the Queen Mary. The private wing's held by a bunch of gangsters and they've taken the generator room over. They say they want ransom for a guy called Lord Driver. But it won't end there, sir."

"No it won't." Vance was standing behind his desk, shock clearly evident on the heavy face. "We'll never have that kind've luck. Goddam!" He suddenly struck the desk. "Do the police know who's involved?"

"Special Branch do. They're playing it close, but they've advised a guy called Gifford, who's chief of their Serious Crime Squad, that we have a top V.I.P. in there. They haven't named him."

"It mustn't leak out. There's going to be hell to pay over this." He glanced at his watch. "Almost seven a.m. Washington time." He stared bleakly at Caplan. "I must ring the President." He reached for the phone. "He's not going to like this on top of everything else."

Caplan considered it the understatement of the year. As if aware of his inadequacy, the Ambassador added: "Make sure they put their very best men on to it. Get down there and keep an eye on things. Keep me posted."

Caplan nodded, "Okay."

The Ambassador gripped the phone as if it was a lifeline. His eyes searched Caplan's in a last, desperate effort to avoid his course of action but there was nothing else he could do. Very quietly he said, "Get me the President. Top priority."

Caplan left the Ambassador to his misery, glad to pass on the enormous responsibility.

* * *

Inspector Erskin saw the gun muzzle, hesitated fractionally, then forced himself to continue another few paces. A voice came through the slats as if the gun itself had spoken.

"That's far enough, daddio, or they'll measure you for a box."

Erskin halted, his nape prickling. There had been no panic in the voice, no fear. The melodramatic cant had been uttered from someone who lived with that kind of expression. Erskin realised that he was not up against the usual hothead, not the type who needed a gun for reassurance like a baby needs its mother's breast. This one was for real.

"What's your problem, son? Why don't you come out and talk about it? I'm not armed."

In the generator room Beatty couldn't believe his ears. The stupid old bugger was really asking for one. He yelled, "I bet you used to go round the beat bashing kids' heads in. A belt round the ears and send 'em home, eh! Grow up, copper. You can't send me home to momma, I never had one. Now piss off."

Erskin stood his ground and kept his voice level. "How far do you think you'll get with this? The whole area is surrounded. Give up now before things get out of hand. Come on, at least talk it over."

It was pathetic. Two coppers at each corner and this old hasbeen patting him on the head and giving him a lump of sugar. Still, it passed the time. He'd give the poor old sod another minute or two.

"What've you got to lose? You've got the gun. Just talk it over before things get really out of hand."

"Copper, I won't tell you again. If you want to draw this week's old age pension get moving now."

"Come on, laddie. Don't be foolish. You can't take on the whole police force. Now come on out."

Laddie! Beatty bristled, itching to squeeze the trigger. The patronising bastard. Then luck favoured Erskin and Beatty saw the funny side of it. "Copper, I can shift you now and I could've got rid of those four monkeys up the end as soon as they arrived. Now be a good feller and save your life."

"You can't shoot us all. Be sensible."

"Want to bet?" The old fool must be as thick as a plank. "Now listen to me. I'm staying here as long as I want. Any of you step out of line and I'll switch off the generator. You know what that means? It means that people in that hospital are going to die because you balled it up. So don't make me do it. Any of you."

Erskin had every excuse to leave. At first he had been convinced that he could handle it, talk the man down. Then he had shown his men how to face an armed man and retain his dignity; that he had certainly done. All this was against police procedure and could be justified only if successful. And it had failed. He had known it would as soon as the man had spoken. But no one had really taught him to retreat once entrenched. He'd try just one more tack, a different approach.

"Feeling brave, are you? Unarmed men and sick people? That your mark?"

The single shot took him in the stomach and he collapsed as if his legs had been whipped from under him. He swore as he hit the ground, aware that the pain in his guts was cauterising the one already there. His cap fell off and he thought Christ, what a mess.

The four policemen heard the shot and, after signalling, one from each corner rushed down, using the double line of cars for cover. There came the moment when they had to decide whether to rush into the open for the writhing and groaning inspector.

Beatty enjoyed the scene, aware of the policemen's fears but unwilling to put their minds at rest. They could find out the hard way, the bastards. When they finally rushed out he was sorely tempted to fire but he might yet need all his ammunition during the hours ahead. They pulled back the old codger unceremoniously and he was glad about that; he'd asked for it. When they were behind the cover of the cars he shouted, "I could've let him have it between the eyes, so get the message. You want his cap?" He couldn't resist it. It was an opportunity to show them they were up against a crack shot. He fired and the cap went towards the line of cars sheltering them.

The two policemen carried Inspector Erskin awkwardly, bent as they were to keep below the line of car roofs. He lay drooped between them, holding his stomach with clasped hands, his head shaking from side to side.

5

THE HONOURABLE MARK DRIVER sat in his office and tried to concentrate. With disaster staring him in the face it was difficult. The next five days would decide his destiny, would make a difference of almost five million pounds, which represented sixty per cent of the existing estate duty. God, the old man had been wealthy in his day. The fool. His liabilities were enormous, they would take months, perhaps years to sort out so confused were his affairs.

But the extra five million should be safe. He'd need every penny, and on the strength of that and the balance of the estate he should be able to raise the rest. Enough to squeeze through his difficulties. The secret was how to survive the next few days.

He saw money as his right; he had been born into a vast but depleting fortune, one of the wealthiest families in the country. But the inheritance of wealth wasn't necessarily accompanied by the ability to handle it, as he'd discovered; he would never admit it. He was young and arrogant and entirely self-centred. He had no respect for a fine-looking mother who was far too soft for him to take it all seriously. And he had only contempt for a father who had messed up his life and handled his affairs with unbelievable naïveté; nor did he see any parallel between his father and himself.

Mark Driver strummed his desk, unable to work and unable to return home to face the questioning eyes of his troubled wife; nor could he go down to the family seat at Panbury to watch the incredible innocence of his mother. He rang for his secretary. For sanity's sake he must occupy his mind.

*   *   *

Allbright worked quietly and quickly. He entered the first room to find two blacks, one of them with a beard, and one white. They all looked seedy and they were afraid. Bed is not the best place to feel brave.

"Just behave yourselves and you'll come through all right." He rattled the Sterling to follow up the assurance with a threat.

"If you need a nurse, ring in the ordinary way." He didn't want involvement with any of them, it could make it difficult later. He crossed to the windows and opened one. Even six floors up this was the vulnerable, unprotected flank. It had been agreed from the outset that this part of the operation should be in his hands. He was the most experienced, he knew what to look for.

He could see across the square. The falling leaves spiralled down casually from the trees as if they knew they were early and were slightly embarrassed by it. The rectangle of grass behind the railings looked wet and speckled with dead leaves that would eventually hide the green completely. The cloud mass was still low, grey and sluggish, its belly drooping.

By leaning out he could see the hospital entrance and the police car directly below him. Another was at the corner of the square and he suspected that the other two corners, obscured by trees, were also blocked. As he watched, a big, ugly vehicle turned into the square and stopped just beyond the intersection to his left. A police mobile headquarters. Almost certainly that meant the Yard. And when it meant the Yard it also meant the various sections of the police they considered necessary; the Serious Crime Squad and a Firearms Squad. They'd all be crawling out like maggots from cheese. Coppers. Things were moving; it was no more than he expected. He closed the window, gave the patients a last look of warning and went next door.

The face on the pillow was tantalisingly familiar, yet unfamiliar, a contradiction Allbright explained to himself as something missing like a moustache or beard. Whatever it was made the difference, for he couldn't place it. The man was asleep on his back. As the gunfire had clearly not roused him, he must be drugged or seriously ill. Allbright took a second look without finding an answer, examined the windows, opened one and looked out, closed it and left the room. Across the corridor he intercepted intent stares from the two doctors. They were worried. So would he be in their shoes.

Allbright did not intend to leave the hospital empty-handed, whatever Shaw might want to do. As he went to the next room he was finding the light rubber gloves warm. It was going to be a long time before air cooled his hands.

The four bodies were piled neatly—if ever the loose-limbed puppetry of the recent dead could be called neat. Barret was on top, face upwards. That made it a quarter of a million each. The cold-bloodedness of his reflection caught Allbright unawares. But *he* might have been lying there instead and he wouldn't have thought the worst of Barret for a similar reaction. He opened the window, looked out; another police car was drawing up behind the mobile. When he stepped back his foot caught Barret and one of the dead man's arms flopped down. He bent to put it back across the chest, then decided to leave it there; what difference did it make? He stepped back, careful not to tread on the outstretched hand.

The next room contained Lord Driver; the machine was humming quietly. Allbright stared down, saw how close to death the man was and thought of his own wife. She must have looked like that but he'd never been allowed to find out. When he remembered that, everything else became easier.

He checked the rest of the rooms, opening the windows and looking out each time, paying attention to ledges, and water drainage pipes. The fifth room contained an attractive, early-middle-aged woman cocooned in an expensive blue nightdress, who looked as if she might be an actress; she had applied her make-up to give herself an over-pale face. Her delicate hands fluttered helplessly when Allbright approached her bed but not all her expression was fear; her widened, beautiful eyes engulfed him. It was clear that he did not repulse her.

You randy old bag, reflected Allbright. In hospital too. He gave her a lecherous grin and was amused when it didn't dismay her. He couldn't know that her sex life was finished, that all that remained to her was a half useless body and bravado.

There was a sedated youth in the last single room; he couldn't have been more than eighteen and by the look of him Allbright wondered if he would ever reach his twenty-first. You never knew, luck might swing his way. As he went from room to room he had to admit that Shaw hadn't been fooling with the telephone wires; no calls would be made from these rooms.

The three-bedded ladies' room was much the biggest and brightest. A young, emaciated girl with bright red painted toenails fringing open-toed sandals lounged in one of the armchairs. Her housecoat was rich with embroidery and her over-exposed legs were as thin as twigs. The other two women were elderly, one obviously too ill to care much about what was happening—unless the firing had worsened her condition to a point of near-collapse. The other was superbly groomed, splendidly regal, sitting straight-backed with pillows to support her, grey hair tinted with a blue wash.

"It must make you feel very brave, young man, terrorising helpless, sick people. Is that all you're fit for?" Her disdain was cutting but it was wasted on him.

Allbright was not thick-skinned. The old girl was probably right; she had guts and poise and he liked her on sight. He gave her a crooked grin and said, "Shut up, duchess," and turned to the girl. "Back to bed," he ordered. "Everyone must stay in bed."

"The poor girl can hardly move. She needs help." The duchess again.

The girl was afraid of him yet she smiled. It was a gutsy

smile which concealed most of her terror and somehow conveyed courage and a sweetness of nature. Inexplicably it touched the hardened Allbright, who inwardly recoiled from its impact. He was suddenly aware of his crudeness. He thought she was blind, or partially anyway. She was still smiling bravely in his direction and was half out of the chair but he could see that her legs weren't going to hold her. Her jet-black hair was falling across her elfin face as she strained to lift herself from the chair.

The duchess was haranguing him again but Allbright hardly heard her. He saw the girl's pain, rammed the Sterling under one arm and hurried towards her. As she collapsed back into the chair he couldn't be sure whether she could no longer hold herself or whether she'd recoiled at his approach. "Don't worry, love. I won't hurt you." The lie unsettled him; he would kill her or anybody who tried to interfere with what they were doing. One rough hand gripped her arm and immediately he released his grip, afraid of breaking a bone. With his other hand he took one of hers. He'd never felt skin so soft, velvet, no—rose petals—softer even.

She was gripping his hand fiercely, whether from need or desperation, he couldn't decide. Close up her deep brown eyes were almost luminous, the edges to her widened pupils fuzzed, like a dog's. He guessed that her depleted strength was from the waist down. His effort at getting her back to bed was the most delicate he had ever performed. He felt clumsy, yet he knew he wasn't hurting her; there was no weight to her at all. As he laid her on the bed the Sterling slipped to the floor and he put one foot on the stock to keep it there. He pulled the sheets up around her frail body, hiding the pity he momentarily felt. He pushed a glass of orange juice on her bedside table nearer to her and turned away to the windows. While he searched the pavement below the ghost of her fragile face floated in front of him.

Allbright didn't like the girl seeing the transitory softness in him; he didn't want to mislead her; she had enough troubles and there could be more, worse even than she'd known. As he left the room he was aware of the duchess staring at him.

In the corridor he easily shook off his mood and gazed across at the office halfway down. They were all looking at him, fixed, like a waxed tableau. There was something unnatural about it.

Allbright walked slowly along the row of doors, all of which he had deliberately left open so that not only would it be easier to keep an eye on the patients but also the windows beyond them. He checked on his mates. McQueen was hunched on his chair in front of the open lift as if he was waiting for the bell to sound for the last of a ten-round bout. The Sterling was draped across his knees. Allbright was beginning to change his mind about McQueen; the London-born Scot may not open his mouth too often but, when Allbright considered it, he'd rather have McQueen with him than against him; look how sharply he had reacted to the copper at the door. McQueen wasn't going to fall asleep on the job even if he looked like it.

At the other end stood Ginger Shaw, Barret's Sterling crooked in his arm, too restless to sit on the chair at his side. Allbright had never met a man so determined, so completely single-minded. It was one of the things that had persuaded him to work with an amateur, something he would not normally consider.

He stopped outside room two and again studied the sleeping form; something stirred in him, a recollection. He walked over to Shaw.

"I think you ought to look at the bloke in two."

"Why? Is he dead?"

Allbright grinned. "None of them are. And they're all harmless except an old duchess down the end. I'd need a bloody steel helmet if she had a walking stick within range. Just take a quick look."

"I don't like leaving these doors after the last lot."

"It'll only take a second. I'll keep an eye on the doors."

The two men walked across to room two, Allbright hanging slightly back to satisfy Shaw that he was watching the exits. Shaw entered the room and Allbright leaned against the doorway. Shaw's reaction was immediate when he saw the figure in bed but he kept strict control over his facial muscles, something he had learned to do almost perfectly over the past few months; like Allbright, he noticed something missing but it had not deceived him, not for one moment. He did not think Allbright had spotted his alarm. "Well?"

"Well, Christ, look at him." Allbright was perplexed.

"I am looking at him."

"Doesn't he remind you of anyone?"

Shaw turned away from the bed. "What does it matter who he is? We're not here to collect autographs."

"You're dead right we're not." Allbright was annoyed at Shaw's indifference. Then he read more into it. Shaw was *too* casual. It was human nature to want to know who Allbright thought the man was. Shaw hadn't even asked him. "You're having me on, you bastard. You know damn fine who he is."

Shaw shook his head, not wanting complications. He kept his voice low so that those in the Sister's office couldn't hear him. "I don't know and I don't care. It can't make any difference to us."

"Can't it by God." Allbright strode into the room, rounded the bed and started ferreting in the side-table drawer. He gave a wicked grin of triumph when he found a pair of horn rimmed spectacles. Opening them he carefully held them over the eyes of the sleeping patient. "Now bloody well look." His fingers were trembling slightly, the spectacles wavering. "Imagine his eyes are open."

Shaw hedged. "I think I know who you mean: there is a similarity, I suppose."

"Don't try to con me, matey. And stop conning yourself. I know that this scheme is only *partly* for money so far as you're concerned. But whether you like it or not you're bent like the rest of us, so turn off the bloody switch that tells you you're not."

Shaw was shaken at the accusation. "I'm not trying to con you." But he knew he didn't sound convincing, that he couldn't leave it there. He'd have to take a chance. There was no chart at the foot of the bed; it must be in the Sister's office. He went to the door, forcing Allbright to step out with him, and he called across the corridor.

"Prof. What's the name of this patient?" It was a calculated risk but there was nothing else he could do. It was the Sister who answered.

"That's Mr. Singer."

"Singer? Let's have his card." It was the only way to keep Allbright quiet. Shaw stepped towards the office and Jean Sandingham handed him the temperature and pulse-rate graph. There was an almost comic silence from those in the office. Shaw was well aware that he had suddenly entered into an unlikely liaison with them and that they must know it. Shaw handed the card to Allbright. "It's a common enough name."

Allbright stared at the name on the card, feeling that in some way he was being duped. "They've made an alteration. They're not going to bring him in under his own name, not someone like that." The persisting seed of doubt restrained him from using the actual name. His certainty was not yet complete.

"Let's get back to the doors."

They walked there together, Allbright still holding the card, frustrated and angry. He did not like the feeling of being misled; it would be easy to falsify the card. Shaw did a check at the spyhole and then turned back to Allbright.

"Supposing you're right? What possible difference can it make to us?"

Allbright was astounded. "Now I know you're a bloody amateur. You know what's going to happen? The whole bloody police force is going to come down on us. Uncle Bill with all his sons and nephews. Christ! And they'll have the army out. The security will be so tight that it'll be like being inside a can without an opener."

"It's going to be like that anyway. We knew that when we took it on."

"It'll be far worse than we realised."

"If you're right it'll be better to give them the impression we don't know who he is. We just stick to the original plan. We don't want complications."

Allbright ran a hand over his face in exasperation. "We've already got 'em, cocker. The fuzz'll have to take the worst view. I know that bugger's face." He was straining to keep his voice down. He stared across the corridor. "Look at that bunch over there. Guilt written all over them. *They know*."

*   *   *

"The thickset guy knows," observed Ed Grann through almost closed lips.

"I'm inclined to agree." Professor Bowyer eased himself on his chair. "I have the feeling that he's trying to argue the big fellow out of recognising the patient."

"An interesting hypothesis. Why should he?"

"They're arguing about something. You disagree?"

"No, sir. I think you're absolutely right. I'm just curious about why he should want to back off from a situation he could use to his own advantage."

"It's puzzling me, too. Find the *real* motive why he's here and you'll have your answer."

Jean Sandingham said, "He *hates* Lord Driver. There must be a reason."

"Or hates his kind," suggested Ed Grann.

The professor looked up sharply at the younger man. "You have a reason for saying that."

"Just an impression. I don't think he's ever met Lord Driver. Would you agree, Jean?" Ed Grann did not miss the quick look of disapproval from the professor. They could be pretty starchy in these English hospitals. He would call the professor sir, because that's how he rated him; the man was a near genius and he reckoned himself to be lucky to be his houseman. But Jean was different.

Jean noticed the professor's glance. She was more concerned about the reaction from the two nurses than from the professor. Long after the American doctor had gone she was still likely to be here; she would miss him. He brought a touch of fresh air, something different to the daily routine of hospital life; he was a benevolent revolutionary, but a good doctor who was at least as interested in the patient as in the disease. She remembered the gun he carried and shivered. "I thought he was fascinated by Lord Driver. There was no recognition, no sign at all when he first saw him. Then his hate showed and it was quite frightening."

"Has anyone any ideas? Anything we can do?" asked the professor.

It brought them all to an uneasy silence. What could be done against three sub-machineguns in the hands of men only too willing to use them?

* * *

Ginger Shaw was still trying to pacify Allbright; he had calmed down a little, though he was still clearly dissatisfied. Shaw knew exactly what was in Allbright's mind and he did not know the remedy. He himself was here for one reason only.

Allbright said, "It doesn't alter the situation but it bloody well changes our demands."

Shaw froze. He'd been expecting it, dreading it.

"That would be stupid. Invite trouble."

Allbright swore. "Why? We're already in up to our necks. Let's cash in on it."

"We could only do that if you're right and you're the only one who thinks you are. For God's sake, you've seen people you've mistaken for someone else before. We all have. And the likeness isn't all that good." The same arguments, round and round. Allbright was like a dog with a bone, he wouldn't let go.

And then suddenly he seemed to, as if Shaw had finally hit the right key, raised sufficient doubt. Allbright shrugged unhappily, still annoyed but possibly now more so with himself. He flipped his hand in a helpless gesture and realised that he was still holding the medical chart. He looked at it again, and noticed the date of admission was missing. He went to the Sister's office and asked Jean Sandingham when Mr. Singer had been admitted.

She stared at him, trying desperately to recall what she had put on the card; it had all been done so quickly and under difficult circumstances. What date had she put down? "I really can't remember the date."

Allbright studied her shrewdly. "I don't want the date, lady. I want the day. How long has be been here?"

Jean Sandingham knew she was in a trap. She had set up

a false temperature and pulse graph for how many days? She tried to remember and knew that any answer was better than none. No one could help her, no one knew what she had written. "He came in last Wednesday, I think."

"You haven't got that many patients here that you don't know exactly."

"It's important only to the doctors. We just take them in and put them to bed. We don't keep the day in mind."

"But you'd enter the date even if you didn't remember it?"

Her heart sank. Had she forgotten to insert the date in her hurry? She had the strong sensation that Dr. Grann wanted to reassure her. At a time like this it was a silly intrusion; any intervention from any of them would be a complete give-away. "Of course I'd enter the date."

Allbright grinned widely. He waved the Sterling as if it was a toy and held up the card. "According to this he's been in for four days. That puts it back to last Friday."

"So, I'm wrong. I've no reason to recall the actual day."

"You're cool, lady, I'll give you that. And I like it. What's more I'd go along with you but you left out the bloody date as well."

There was no answer. To have left out the date *and* to forget the day of such a recent admission was most unlikely. Jean Sandingham instinctively knew that any excuse she attempted would point to her guilt. It was better to say little or nothing but the silence was unbearable and Allbright wanted her to sweat.

"I can't explain," she finally said lamely. "It's one of those things."

"*Two* of those things, lady. Hand over that bin."

"Bin?"

"Come on, the game's up. Hand the bloody thing over."

"He means the trash can." Ed Grann had never felt so useless. And yet he knew, as he suspected they all knew, that any interference could do more harm than good. There was no escape. He picked up the swivel-topped plastic bin to save Jean further anguish and passed it over.

Allbright knocked off its lid and emptied the contents on to the floor. Amongst the pile of screwed up paper, he saw what he wanted. Quickly he picked up the pieces, seizing on those that were really relevant and dropping the rest back on to the floor.

"So he came in today." He started to laugh, turned and waved the pieces at Shaw. "You damn well knew, didn't you?" But being proved right had restored his ego, left him good-humoured. He retained the three pieces of paper he wanted and told the nurses to clean up the rest. He was still smiling when he spoke again, looking slyly at Jean Sandingham.

"Not only pretty but a clever little bitch, too. I should knock your bloody head off. But you all know, don't you?" He glared at the two doctors. "Crafty bastards; those bodyguards weren't waiting for his arrival; *he was already here*." He sauntered up the ward towards a poker faced Shaw. "Look at these," he demanded. "Just you look at them."

Shaw didn't want to, he'd known the answers all along but he went through the motions and handed back the pieces of graph paper. "So you're right."

"You knew bloody well I was right."

"Have it your own way."

"We up the ante."

"Who's going to pay?"

"The bloody government; the Yanks. Let *them* sort it out between them. All we have to do is tell 'em to pay."

"How're you going to get it? We had problems enough sorting out the million. Isn't that enough for you?" It was true. They had first decided on demanding a million in one-pound non-sequenced notes, until they'd found out that it would weigh nearly nineteen hundredweight without any form of container.

"How much is enough? We'd be doubling our chances. There'll never be another opportunity like this, not in a lifetime. It's been handed to us on a plate."

"No," said Shaw abruptly. "It's inviting more trouble than we can handle. Instead of national we'll be worldwide headlines. Every bastard on earth will be looking for us. We'll never be able to enjoy the money, never get a chance."

"And I say yes. We've got time to work something out. We'd all be millionaires."

"How much were you thinking of asking for?"

Allbright had already considered, his brown eyes bright. "There's almost no limit with him but let's keep it reasonable. Let's say three million quid. With the other that gives us a tax-free million each." He started to grin.

Shaw realised he had his back to the wall but he couldn't see how to manoeuvre. It wasn't that Allbright was particularly greedy, but the professional in him couldn't resist a God-sent opportunity. It was like a poker player discarding a royal flush. If Shaw was a criminal he'd think the same but he didn't see himself as one. The righteousness of his cause was safely locked in his head, unassailable. In rare moments of clarity he knew that if he ever let the idea go he would fall apart. What Allbright was advocating was blatant crime against someone with whom he had no grudge. And with this man the dangers were very real; if not here at the hospital then certainly later. Yet, as Shaw considered quickly, he accepted that he would have to concede, at least ostensibly. His whole thought process became a series of self-justifying forays.

He said, "There are four of us. We can't consult Beatty over the air but at least we can ask McQueen. Hold on here and I'll have a word with him."

"No you don't, you crafty devil." Allbright sensed that things had swung his way. "We both know Beatty's answer without asking. You're able to talk McQueen out of it and then we're split. *I'll* talk to McQueen and give it to him straight so he can make up his own mind."

"So you don't trust me?" A last, futile effort.

"I trust you all along the line, Ginger boy, to get anything you set your mind to. But this ain't it. No hard feelings, mate. Anyway, we both agreed that we'd never be undercapitalised again." Allbright punched Shaw playfully on the arm. "This'll set us up."

He strode up the corridor to McQueen while a troubled Shaw checked on his spyhole. Shaw realised he had lost some of his authority, and yet to have given an unequivocal "no" could have led to Allbright taking over. He would have to play it as he saw it and keep his main objective in mind at all times.

Their present disguises were flimsy but adequate. Identification was always difficult; there were always variations of descriptions from witnesses. They had their wigs, cheek pads, nostril dilators. It had taken some time to get used to them. Allbright was wearing corsets to pull in his belly and Shaw had padded himself out, made himself look heavier. But if they went ahead with Allbright's idea they'd need facial surgery and that would lead to complications and new witnesses. Allbright was too carried away at present. Shaw reckoned he'd have to bide his time.

At the other end of the ward Allbright presented the case fairly to McQueen. The only influence he used was subconscious inflection; McQueen couldn't fail to miss his enthusiasm. And all McQueen could see was an extra three million pounds. That's what it was all about; always had been. Threatening the life of one man or a dozen was all the same to him. He nodded eagerly with an instant vision of beaches and women. It hadn't been boxing that sent him to hospital but women who had gradually depleted him until he was getting knocked around in the ring too much and had retired to save himself; he wouldn't have minded so much if he'd got more from the women but the only free gift they'd handed out had K.O.'d him.

With *that* much money *they'd* find him; good-lookers; the right kind. It wouldn't matter that they were after his money; he could afford it and they'd have to work for it. *They* wouldn't complain at his roughness because they'd know which side their bleeding bread was buttered. He'd always been sensitive to their harsh remarks even when he'd been paying for it. Now he'd be able to pay enough to keep a smile on their faces. It wouldn't matter that they were acting, as long as they gave a good performance he could call the tune.

"Okay!" he said. "I'm in."

Allbright slapped him on the shoulders and turned away.

"Just a minute." McQueen checked him, scratching his beard with the butt of the Sterling. "Who *is* this bugger who's worth so much?"

Allbright grinned. "He's worth a lot more, cocker, but we're making it easy for them." He watched McQueen's battered face, the slightly dulled eyes at the moment dreaming, and he laid it on thick, bowing slightly from the waist. "Why, my dear old mate, he's the Secretary of State for the United States of America."

6

ON THE WAY to the hospital Commander Jack Gifford sat beside Assistant Commissioner Roberts thinking about what might lie ahead. He knew that Roberts would leave the handling to him and his first task would be to cut through the inevitable early confusion, get complete control as soon as he could, and seal the hospital up tight. He wanted no interference, no red tape. His right-hand man would be Superintendent McDonald, who was already at the hospital forming a firearms squad, grabbing men from any division he could lay hands on.

Gifford smiled grimly as he thought of the tall spare Scot the lower ranks referred to as MacDracula. But Jock McDonald was far too good a shot to draw much blood from anyone. So would his men be. With the regular police force unarmed in Britain, the comparative few that carried guns were marksmen. As the police car scythed through the traffic with its siren howling and the flasher gyrating, Gifford wondered again about the V.I.P. in the private wing. One way or the other he would find out who he was either officially or unofficially; he had no intention of operating blind, whatever the politicians said.

Jack Gifford was not armed. But he *was* chief of the Serious Crime Squad, which dealt with all the big crimes; he was a tough, hardened copper who had one burning ambition in life, to catch as many villains as he could without bending the rules. It wasn't always easy; sometimes it was difficult to know when one crossed the line, as mixing with criminals was an essential part of detective work. But Gifford knew, always had. He had graduated from beat copper in London's dockland, through C.I.D. and Flying Squad to his present position. These days more than ever he realised the importance of going by the book; he overcame this clear disadvantage by a tremendous application to work, together with a formidable memory, a sense of anticipation that had bewildered many, and an ability to use the right man in the right job.

Delegation was a talent missing in many top-level men who imagined that nobody could handle the matter better than they. Jack Gifford suffered no such delusions; instead he drove his men hard. If he had a fault then that was it. Unmarried, he gave himself body and soul to his profession; he didn't want spare time and tended to think that everyone should be the same. Every so often the Assistant Commissioner would give him a nudge and he'd temporarily ease the reins, but he would soon revert back to type again. Fortunately his men thought the world of him and drove themselves into the ground for him. This was his saving grace—even if one or two of their marriages suffered. But even then he well knew how to put a sense of pride into the long-suffering wives and to hold things together. He looked exactly what he was, a dedicated, tough copper with bitter experience showing on his jaw-jutting face.

When the car pulled up behind the mobile close to the hospital, Gifford climbed out, his features quietly aggressive. The fringe of his close mat of greying hair was vaguely stirred by the beginning of a soft breeze that squeezed between the buildings. His eyes were cold and sharp and concentrated on the sixth floor of the hospital as he climbed from the car.

This was one case he could not delegate. He must hold all the strings, to know precisely what was happening and where. And he must gather them up quickly.

As the long frame of Superintendent McDonald raced

forward Gifford called out, "Hello, Jock. How many peashooters have you got?"

"A dozen. We need far more. I'd like two armed men at every lift and stairwell on every floor. I've got two on the roof; two each end of the private wing hallway between the fifth and sixth floors. Four are covering the ground floor and fire exits and the other two are keeping an eye on the generator. As more arrive I'll deploy them."

Gifford nodded quickly. "I'll take a look at the roof later. When you have more men get some down in the basement."

McDonald looked surprised but didn't argue.

Gifford said, "I'll bring you up to date once I've checked with the hospital management." He ran up the hospital steps. Inside the cheerful hall he located the plain-clothes men without difficulty and spotted a uniformed sergeant leaving the Secretary's office. He went up to him and produced his warrant card. The sergeant looked relieved.

"What's happening? Where's Inspector Erskin?"

"He's been shot, sir. Just before the mobile arrived."

"Good God! Dead?"

"No sir, but it's bad. In the stomach."

"Up on the sixth?"

"By the man in the generator house, sir."

"*You mean he tried to get in?*"

"Er—no, sir. He tried to talk to the man."

Gifford could see that the sergeant was trying to protect his superior. But he wouldn't criticise in front of the sergeant. The inspector had broken a cardinal rule. "Where is he now?"

"They've screened off part of one of the wards, sir. I'll take you."

The ward was on the first floor. A series of screens had been erected just inside the door. The two beds in the makeshift cubicle contained the Special Branch men, Naylor, and Inspector Erskin. Both had suspended drips and Naylor also had an arm in a sling. Neither looked too bright.

Gifford smiled with an effort. He was livid that two police officers had been shot but this was no time to show it. "I'm Gifford of the Serious Crime Squad. We're here to relieve you of your worries. How long have you been in here?"

"Just a few minutes, sir." Naylor, the younger and obviously the stronger smiled weakly. The inspector was deathly white, in a bad way.

"Is there anything you can tell me without distressing yourselves?"

"There's a character on the sixth, arm in a sling, beard, mass of hair like an ape." Naylor smiled ruefully. "And bloody quick reflexes. Looked like an ex-pug."

"If I send an identikit along do you think you can knock something up for us?"

"I can try, sir. It was largely profile." It was hurting him to speak.

"What's happening to you two?"

Inspector Erskin tried to speak but Naylor took the chore from him. "We're waiting to go to X-Ray. And I believe there's a surgeon on his way. They've been very good."

Gifford nodded. "Good luck to you both. If you want anything let me know through the nurse. I'll be in the mobile outside." He addressed Erskin specifically. "I know it's difficult for you but has the Driver family been contacted yet?"

Erskin's every word was an effort. "I asked the hospital Secretary to contact Lady Driver." The words were slow and horribly spaced out. "I've—been on my own." He managed a ghastly smile. "Got rid of my ulcer."

"I understand." Gifford was not a sentimental man although he was known to have shown moments of softness. He didn't like Erskin's greyness. Against his judgment he said, "What you did was a very brave act, inspector." He could have added "but stupid". He left them with a smile that lasted until they couldn't see him. Outside the ward a doctor and a nurse were waiting.

"What're their chances, doctor?"

"The young one's as strong as an ox. A nasty wound. Smashed ribs and we've yet to locate the bullet. But he'll survive and finish up back on duty. The older man is more serious. His wound is deep and his general condition is not good. Nor does he seem to be fighting it. Very much touch and go, I'm afraid."

Gifford ran down the stairs, sad and angry and very determined, the sergeant half a pace behind him. At the foot of the stairs Gifford stopped. "Have any of your lot tried to contact Mrs. Erskin?"

"There hasn't been a moment sir, the Chief Superintendent——"

"I know," Gifford cut in. "But apart from the unavoidable dispersal of your senior officers it seems to me to be one big balls-up. Have another shot at raising some of your brass. Mrs. Erskin ought to be told quickly. She should see him before the operation."

Gifford knocked discreetly on the Secretary's door and went in. There were four people inside who Gifford assumed to be hospital administration but he went straight to the man behind the desk. He had enough presence to cut the animated dialogue dead. He introduced himself and flashed the card, noticing that the telephone had been taken off its cradle. "You're having a rough time, sir."

The Secretary had not a hair out of place; he was young, extremely efficient, and, right now, overburdened with questions and problems from all parts of the hospital, not least of which was curiosity. His one concession to strain was a blue tie very slightly askew.

"It's not my metier, Mr. Gifford. At least the Electricity people are on their way. Will you be able to get those men out of the private wing and generator room?"

"It will be a long job, sir. Their deadline is five o'clock and I doubt that much will happen before then. All we can do, unless other developments make us change our mind, is to contain the situation; keep them there. But they're in a very strong position until they move. I wondered if you could provide a surveyor's plan of the hospital for us. It would be useful to know the general layout; particularly of the roof and the basement."

"I'll see what I can do."

Gifford gazed round at the other three standing figures, their faces turned to him, waiting, as if for some magic words of reassurance. He had none to offer. "Has the Driver family been contacted yet, sir? I believe it was left to you?"

The Secretary appeared nonplussed, then recovered quickly.

"There's been so much confusion—We have rung Cleats Hall but Lady Driver is out. She's expected back shortly. We left a message for her to ring back."

Gifford glanced at the phone off the hook and the Secretary explained, "The gunmen demanded that we leave it off, presumably so that they have immediate access; they'll flash if they want us."

"Forget about the Drivers, sir. We'll follow it up, if you'll give me the number. We have a mobile headquarters outside. Am I to understand that you're acting as runner if the villains call?"

"The sergeant went off to get someone to stand by the phone."

"One other thing, sir; you won't like it but it can't be helped. May we take over your office? We may have to negotiate with the gunmen over that phone and policemen will be coming and going and making it impossible for you to work."

The Secretary smiled ruefully. "Tactfully put, Commander. You mean I'll be in your way, that you'd prefer me not to know what's going on."

Gifford grinned apologetically. "It would make a convenient on the spot H.Q. while the routine work is done from the mobile."

The Secretary started to gather his papers. Gifford thanked him, nodded to the others who hadn't spoken, and left the office. A policeman was waiting outside the door.

"You the chap the sergeant nominated for the phone?"

"Yes, sir. I was waiting for you to come out."

"Right. Stand by the phone and don't leave it. When you hear it flashing, pick it up, listen, acknowledge, then tell them you're sending for me. I'll send another officer in as runner. Do you know who I am?"

"Yes, sir. The sergeant told me."

"Good. If I'm not in the mobile the Assistant Commissioner will be."

Gifford hurried across the hall. The Secretary shouldn't have been involved, he had more than enough of his own problems. On the steps outside he told the nearest uniformed man to stand by as runner to his colleague at the phone. He considered taking the uniformed police away from the entrance; they attracted too much attention to a critical situation. Then he realised that with the mobile, the squad cars and the increasing rate of activity, it would make no difference.

Gifford entered the mobile, said, "Hold on a minute, sir," to A.C. Roberts and turned to the operator on the panic frequency. "Contact the Panbury Police and ask them to locate Lady Driver quick. If they can't find her in half an hour tell them to let us know——" He then instructed a sergeant to take an identikit up to Naylor at once. He gave the A.C. the news about the two wounded men and checked with an inspector on how many of his own men were available.

The mobile was cramped. Two fixed benches ran down either side. At the end, back to back, sat two radio operators. One was on a panic or incident frequency which had been cleared of all calls except those pertaining to this particular crime. The other was on normal frequency. A sergeant with his jacket off sat at the far end of the nearside bench, an incident log book open on the table in front of him. Every single event connected with the case would be entered. His work might ease later but at the moment he was writing as fast as he could. A bank of six G.P.O. telephones was spread along the table waiting to be connected to the main telephone system by Post Office engineers already on their way. When the identikit was despatched Gifford squeezed himself on to the bench opposite the Assistant Commissioner.

Superintendent McDonald came in and without difficulty sat beside Gifford who was cramped on the bench. Gifford, anxious to get on, addressed the A.C.

"We have an unknown number of men armed with submachineguns holding the private wing on the sixth floor and threatening to kill Lord Driver unless they receive one million pounds by five this evening. We have their additional threat to kill patients if a policeman comes in sight. They have disrupted the electricity supply and one man only is believed to be holding the generator room so that the remaining power to the hospital is in their hands. We also know that an unnamed V.I.P. is in the private wing, as far as we know, at the moment without the gunmen knowing. Is there anything we know about these men apart from what we hope Naylor can supply through identikit?"

"The man in the generator room is a crack shot." McDonald's words were as sparse as his frame. He related his enquiries with the police who had rescued Inspector Erskin. "An exceptional shot by the sound of it. And judging by his voice they reckon him to be young and a Londoner." McDonald was rubbing his hands together though it was warm in the big van.

"We'll run a check with C.R.O. Young brilliant shot with London accent." Gifford gave the nod to the inspector who set it in operation. "But no sight of him?"

"No. I've had a look myself."

"Can you get your marksmen on it?" Gifford already guessed the answer but wanted it from the expert.

"It would be random shooting and we're answerable. There are also two grave risks; one, we hit a vital part of machinery and, two, he switches off the generator as retaliation. Without seeing him, the chances of killing him outright are thin. It's my impression these men mean exactly what they say. They've already proved it by shooting two police officers. If we touch him they'll start killing patients in the private wing."

Gifford nodded agreement. "By taking over the power they've taken out a double indemnity; they've got us both ways. Do we yet know how seriously ill Lord Driver is?"

"He's dying." The Assistant Commissioner folded his arms morosely. "I checked with a member of the hospital board. It's a miracle he's still alive."

"So they couldn't have known whether he'd still be alive when they arrived. With a double threat they're making damned sure they get their money from somewhere. It's queer, though; there's something about Lord Driver we don't know."

Gifford didn't pursue it because it wasn't the immediate problem. He looked squarely at his superior.

"They've got us by the short and curlies. I'd feel happier if we knew who the American is. At least we'd know what we're in for. The security clamp can only indicate someone very big. Perhaps you can pull some strings for us, sir? Meanwhile there's little we can do but put the lid on the hospital and lock it up tight. We daren't use tear gas with so many hospitals around. It might kill some patients."

Gifford faced his colleagues in turn, noticing the bulge under McDonald's jacket as the Scot thrust his hands in his pockets and narrowed his shoulders. "We all know that anything we do may be a complete waste of time."

The three men exchanged grim glances. They knew. Gifford said, "A plan of the hospital is on its way. Let's get some local experts on the scene; drainage men, electric cable layers. And we'd better get some patrol cars out of the way; they're beginning to block the square." He glanced at his watch. Less than five hours to go. He rose, impatient to get on.

* * *

Shaw could judge from Allbright's face that McQueen had agreed to the new plan. Allbright was going to try to make him move before they had thought it through. When Allbright reached him he was ready for the pressure but not for the answers.

"That's it," said Allbright when he rejoined Shaw. "Three to one."

It was not worth arguing about Beatty not having his say. Shaw knew that Beatty would vote for further extortion. "What form is the money to take?"

"Same as now."

"It would weigh too much."

"We've got time to sort it out. There may be another way but let them know we're on to it first."

"All right. Hold on here." Better concede than fall out; avoid that at all costs. Shaw reflected dryly that Allbright would now see *this* as the main plan; the original was petty cash. He went to the Sister's office, remaining outside as he always did, and reached for the telephone.

"One moment." The professor courageously put a hand over on the cradle as Shaw lifted the receiver. "Do you realise what you're doing, young man?"

"Take your hand away."

"You have more sense than the others. I don't believe you want to do it."

"It makes no difference."

"Dissuade them."

"You dissuade them; you're not doing very well with me and I'm the easiest."

"Please, think it through; think of the consequences."

"I have thought it through, prof. Take your hand away."

"You're intelligent. You surprise me."

"Prof, if you don't take your hand away I'll have to shoot you. Have *you* thought *that* through?" Shaw was well aware that he couldn't weaken, not ever again. Allbright and McQueen were watching, they'd probably have finished it by now.

Professor Bowyer kept his hand on the cradle and Ed Grann interceded as Shaw's eyes narrowed and his trigger finger tightened.

"Let me talk to your men."

"Don't be ridiculous."

"There's a lot they don't understand. You'll never get away with it."

Shaw gave Grann a quizzical look. "Don't get confused, Yank. We'll get away with it. You've got three seconds, prof." He meant it.

Professor Bowyer hesitated. Ed Grann leaned sideways and gently lifted the professor's hand. "Let them make their own mistakes." Then, to Shaw, "You've yet to get out of this place."

"Is that something new?"

Ed Grann had to force his next words out. "If you really mean to get the money you've got to be ready to go all the way, kill him if necessary."

"That hasn't changed."

"The target has."

"We've merely increased the numbers. And we won't stop at two; we'll do what we have to."

"The repercussions will be vastly different. I feel sorry for you guys."

"That's immoral, doc. You're saying that more effort will

go into protecting Charlie over there than Joe Bloggs." Shaw flashed the phone angrily.

Grann realised that he had said something to harden Shaw. He hadn't expected to worsen the position but he felt strongly that he had.

Shaw listened to the officer who answered the phone and waited impatiently. The voice that eventually came over the wire was a little breathless but cool, very steady. "Who're you?" demanded Shaw.

"I'm Assistant Commissioner Roberts. And who are you?"

"Don't be funny." Shaw was suddenly pleased. The American had touched on an exposed nerve but at least the top fuzz were here at last; they would now get places. "What's happening about Lady Driver?"

"She's being contacted. It shouldn't take long now." The A.C. had considered verbal tactics; threats, pleading, but these men wouldn't be here at all unless they were prepared to go all the way. Much better to let *them* do the wondering. "Are the patients and staff unharmed?"

"They're okay for the moment. Their safety depends on you. I'll spell it out. If you try any funny business like trying to bore holes through ceilings, floors or walls and putting us all out with gas let me tell you what will happen; at the first sign of drowsiness I'll radio my man in the generator room and he'll switch off. Even if you rush him some of your men will die and so will some of the patients. So you'd better pray like hell that I had a good sleep last night."

"We can't risk the lives of the patients by using gas."

"Let's not kid ourselves. I'm just warning you not to try. Any threats to us here and the generator goes. Any threat to him and the patients up here go one at a time. We're in all the way, commissioner. Do I make myself clear?"

"Perfectly. You have no cause to harm anyone."

"Keep it that way." Shaw was feeling settled again. He had never doubted that his scheme would work; the precautions had been considered again and again. Now he was faced with the other issue. "There's a second demand," he said bluntly.

"Oh? You think the Drivers can stand it?"

"Don't play silly buggers with me. We reckon the safety of the American Secretary of State is worth an extra three million."

The silence was so prolonged at the other end of the phone that Shaw began to think that the Assistant Commissioner had gone. He had heard the first sharp, involuntary drawing in of breath and then nothing.

"Are you there?"

"Yes . . . I'm here. I believe you said three million."

"Peanuts, actually. We try to be reasonable." Strangely, Shaw was enjoying the situation. He shouldn't be, not over this, but he was and he was slightly bewildered at his own reaction.

"How do you want it?"

The Assistant Commissioner's words were so hesitant that Shaw came to the conclusion that the man was in a state of shock. Surely someone that high up would know who was here?

"We'll let you know later. We might even want advice on it." The possibility of an enormous irony struck him. "The Honourable Mark Driver might be interested; he's a banker. Meanwhile I want the principle and the figure agreed. The same deadline will apply."

"That may not be possible. It's a huge sum of money."

"You'd better make up your minds what this joker is worth. Five o'clock. No compromise."

"I'll tell my superiors."

"You've got just under five hours left. After that we kill him." He made the threat so that all could hear, so that all would be totally bound by the strength of their shared knowledge. They would see it through or fall apart and there was no possibility of that. Allbright flashed a grin of approval and McQueen settled his Sterling across his knees and gave the thumbs up sign with his good hand. It was time Beatty had some inkling of what was happening. Shaw flicked the switch of his radio. He didn't reveal the name of the new victim but simply told him that there was now a million each in it for them due to an unforeseen inclusion but the extra would probably be deferred payment. They were on the air; Shaw, like the police, had no desire for sudden panic messages that would be picked up and flashed around and create confusion. Both parties wanted a controlled situation for quite different reasons. When he switched off he was feeling surprisingly content.

7

THOSE IN THE Sister's office exchanged uneasy glances. Once the phone had been put down it was utterly quiet. They knew that in the wider threat they were all involved; they dared not put a foot wrong.

Ed Grann had the wild desire to fling the gun in his pocket out of the nearest window. Suddenly it was a lump in his side, an obstruction, a constant danger. He sought and squeezed Jean Sandingham's hand. He did not look at her, could not trust himself to look at anyone just then; he simply squeezed it to offer comfort although afterwards he wasn't sure if it was to comfort himself. There was no self-consciousness in her return grip but there was a kind of communication he had not really sought nor expected. He wondered if she felt it too; then he was afraid because of it.

The turn of events affected him deeply. He was not usually politically orientated, but it was now all too close, he was too involved. He had still been at medical school when John Kennedy had been assassinated. But he could remember the grief, the unbelievable shock that reverberated right round the world. The man in room two was not the President; in line he was the third most important person in America. Yet there were many hard-headed realists who considered him *the* most important. Ed Grann had never been a fervent patriot, yet now he was becoming aware of a strange sense of responsibility and it touched him with the stealth of a pickpocket so that he was almost unaware of what was happening.

The two nurses moved closer together, wanting to touch yet shy to reveal the necessity. They were both Irish. Nurse O'Connor came from the suburbs of Dublin and was a devout Catholic. Nurse Cummings was from the firmly Protestant town of Ballymena in Ulster.

Two things had discouraged possible friction between them. Their work, of course, a dedication to their job; and a peculiar solace in a country that accepted them both without question yet largely took the blame for their current differences. Now another factor pushed them closer. A very real danger outside themselves made their differences inconsequential. This was aided by their age and rank, setting them slightly aside from the two doctors and the Sister. Unexpectedly they needed each other for what they were and not for what they believed. As they saw Shaw's grim, unrelenting face, heard his hard, uncompromising demands that somehow included them, their hands touched first, then encircled each other's waists.

* * *

The Prime Minister was furious. He masked his feelings behind a bland expression betrayed only by a stillness of eye the public never saw. His voice was carefully controlled as he spoke on the hot line.

"You have beaten me by a fraction of a second. I was about to call you. I understand your fears completely, but *we* have the problem. It's on *our* doorstep and I've been gathering reports. So far nothing has happened but I agree we must plan for the worst."

He listened for a while, not a muscle moving and then said, "Of course we have our best man on it, Commander Gifford. He has a splendid team of top policemen. Army units are on stand-by. The Commissioner is on his way and the Assistant Commissioner is already there. Everything that can be done is being done. We want a calamity no more than you as I'm sure you're aware. Yes. I'll personally keep you in touch with all developments." Then, "I know his physician is on his way, he should arrive late this evening; I didn't know his wife was coming. Give me the details and we'll have her met."

When he put down the phone he was still for just a few seconds. Why did it have to happen here? He well understood the President's deep concern; the outcome would be disastrous in every possible direction; only the extent was unpredictable. He picked up another phone.

"Get me the Home Secretary." His voice was quite different.

* * *

Edward Stannard, M.P., Under Secretary of State to the Home Office, fingered his Old Etonian tie. Old Unflappable, the Home Secretary, wanted to see him. He adjusted his tie once more, the right amount of cuff fluttering white wings against his dark suit, and entered the Minister's office.

Harvey Reeve was sitting immobile behind his desk, his jowls pasty, his pale eyes veiled with speculation. Stannard rightly assumed that the Home Secretary had received a shock; he had never seen him look quite so shaken. A big man, the minister had meticulously controlled his weight and could still boast a full, neatly trimmed head of hair. His few suits were made in Savile Row; he had been voted the best dressed politician by the *Tailor and Cutter*.

"Close the door, for God's sake." And when Stannard had complied: "Operation Woodcutter's in a complete mess. The hospital is in the hands of armed men."

Stannard, unbidden, sank to a chair.

Harvey Reeve gestured impatiently towards his telephones.

"The P.M. was just on, making sure we have the right man on the job. We have, of course, a fatuous enquiry but what one might expect." There was bitterness in his tone. "Special Branch informed the Americans, the Foreign Secretary and myself. The American Ambassador contacted the President who immediately raised the Prime Minister on the hot line. The P.M. was annoyed because he didn't get a call in first, he said he was waiting for further information from me. He already knew what there is to know. At the moment there's nothing else I can tell him."

Home Secretary was no longer the relatively cushy number it used to be. What with bombs and demonstrations, crimes of violence on the upsurge, the problems were constant and trickier than they had been. But Harvey Reeve had obtained the post he wanted. For the first time since his appointment three years ago he was sorry that he had. Nothing but trouble would come from this; there could be no winners. Relationship with the United States was on one of its downward trends. It would always be undulating, like the squabbles of a family, but lately it had become rather bleak. Domestic problems both sides of the Atlantic hadn't helped and the Middle East had managed to stir the old cauldron of discontent between the two allies. Something like this couldn't have come at a worse time.

Stannard asked tremulously, "What ransom are they asking for the Secretary of State?" He could see no reason for using a code name in this office.

"None." Harvey Reeve looked up bleakly. "At the moment they don't know he's there. They're holding out for Lord Driver, the multi-millionaire who, at the moment, I gather, is hanging on to life by a thread."

Stannard looked hopeful. "Then they might never find out."

"I've heard better definitions of optimism. We can't afford to take the view that we'll be lucky. Discovery of the Secretary's presence at the hospital is inevitable. And then Lord help us." Harvey Reeve rubbed his already bloodshot eyes. "How strong are you on prayer, Edward?"

Stannard smiled nervously. "Have they set a deadline?"

"A million pounds by five o'clock from the Driver estate. God knows what they'll ask for when they find the golden egg."

"But time is on our side."

"I don't agree. Had they gone in and out quickly we might have got away with it. They have too long; they'll recognise him, or it will come to light in some other way."

"Who's down there?"

"Gifford of the Serious Crime Squad; he should satisfy

the President's demands. Then there's Assistant Commissioner Roberts, and Detective Chief Superintendent Evans of Special Branch, who's already involved. The Commissioner is on his way. But Gifford holds the reins."

"Would you consider operation Straitjacket?"

"I'll consider anything. It will probably come to that but in any event Army units are standing by. We must first give the police an opportunity to sort themselves out." For a moment the Minister lightly drummed the desk with his finger-tips. The very speed of the movement indicated the pace of his thoughts. "Think about it carefully, Edward, and then realise the tremendous implications if the Secretary is recognised and held hostage. It would be disastrous. Now this is what I want done," he added quickly. "First, I'll speak to the Ambassador. While I'm doing that I want a D notice issued to the press and later I'll speak to each editor of the Nationals personally. I don't mind them printing the Driver business but I want no breath of suspicion of anything else. I'll then speak to the Police Commissioner, he'll have to be told who's involved, but only him. You keep in touch with Special Branch. I want to be informed of all developments. I've got to make that statement about prisons this afternoon; it's a nuisance, but I can't get out of it. Don't hesitate to pull me out of the House if it's necessary."

Harvey Reeve paused, obviously distressed. "There's something else. The three security officers are believed to have been shot dead."

"Good God. Then they have nothing to lose. They'll kill anyone to get their way." Stannard fingered his tie and subconsciously got it right. There would be no soft route out of this jungle, no diplomatic manoeuvre, no bargaining, no room for play. It would come hard to Old Unflappable, even if he had talked himself out of almost every adverse situation imaginable. Suddenly they were both confronted with basics.

"I'll get on," murmured Stannard, and left the room.

Harvey Reeve reached for a telephone and asked for the American Ambassador. He had dealt with thugs before, many times, but this was going to be difficult; his instinct warned him that far worse was yet to come.

It had all started innocuously enough. The Secretary of

State had flown in from a Nato meeting in Brussels to address the Pilgrim Society that evening. He had discussed the relationship between Europe and the United States and there had been no problems until late that night at the American Embassy. He had collapsed without warning and created a panic. As Harvey Reeve mused over it he considered it a wonder that the fellow had not collapsed before. At the crack of dawn he had been moved to the Queen Mary where tests could quickly be made and a diagnosis formed. He probably needed nothing more than a really good night's sleep. But a check-up was essential in the circumstances. Most likely he would have been discharged later in the day or the following day when a discreet press release would have been arranged. And now this.

Behind closed doors Harvey Reeve was tempted to loosen his collar in the sudden need for more air. But he had nurtured his image for too long to relax it, even now. The telephone rang and he sank behind a bland expression as he lifted the receiver. "Hello, Russell. You were just about to—yes. Dreadful business. My dear chap, I can't tell you how we feel here. But it's under control; in the best of hands. Things moved very rapidly as you'd expect . . . Yes, I know the President has been on to the Prime Minister. We're in this same boat—all of us. Let's pray the foreign press don't pick up a whisper . . ."

* * *

When Assistant Commissioner Roberts had finished talking to Ginger Shaw he was in a quandary. It was worse than he expected. The demand had to be relayed quickly but he didn't want to do it by radio and in any event he didn't want the staff of the mobile hearing what he had to say; not even Jack Gifford. He was glad now that Gifford had been away from the mobile when the call had come through.

The G.P.O. engineers had arrived to connect the mobile to the main telephone system. They were still working at it. In any event, if it was ready, it would mean using the mobile. He located the hospital Secretary and asked where he might make a confidential call and he was shown to a near-by office. After suffering the usual delays through the over-busy switchboard he asked for a line and called Detective Chief Superintendent Evans of Special Branch.

"Taff? This is A.C. Roberts. I've got to be careful how I say this so let me know if I'm obscure."

"You just caught me, sir. I'm on my way down."

"The balloon's gone up. The one you thought might leak. I know who it is now but so far I'm the only one. They want three million by five. Will you pass this on to the Minister and the Commissioner? They want an answer in principle and they'll give details later. I could have told them then but I'd better have it officially. It will tie you up a little longer, but there's not much you can do here. We're sealing up tight."

Evans sighed resignedly, "Right, sir. I'll get down when I can. I've warned those who matter." He paused then added wearily, "Expect some irate American security brass headed by Art Caplan. They're breathing fire and brimstone."

"To show us how it's done?"

"They haven't too much confidence about what's happened so far. They wanted more men there and we restricted them."

"No one could have foreseen this."

"They believe in preparing for the worst. I have a certain sympathy."

"You're the eternal pessimist, Taff. If we'd slipped him in without an escort we'd have got away with it. Nobody would have been the wiser."

"Maybe. Anyway, they're on their way, sir. Where shall I ring you?"

"At the mobile. The phones should be ready soon but speak to nobody but me. I hope they don't get up Jack Gifford's nose; he's not so good on entente cordiale, if that's the right expression. But still, they certainly have something to worry about. Had a rough time?"

"Not only from them. And it's only just beginning."

* * *

The hospital was quickly being sealed, as thoroughly as it was possible now. There were too many nooks and crannies in these old buildings, no matter how modernised they were. The villains already knew how they would get out, but Jack Gifford had yet to learn. He was also getting impatient for the hospital plans that were now being raised in the maintenance office. He'd been reluctant to do the full rounds until he'd sorted out the detail and he badly wanted to use the phones, now almost connected to the underground cables. They'd been forced to reverse the mobile thirty yards to find the nearest linkage point. When he returned to the mobile the Assistant Commissioner was missing so he listened to the two radio operators quietly busy, their tones subdued and normal even under the mounting pressure of increasing calls. These boys made it sound like a radio operator's exercise; he was grateful for their unassuming normality.

When the A.C. entered the mobile Gifford immediately knew that something had happened. The A.C. was poker-faced and Gifford had known him for too long. "Do you want to tell me, sir?"

The A.C. smiled briefly. "You sound like a damned detective. All right, I'll go so far. No names, Jack. They're demanding three million for their new discovery."

Jack Gifford stuck his chin out, studying his superior and gaining a little more knowledge from the tone of his voice rather than what his face told him. "You give me the impression they're not asking too much." It was a shrewd observation.

"Right, so let's drop it right there."

One of the G.P.O. engineers poked his head in and told them they were linked up and Gifford wedged himself in front of the nearest phone. Lady Driver had still not been found. He pulled a piece of paper from his pocket and dialled.

"Is Lady Driver back, please? This is New Scotland Yard." He waited. The A.C. sat thoughtfully opposite him.

"Lady Driver? We've been trying to get you. I'm Commander Gifford of New Scotland Yard and I'm telephoning you from a mobile unit near Queen Mary's Hospital, London. I have some difficult news for you . . ."

* * *

Lady Moira Driver replaced the old receiver on its massive antique cradle and gazed thoughtfully through the latticed windows to the enormous spread of lawns haphazardly flanked by well-kept roses. She had only just returned to the house when the phone rang and she still wore her top coat. She was dazed but not unduly upset, bewildered more than concerned. The Commander had been very kind, very gentle, at pains to keep the natural gruffness from his voice. What did it mean? What kind of men could make such a terrible threat? At first she hadn't believed it, had considered it some horrifying joke. Then the Commander had quietly explained why he had refrained from asking the local police to call on her; he had told her to ring him back if she wanted to be sure. Well, she was sure.

A striking woman with a title in her own right, she had once been debutante of the year. In her late forties, she was, if anything, more beautiful than she had been in her youth. Money had enabled her to ward off the wrinkles, yet the few that had persisted added serenity to her looks. The sudden and premature illness of her husband had shocked her but the knowledge of his many mistresses over the years had been much more difficult to bear and had somewhat deadened the blow. She sat on a brocaded Louis XIV chair unaware of her classic, straight-backed pose, that was only minimally spoiled by a slow, unconscious intertwining of her fingers.

She gazed around her and felt the loneliness of the huge house; she hated it, but it was the family seat. Because of her dislike of what she called the Driver mausoleum she had surrounded herself with things to her own taste which were the envy of her friends. She sat on committees, she busied herself with charity work, she tended her gardens lovingly; but none of it was compensation for the solitary life she had always led, even before her husband fell ill. Her son and daughter lived in London, and she saw them hardly at all. She had married at nineteen, full of dreams, but they had never matured. The wealth she had inherited from birth had never given her the happiness she had always craved. She would rather have been poorer and carried off on a white charger. Still she had her dreams; but now she knew that that was what they would always remain.

As she sat on the chair tears pricked her eyes and ran down her face. It was a little while before she realised that she was crying and then she did not know why. It was not done. Any tears she had previously shed had been in the privacy of her own room. She was not crying over the threat to her husband, much as this distressed her; perhaps the news was the culminating point of an empty life, of years of wasted beauty. For what? Self-respect had deserted her many years ago when she should first have walked out. But it was unnatural of her to feel self-pity, she possessed too much dignity for that; perhaps it was for her own failures. Failure to hold a husband's love, if it had ever been there, failure to confront him with his unfaithfulness and, above all, failure to produce children for whom she had any admiration; her husband's genes were predominant in them, even in the girl Annabel. Her brief spell of weakness passed as quickly as it had begun. She reached again for the telephone. By the time her son was on the line her tears were dry, her face composed.

"Mark? Something terrible has happened, dear. Some gangsters are holding your father to ransom. They want one million pounds or they will kill him." Her voice was shaking slightly. The silence was prolonged. And then:

"Mother, are you all right? What on earth are you talking about?"

"If you ring Commander Gifford he will give you the details. I have the number. They want the money by five o'clock."

The Hon. Mark Driver still floundered, but he knew his mother could not be joking. He held the telephone away from his pale, narrow face, a supercilious smile locked on thin lips as he gazed with cold eyes at the shapeless image of disaster rising before them. In an instant he saw the many and dangerous consequences of his father dying before another five days had elapsed and each one was like a savage attack on his sanity. His mind was blood-filled and reeling. "*Shit*," he said savagely.

Lady Driver cringed. "Must you always be so foul?"

"Mother, you don't understand."

"I understand that your father's life is in danger."

"Oh, Christ. He's dying anyway. It makes no difference.

Only the next five days make a difference."

"Is that all that concerns you? Have you any thought for *him*?"

"What good would it do, for God's sake? He doesn't even know what's happening. It'll be *us* who are landed with the consequences."

"And that worries you, of course."

"It worries me sick. And if you didn't place yourself above it, it would worry you sick too."

"You mean the will?"

"The deed of gift, mother. We've told you often enough; you didn't want to know. Now you'd better listen."

"I'm not bothered by the deed, Mark. Money is not *my* God. If those men turn off that machine it would be a blessing for your father."

"*Are you mad?* Money doesn't mean a thing to you because you've always had it. You'd sing a different tune if it was taken away. Stop living in a dream, mother. If father fails to last out the next five days it will be disaster for all of us. *Five million* in death duties. All because the old fool failed to recognise the possibility of dying before his time. The rate he drank he should have seen the writing on the wall."

"Don't talk like that; he was always good to you."

"Rubbish! He looked after himself, and that's what I intend to do. After the way he's treated you over the years I find your defence of him extraordinary."

"Speak to Diane. Ask her why she defends *you*; why she tolerates you as a husband. Whatever he is or was I see no reason for prolonging his suffering. It would be merciful to let him go."

"He's *not* suffering. Mother, are you actually suggesting that we refuse to pay the money, that we allow these men to murder him?"

"What would be your attitude if this were happening a week from now? Would you recommend paying?"

"That's hypothetical. We're dealing with now." He was unable to answer truthfully. "How do they want the money?"

"You disgust me."

"Mother, there are matters you don't know about and you wouldn't understand if you did. The bank could be in difficulties if we pay those death duties. We need the money desperately. *We've got to have it.* I've been sweating blood these last days and the next five will be a living nightmare. For God's sake try to understand."

"Even after death duties there should be enough for us all to live comfortably. It's wicked to keep him hanging on; I've thought so for some time."

"Oh, Christ! I'm not getting through to you. *We are not keeping him alive.* It's nothing to do with us. We have no control over it. The bloody doctors are keeping him alive; it's coincidence that it's to our advantage. If he dies now there won't *be* any estate left. It's in hock up to the eyebrows. If we don't get that money a lot of people are going to lose theirs; people who depend on us; people who cannot afford to lose their life savings." Desperation was forcing him to give information that should never have been revealed over an open telephone but he could not help himself. As he saw it he was pleading for his own life.

"Virtuosity rides badly on you, Mark. You're not thinking of them. But is it true?" She spoke very quietly, calm now that responsibility was at last forced on to her.

"As God's my judge. Speak to Annabel, but we must go ahead meanwhile. Time is short."

She stood holding the phone, deliberately gazing through the window, then again, slowly round the room. She knew her son to be a crass liar—he was, after all a reflection of her husband—but there was a desperate cry for help in his tone; it was this, more than the strong ring of truth in his final plea that swayed her. Yet she could not resist a final condemnation. "So you've been playing with other people's money?"

"Mother, *please. How do they want it?*"

* * *

Commander Gifford finger-combed his hair as if it made a difference to its wiriness, and sighed impatiently. He had to wait for the return call because he wanted nobody else to deal with it. From the early stages of near chaos, of the overlapping of the local division with the Yard and Special Branch, each originally ignorant of the other's involvement, a pattern was emerging, a steady professionalism plugging all the holes and closing the gaps. Even now there was nothing straightforward about the case with its mystery V.I.P. A double ransom. That in itself was unusual if not unique.

Gifford was qualified to be armed but was such an indifferent shot that he had declined Superintendent McDonald's offer of a choice of weapons. Jock could shoot the ash off a cigar and he was welcome to it. Gifford didn't like arms in any shape or form; he'd have been happier getting his powerful hands round a gunman's neck. Meanwhile a description, compiled from the identikit that Naylor had constructed before entering the operating theatre, had been passed on to C.R.O. and they were waiting for a result. Thought of the operating theatre roused him to rush back to the Secretary's temporary office after leaving a message where he was going.

The Secretary was still being harassed from all sides but had at last managed to get a hot cup of coffee in front of him; Gifford eyed it enviously. "What actually happens if the generator is cut off?"

The Secretary finished the call he was on and left the telephone off the hook. He nodded wearily: "In spite of what you're thinking it's the only way I'll be able to answer your questions."

"I know, sir. They must be driving you mad."

"I'm beginning to find out how inadequate some people are and how splendidly efficient are others; most of them, I'm happy to say. If the generator's cut off we have no power. As simple as that. No lights, no lifts, no machinery working, no heat and no essential refrigeration. One does not realise how one depends on power until it's no longer there."

"I realise that, sir, but how will it affect patients?"

"You mean will any die?"

"That's what I'm getting at. Without the technical detail, sir."

"We've just gone into this." The Secretary leaned back, still outwardly unruffled except for the smudges spreading under his eyes. "Five will almost certainly die. In some cases we can maintain the machines by hand; other we can't."

"What about the operating theatre?"

"It will depend on what's going on. We do more than our fair share of brain surgery. Fortunately, we have become so used to strikes and threats of strikes that we have developed a certain resilience. We have compressed air drills for emergencies."

"But you'd still lose your light, those huge things over the operating tables."

"Oh, it would be undeniably tricky. Very tricky indeed. Were you considering attacking the generator building?"

"Obviously we can't. I was just checking how serious it would be if we did."

"Far too serious, Commander. At the moment at least the essentials are still functioning."

The A.C. had returned to the mobile when Gifford got back. The atmosphere inside was quietly becoming charged, giving the sensation of a gradual build-up to crisis point. The sergeant was still hunched over the incident book and the radio operators were constantly taking and relaying messages under the supervision of an inspector. As Gifford arrived a routine check-in was being made of the men positioned throughout the hospital.

Lady Driver rang and Gifford passed on the news to the A.C.

"They'll pay up. Her merchant-banker son is organising it now."

The A.C. raised his brows. "Even a merchant bank will have its work cut out to raise a million in twenties by five." He paused. "Did she say why?"

"Yes, she must have realised we thought it odd. It's something to do with estate or death duties. He has five days to go before the seven-year clause becomes fully effective. This way they lose one million instead of five."

"Phew! I thought those days of affluence were over."

"I never believed it myself. Someone's keeping our pay down. Shall I ring up the private ward and tell them?"

The A.C. smoothed his bald pate; he was smiling faintly. "Think you might find out who the V.I.P. is that way?"

Gifford looked innocent and placed a hand on his heart. "Never crossed my mind sir. I'll find out anyway. The secret will come out as the day goes on."

One of the phones rang and an inspector held it out to the A.C.

"The Commissioner for you, sir."

Gifford eased out from his seat and said, "Time to go," and left the A.C. to deal with the most powerful policeman in the country. He went back into the hospital, noticing that the collection of police cars had dispersed to double park elsewhere. He located Superintendent McDonald on the ground floor and insisted on inspecting the positioning of his armed men.

"Och, I've just done it."

"You can do it again. It'll keep your circulation going; you're too thin-blooded, Jock. You're rubbing your hands away."

McDonald had positioned his men faultlessly. All stairs, lifts and emergency exists were covered but it was still debatable whether there were enough men. More were still on their way, armed men from any division they could be scrounged from. On the roof it was cold and damp, the rising wind more noticeable. The surface was littered with pipes and outhouses although from below it appeared flat. There were four men up here and both senior officers agreed that this was not enough. Long before the money arrived they would need far more.

Neither liked the way the building was annexed to others. Three main adjoining buildings covered such a wide area that security would be difficult at any level. The number of men required to seal off all the buildings at street level would be enormous. Yet it had to be done. They walked round the parapet together and looked down on the short narrow canyon that cradled the generator housing. It looked no bigger than a shed, its six-inch-thick concrete roof innocuous from this height. The two short rows of cars spread either side like a mechanised escort.

Gifford gazed down reflectively, the breeze making no impact on his wire wool hair. "Do you remember that case in Holland? The Dutch lifted a bloody great concrete block by helicopter and dropped it on the roof."

"Aye. But there wasn't a generator inside."

"Right. From up here you get a better idea. I'll have to

call out all the uniformed men I can. I was hoping not to but I daren't take the risk. I'll have to flood the square and these other surrounding buildings."

They did another circuit, locating the figures of their men on the streets and spotted areas of weakness. But at least the hospital itself was tight. They stopped behind a brick shed and faced each other. McDonald had a suspicion of what was coming.

"Jock, I think you ought to pull your men off the intermediate floors and concentrate them up here and on the ground floor and basement."

McDonald was silent, feeling more cold than usual. He said nothing.

"I know you've done it right but we're not dealing with a standard situation. They'll come out from below or up here."

"Helicopter?"

"It's possible. I've seen flatter roofs but there's an area beyond that double run of pipes where one could put down without too much trouble."

"I agree with you about the helicopter. But why a concentration in the basement?"

"A hunch. I'll have a better idea when they finally raise that bloody plan. I've got men rousting the London Electricity Board and the Main Drainage Service. There are sewers all over the place and some of these electrical cable tunnels can take a man standing up. That's why the basement. This is an old building."

"You've been doing your homework."

"It's old hat, Jock. There are times when I feel as old as London—and as ravaged."

"I'll admit I've often wondered if you have mice in your hair,—sir. Glasgow used to have the same effect on me."

Gifford pulled out the radio he had tucked into his raincoat pocket. "Channel four, Commander Gifford. That you, Jenkins? Get on to the Yard. Tell 'em I want two hundred uniformed men down here at once. And send someone down for crowd control; they're beginning to build up." He gave a quizzical wink to McDonald. "I might get a hundred. God knows where they'll get them from. But I want to net those bastards."

McDonald was shivering so much that Gifford pulled his own coat tighter.

"You're the original skeleton on a tin roof; I can hear you rattling from here."

"I need a very large Scotch."

"Let's see what we can do."

On the way down McDonald asked, "Have you considered the possibility of them all walking out by the front door?"

"I have, Jock."

The two men exchanged glances. Gifford added, "It scares me silly. If they do that your hired guns won't be of much use to you. Nor my two hundred coppers."

There were just under four hours to go.

8

GINGER SHAW TOOK the call from Assistant Commissioner Roberts and said, "Right. One down and one to go." When he lowered the phone he kept his hand on it. His feeling of elation was indescribable. For a moment he was lightheaded, as if he'd swallowed a drug and it was racing through his veins. In a terrible moment of recklessness he almost tore off his wig and threw it in the air. This was what it was all about and it was working. One million pounds. But more than that; much more. How did one value that immense satisfaction that came from those weeks of careful preparation?

He straightened, and, as he did, realised he was smiling. It was the first time he had smiled for months. Even after the collapse of all he'd worked for he had still managed occasionally to smile. But never after Ruth had gone; never again, and now he was and it was strange and wonderful.

Allbright called out. "You've swallowed the canary. So they're coughing up?"

Shaw nodded, still smiling. McQueen shouted, "Yippee! Give me the sunshine——" And tailed away the song horribly off-key. The morale of the three men rocketed. From a bad start things were now humming. McQueen, sitting on his chair, followed up his disastrous venture into melody and did a Cossack dance with his legs as if he were squatting unsupported. Shaw raised Beatty on his radio. "First stage okay. It's on its way." Everyone in the ward heard Beatty's yell of delight through McQueen's radio, which was set permanently on receive. Shaw added carefully, "And that's only part of the packet. Whatever was discussed before is quadrupled." He switched off.

Ed Grann picked up an innuendo that he couldn't pinpoint. He was puzzled. Something else had subtly happened apart from the obvious agreement to deliver the money. Jean Sandingham thought the stocky man looked quite different when he smiled. Nurse O'Connor and Nurse Cummings felt the tremendous surge of excitement sweeping the three men; it was inescapable, so acute that they felt part of it until they remembered.

*   *   *

When Gifford returned to the mobile it was crowded out and buzzing, as if a special demonstration was being staged for the Police Commissioner who had now arrived and was talking to the A.C. All phones were manned and there was barely room to squeeze through. Calls were being made to and were coming in from other divisions, records, the Home Office, the U.S. Embassy, who had been given the emergency number, Main Drainage, London Electricity, the Gas Board and other sundry sources. Space was so tight that the Commissioner, the A.C. and Commander Gifford stepped outside.

The Commissioner was the only man of his rank to have

come up from the beat. He was straight and direct and he knew that he was in the damned way. But with the way this incident had blown up and with the knowledge of the American involvement he well understood the value of flashing the scrambled egg braid of his cap. No one could later say that the top copper had shown no concern.

While the three police officers were talking and the disposition of the men being explained to the Commissioner, a Cadillac the width of an armoured car drew up and captured everyone's attention; it made the mobile look shoddy as it double parked beside it. A worried-looking Art Caplan and a colleague got out, saw the small group and the scrambled egg on the Commissioner's cap and came up demanding to speak to the Chief of Police. The Commissioner had yet to be warned that American security men were on the way but their accents were enough to persuade him of their purpose; he switched to his diplomatic channel while the wily Gifford excused himself from the group; what else were the Police Commissioners for?

The Commissioner and the A.C. conducted the American security men to the hospital to show them the arrangements and Gifford was grateful. Back in the mobile there was information for him.

Records had produced five likely possibilities of the identity of the man who had shot Naylor. He rushed back to the hospital, passing the Commissioner's group on the way and catching the odd word that convinced him that the Commissioner was a smooth old bastard currently doing a good job on Anglo-American relations. He ran up to the first floor, dashed into the ward where Naylor and Erskin had been, to find both beds empty and a nurse remaking them.

"Where've they gone?" He was panting after his run.

"The operating theatre."

"Fifth floor?"

"Yes, sir."

Gifford lost a few seconds locating a lift and when he did he pressed the button, flapping the reports against his legs impatiently. On the fifth floor he dived into the nearest ward to seek direction to the operating theatre. By the time he found it he was breathless. He pushed through swing doors to the smell of ether and the sight of white walls and of Naylor on a trolley with a nurse by his side holding up a drip. It was some form of pre-operational ante room. He strode quickly to Naylor, ignoring the nurse's frantic signals for him to go away, and saw at once that the Special Branch man was comatose, obviously having had a pre-operation shot of Pentothal.

"Can you rouse him?"

The nurse looked horrified, glancing back at the closed door behind her. "Who are you? Go away."

Gifford flashed his card. "I've got to speak to him for just a second."

"You can't. He's ready for an op."

"Is the other one inside?" Gifford jerked a finger at the inner doors. They opened as he spoke and a doctor cloaked in operation smock, gloves, surgical mask and cap came through, saw Gifford and stopped, his hands held high as if he was drying them. Two eyes stared at Gifford above the mask. "What do you want?"

Gifford again explained who he was. "I want to speak to this one before he goes in."

"That's impossible. Can't you see he's unconscious?"

"Can't you bring him round? For a short time?"

"What sort of policeman are you, Commander? This man's been seriously wounded. He's still bleeding internally."

"He's young, he's tough. I only want a second. Give him a shot of something."

The doctor glanced at the nurse; it was clear what they both thought. The doctor turned back to Gifford, his mask pumping as he spoke, his voice slightly muffled. "You make it easy to believe what one reads about police brutality, Commander. Your suggestion is monstrous."

"I'm trying to save other lives."

"I can't believe that a few seconds of talking to this man can save them."

"Then how long will it be before I can speak to him?"

"A few hours, at least. The operation may not take too long but he must have time to recover from the anaesthetic."

Gifford gazed down at the placid features of Naylor and felt like thumping him. The silly bugger should have insisted on waiting for the operation. When he had the bit between his teeth Gifford could only take the shortest cut. He accepted that he was unreasonable, unfair, but in his hand were the descriptions of five men. It was more than likely that Naylor could have pinpointed one of them and that might have proved valuable. He stared the doctor out, gave the nurse a glance that made the hand with the bottle shake, and finally gave Naylor a look of pity he did not deserve. Finally he shrugged and left the room. Once outside he said, "*Sod it*", loudly enough for those inside to hear.

Gifford had a hunch that he was near to something. At the moment he had nothing, no advantage, no information. He didn't even know how many gunmen were involved. Any information now could prove useful. He went to the head of the stairs and sat down. Less ruffled he read each report once more. And then again. On the fifth floor, he was tempted to creep up to the sixth and do what Naylor had done, peer through the spyhole. Then he had another idea.

Back at the mobile Gifford called the inspector, raising his voice against the now constant babble of voices. "Where have you put the dog handlers?"

The inspector climbed over the back of one of the policemen on a telephone and said, "How many do you want, sir?"

"One."

"One?"

"Just one. The best one you've got."

The inspector called out to the operator on the panic line and told him to ask Sergeant Johnson to report. Within a couple of minutes a dog van pulled up behind the mobile and a sergeant climbed out from the passenger seat. He gave Gifford a salute that was an invention of his own, then stroked his heavy moustache with a hairy hand.

Gifford gazed down at him. "Sergeant Johnson?"

"Yes, sir."

"Where's your dog?"

"In the van, sir."

"You're short for a copper, aren't you?"

Johnson grinned still nervously fingering his moustache. "Only just made it for height, sir. Had wedges tucked in my socks."

Gifford smiled back. "So you got yourself a pooch to make up for inches?"

"Something like that, sir. Shall I get him?"

Gifford nodded. "What's his name?"

"Banks, sir." Johnson opened a door of the van and an Alsatian jumped down.

"Banks? That's a funny name for a dog." Gifford kept a discreet distance.

"After the old English goalkeeper, sir. Try to get a ball past him and you'd know what I mean. Sit."

Banks sat between Johnson's feet and Gifford eyed him speculatively. The bright, intelligent eyes stared up at him but the ears were back listening for his handler. The big jaws were closed but Gifford decided not to get too near.

"He won't hurt you, sir. He's as soft as a puppy. Should see him with children."

"I can see he is. I don't want to tempt him. Sergeant, I've got a job for him and I don't know that it will work."

"We can try, sir."

"If I'm wrong you might lose him."

"Lose him?" Instinctively the sergeant's hand went to the dog's head; the dog responded by lifting its muzzle, still sitting.

"I know how you feel about him; you're all the same. But it's got to be faced. It's only fair to warn you."

The sergeant said nothing, scratching the dog's head slowly with one finger. It was something he would never normally do on duty.

"Can you slip a lead on him and follow me?"

They went by lift to the fifth floor and then by foot up to the half landing where three of Jock McDonald's firearms squad were waiting. Gifford told the plain-clothes men to wait on the lower landing. Gifford, Sergeant Johnson and Banks were quite still, silence essential. If they turned the corner the doors near the gunman would be in sight. Gifford prayed that the man wasn't watching at this moment. He knelt down and carefully peered round the corner. His caution was not solely for his own safety; the villains had threatened to knock off the patients one by one if the police showed a face. He had to hope that they wouldn't include a dog. Rolling over, he lay flat on the lower stairs gazing up at the doors. From the low elevation he could see only the tops of the doors and very little of the glass panes; certainly no spyhole. He signalled Sergeant Johnson to join him. The two men lay side by side, uncomfortably placed but out of sight. When Gifford was certain that Johnson had assimilated the layout he signalled him back and motioned him to descend to the fifth-floor landing. Gifford was panting a little.

"I'm too old for this caper." He was barely whispering, intent that no sound should travel up the stairs.

Banks was quietly sitting with his slip chain off, watching his master, taking little notice of the others.

"This is what I want you to do and for God's sake don't let them see you; if you do people will die. As it is I'm pushing my luck with the dog. Go back to where you were lying and take Banks with you. I want you then to send him to the doors and to bark. Can he do that?"

"No problem, sir. What's the risk?"

"It depends on who's the other side of the door. If it's the man I think it is I don't think there's much risk. But if I'm wrong the chances are that Banks will stop a load of lead."

Johnson bit his lip, clearly worried, his gaze straying to his dog.

"When you're on the stairs," continued Gifford, "make sure your voice doesn't carry beyond your dog."

"Dogs have acute hearing. No one will hear. Can I bring him straight back as soon as he's barked?"

"No. He must wait for a reaction. I'm sorry, sergeant."

Sergeant Johnson crouched by Banks, wondering if the animal had picked up a nuance of his deep feeling of fear. The sergeant trod softly to the half landing, Banks by his side, then flattened and wriggled round the corner to lie on the upper stairs as he'd done with Gifford. His feet were still on the half landing. Because of his lack of height he had to raise his head slightly to locate the top of the doors. He turned to

Banks, feeling like a man sending his best friend to certain death. "Go."

Banks padded up the stairs without looking back. Johnson raised himself as much as he dared when Banks reached the landing. "Stop." By stretching he could just see the quiet stationary fawn top of the haunches. With a dry mouth Johnson said, "Speak."

* * *

McQueen was on top of the world. He was in sight of more money than he had ever dared dream of having. On sudden impulse he was grateful to Ginger Shaw; well, he wouldn't let him down that was for sure; he'd earn his part of it whatever happened. Even the ache in his shoulder was more bearable, and anyway, he didn't need two hands to control a Sterling.

When he heard the dog coming up the stairs his jubilation dissipated in an instant. It was doubtful if anyone else would have heard the dog but it was the one sound that McQueen would remain tuned into all his life. Normally it wouldn't have been so bad but he knew it was a police dog, couldn't be anything else in a hospital, especially at a time like this; just the soft sound of its nails catching the stone stairs.

God, that conjured up nightmares. They shouldn't have sent a dog after him. All his life he'd loved dogs; the only thing in life he'd ever really loved. They hadn't complained at his rough handling, they'd come straight back to him asking for more. *They* hadn't been concerned whether he was broke or not, drunken or sober, and then when he'd been holed up in that factory the police had sent one after him to flush him out. He hadn't known then that police dogs were trained to go for the *right* hand. He'd injured his right on someone's jaw the previous night and it was bandaged. His gun had been in his left. When the dog sprang at his sore right hand he reacted without thinking and fired the gun. Christ! How could he hit anything firing left-handed? Time and time again in his cell he was to ask himself the same question.

He could still see the dog halted in mid air, falling sideways with a terrible howl of pain, and lying in front of him, writhing, whimpering in agony until he had been forced to fire again and again to shut out the dreadful sound. That was a mistake too, for he could never shut out the sound. Never. He heard it now, inside his head as the dog reached the landing. When it started to bark McQueen broke out in a cold sweat, unable to move.

They all heard the deep-throated barking. Allbright and Shaw looked to McQueen to deal with it and were astounded by his pale-faced fixation. Shaw hurried up the ward and saw the sweat rolling down McQueen's face, the wild, scared look. McQueen afraid of dogs? Shaw edged along the wall to the door. There might be a man with the dog, in which case they'd have to start carrying out their threat. He crept up to the spy hole and saw the dog in front of the doors barking. It was just standing there; there was no one else in sight. What the hell were they playing at?

Shaw turned to McQueen and said, "Okay. If it worries you so much." It gave him the chance to regain what authority he might have lost in Allbright's eyes; it could convince them that he didn't have the soft spot they might suspect. He swung his Sterling low down at the door.

"No!" McQueen was off his chair and hurling himself at Shaw before a shot could be fired. He crashed into Shaw, who, solid though he was, reeled under the impact and was knocked past the doors on to one knee.

Realising what he'd done, McQueen struggled to straighten his feelings, his face undergoing a variety of changes to settle into an expression of child-like sorrow. In his anguish he took his arm from the sling and wiped the sweat from his face with his mis-shapen, bruiser's hand. "It's only a dog, for Christ's sake. He can't hurt us. I'm sorry, Ging——" He stopped before he could make another mistake. He went forward to help Shaw up, a sloppy smile of apology showing beneath the untidy beard. "Didn't mean to knock you like that. Can't stand cruelty to dogs."

By the time Shaw was on his feet the barking had stopped. Sensing he had to put the record straight McQueen plucked up courage and went to the spy hole. He spun round, his grin now one of triumph. "He's gone," he said happily. "He's gone."

Shaw, feeling ruffled, went to the phone. "Get me the top copper," he demanded angrily.

* * *

Gifford had been standing near Sergeant Johnson on the half landing and out of sight. When Banks started barking he realised how the sergeant must feel. He was straining to pick up any sound beyond the barking which had now gone on for longer than he expected. When he heard the frantic "No!" and the brief scuffle he responded immediately. "Get him back."

Sergeant Johnson said, "Come," before Gifford had finished and Banks came scudding down the stairs as his master rolled round the corner to join Gifford. They went down to the fifth floor and Gifford patted Johnson's shoulder. "Good work. Will the dog kill me if I touch it?"

Johnson was grinning in relief. "He won't bite."

Gifford scratched the dog's head. "Thanks, Banks. You pulled off a beauty. I now know who one of the bastards is."

On the way down in the lift Gifford considered Naylor's description of McQueen. Back at the mobile he commanded a top priority check on all known friends and associates of McQueen, especially recent ones. When that was under way the A.C. came in, quietly fuming.

"Have you been using dogs?" He made an effort to keep his voice down.

"One. Why, sir?"

"Jack, don't come the innocent with me or I'll start throwing rank at you. They've threatened the patients if there's another sniff of one."

"I kept to their rules. There was no policeman in sight."

"You were splitting very dangerous hairs and you knew it. You took one hell of a risk with other people's lives."

"It was a calculated one, and it worked. I've identified one of them. He shot a police dog three years ago and had to have psychiatric treatment when he was inside because of it."

The A.C. was still grim. "Don't ever do it again."

"No, sir." Knowing he had deserved the rocket Gifford

went outside to organise the arrival of some of the uniformed police. As he stepped down a well-dressed, dignified but deeply worried-looking man approached the mobile. As conservatively as he was dressed Gifford knew at once that he wasn't English; perhaps the tie or the cut of the light topcoat gave him away. He wore a homburg and touched it as he spoke. "Good afternoon, my name is Russel Vance. I'd like to speak to the officer in charge."

Gifford recognised the accent, face and name as that of the American Ambassador. Two hard-faced men stood a little behind him trying not to look like bodyguards. Cunningly he said, "I'm Commander Gifford, the executive officer in charge. How can I help you, sir?"

"You can tell me what news there is of the Secretary of State, Commander."

"In that case, sir, perhaps you'd like to speak to the Assistant Commissioner. He's inside. The Commissioner is at the moment showing some of your security personnel our arrangements but he should be back shortly." He held the door of the mobile open and said quietly, "I wouldn't mention who's involved again, sir, if I were you. Very few of us know. Better the press don't get hold of it yet."

"Thank you, Commander. I wouldn't dream of letting anyone know."

Gifford suffered the reaction of everyone who learned the identity of the V.I.P. He had known it was someone big but not *that* big. It made him nervous and nerves had never worried him before. Within seconds the Ambassador reappeared with the A.C. Gifford had known that the A.C. wouldn't remain inside with so many other policemen there. He went back in himself to find that a negative report had come in on the crack pistol shot; he was no known criminal. Puzzled, he said, "Check with the pistol clubs; only their very top marksmen. Yes, and check the services, army, navy and air force. Maybe he learned to shoot in uniform. And I want a chopper to stand by."

Gifford peered outside the van to see the Commissioner and the two Americans returning. The Americans wouldn't be satisfied; they'd prefer the area to be saturated with armed men, but the only way to do that was to call in the army and that was up to the Home Secretary. At one stage he had considered calling in the Fire Brigade to get a police observer with binoculars to scan the sixth floor windows from a turn-table ladder but he'd discarded the idea on the grounds of it being too great a risk for the man who could easily have been picked off. But long before the deadline they had to close the place off so that a flea couldn't get out. The crowd was thickening all the time, particularly as it was now the lunch hour. The uniformed boys were doing their stuff, keeping them back and keeping them moving. It would have been better if they could all have been herded into the central garden and locked in. He turned wearily to the operator on the panic frequency. "Rustle up the press relations officer, Fred Jessel. The press are late in coming."

Just as he was about to leave the operator stopped him. "Message from the Yard, sir. They traced the frequency the villains are using and they've been monitoring their calls."

"So?"

"They seem to think there was something odd about the last call. Here's the script." The operator passed Gifford a piece of paper.

"What's wrong with it?"

"The last bit, sir. About any money so far discussed being quadrupled. They already knew that. The man in the generator room had already been told they'd upped the amount."

Gifford thought it over and was puzzled. The operator saw his frown and went on: "It was the *way* it was said, sir. To a trained operator it sounded as if it was meant for somebody else on the frequency, someone not identified with the private wing or the generator."

A man *outside* the hospital perimeter? Gifford sat down slowly.

* * *

Ginger Shaw allowed the two nurses to make tea all round. He even permitted the patients to be served first. It brought a measure of action and an easing of the tension. There was still over three hours to go. All they now had to do was to sit and wait and sweat it out until the money arrived. There was still the problem of the other three million but he had some ideas about that. For them there could be no relaxing; the fuzz might get up to all sorts of tricks. He had no illusions about all the exits being blocked. It was as good a way as any of tying the police in knots.

While the tea was being distributed Shaw went to talk with Allbright. "I'll have to speak to Driver's son. I'm not a financial wizard; he's at least in the racket."

"Can you trust him? He might try to diddle us."

"This was your bloody idea. Unless you've got a better one that's what I'll do. We'd never be able to carry the weight of the money; it's got to be some other way."

Allbright didn't reply. He'd got his way; he was ready to leave the detail to Shaw.

Shaw went back to the telephone and asked for the A.C. He was getting used to the little time lags. When he came on Shaw said, "I want to speak to Lord Driver's son."

"But he's already arranging the money. Even a banker takes time to get this sort of money together."

"I just want to speak to him. You can give me the number and a line and I'll dial it myself. When I've finished tell the girl to link up again with the Secretary's office." When he had the number he dialled and asked for the Hon. Mark Driver. As he waited he felt an overwhelming hatred for the man. When the girl asked his name he said, "Tell him it's about his father; I'm phoning from the hospital."

When the Hon. Mark Driver picked up the call his tone was immediately offensive. Shaw bridled at once.

"If you want your old man alive watch your tongue, you jumped-up bastard."

"Dammit, I'm raising the money now. I can't do more; you'll have it in time." His aggression changed to smarm.

Shaw felt sick. "We'll have it all right. I'm not phoning about that. There's some other money. How can it be transferred abroad to another bank?"

"There's no problem about that provided it doesn't exceed the Bank of England limit. If it does you'd need their permission." His tone had become so conciliatory that Shaw wanted to spit down the phone.

"Take Bank of England permission for granted. Can a sum

be transferred to a Swiss bank without the money actually travelling?"

"If the Swiss bank is sure of the source it can credit some of its own funds to an account, charge the source interest and receive the money at an arranged date."

"Does the source have to know the Swiss bank account number?"

"That's more difficult to answer. It would depend on the arrangements. Normally only the person credited would know the number."

Normally. That was the rub. Shaw hung up without another word, well aware that the police would have listened on an extension, but knowing that he had given nothing away that could help them. He stood silent for perhaps a minute, sipped some of the tea that had been placed before him and picked up the telephone again.

* * *

Commander Gifford left the mobile and stood at the foot of it, reluctant to join the group of big brass standing a few feet away. From the general tone it sounded to him as if things were getting a little heated; nerves were fraying and as the deadline approached they'd begin to snap here and there. Well, his wouldn't. The hubbub of activity in the confined space of the mobile was still ringing in his ears. He could hear the phones from where he stood. He saw the constable rush from the hospital entrance and recognised him as the permanent runner they had left in the Secretary's office. When the A.C. was drawn aside by the constable, the others went silent. The A.C. said something to the group and then broke away towards the entrance. Gifford timed it, then ran after him and tugged his sleeve. "A moment, sir."

"Can't stop, they're on the extension."

"Let me speak to them."

Both men had slowed to a fast walk. "You know why you can't."

"I know about the American Secretary of State. Let me deal with them."

A.C. Roberts halted. "How did you find out?" Both men were breathing heavily.

"The Ambassador inadvertently told me."

"You mean you tricked him."

"If security was that tight I couldn't have managed it. I agree that the information isn't something to spread around. But I know, and that's it. Look, sir, if it were only Lord Driver involved I'd be speaking to them anyway."

"I can't stand here arguing, Jack."

"Then let me do it. I don't want the bloody credit; I just want to fix those bastards up there."

The A.C. hesitated. He had known Gifford a long time; the Commander had got his teeth on the edge of the rag and wanted to go on chewing until he had it all in his mouth. Gifford's jaw was rigid, his eyes hard and narrowed, his wire wool hair sponged about the square head. Roberts would not have hesitated but for the most unusual circumstances. If his judgment was wrong he'd take the can. He indicated the group behind them with a back flip of his head, "You realise I'll have to explain to them why I've delegated? They'll have my head if it boomerangs."

"All that's changing is my speaking to them. The operation remains the same. I'd have had to know sooner or later. I just might get something from him."

"All right."

Gifford nodded and raced for the hospital entrance.

9

COMMANDER GIFFORD HAD got what he wanted. Not the most tolerant of men, he could not stand split control. He was willing to rise or fall by his own decisions; if one day he made a complete balls-up that required his resignation, at least he wouldn't seek a scapegoat. Now it was his show all the way. It was true that Superintendent McDonald had charge of the armed men but he and Jock knew each other too well to fall out, and he had the final say when it came to the crunch.

By the time he reached the Secretary's office he was so out of breath he decided that after this shindig he'd do something about his weight. He put his hand over the mouthpiece while he eased his breathing and then ejected a very curt, "Yes?"

* * *

Ginger Shaw at once realised he was dealing with someone else and the tone rattled him. "Who the hell are you?"

"I'm Commander Gifford, sonny. They've reduced you to the nitty-gritty. You'll deal with me in future."

"I wouldn't be so brave if I were you, copper. We've a lot of hostages up here."

"So you'll knock them off because you don't like the sound of my voice? That figures. Scum who'll shoot unarmed men don't need a reason for knocking anybody off. But let me tell you this; you harm one more person up there and when you come out I'll turn so many blind eyes that you'll finish up with enough lead in you to be radiation proof. The public enjoy armed men getting shot; it's the only time we're popular. Now what do you want?"

Shaw was rattled. He had been deliberately provoked and it had almost worked. This copper was tough but not stupid.

"We haven't heard about the three million yet."

"You're dealing with politicians; what the hell do you expect? Drop him and concentrate on Lord Driver. Isn't a million enough to go round six?"

Had he got the number right Shaw might have fallen for it. Instead he chuckled uneasily; it was an act he forced himself into. He'd have to watch this one all the way. "You're being too clever, copper. We want the three million transferred to a Swiss Bank. When that's been done the manager of the Swiss bank is to ring me here and give me the account number."

"Right. Who does he ask for?"

"You funny bastard."

"I'll pass on your message. Oh, and give McQueen my regards."

The receiver slammed down on the desk the other end and Shaw snatched his own away from his ear. His hand was trembling. How had they got on to McQueen? Allbright was watching him as he always did during these telephone exchanges. So were those behind the desk; and they must have seen how shaken he was. It was like being under one of their damned microscopes all the time.

But what really upset him was their knowledge of McQueen. He dared not tell McQueen that the police knew he was here, but he didn't want to keep it to himself; he went to tell Allbright.

Allbright didn't like it either.

While Shaw and Allbright were talking Jean Sandingham rose from her chair, straightened her uniform apron and put down her cup. She tried to prevent the professor and the two nurses overhearing her whisper to Grann by speaking close to his ear. "We must hide the gun."

"They won't search us again." Grann felt her breath on the top of his ear as she moved her head.

"He was shaken just now. I don't know what was said but if they get nervous they might do anything."

She bent forward, pretending to adjust the papers on her desk, and her face was very close to his. He saw how flawless it was; the traditional complexion of her country. And he wanted to touch it, he wanted more than that. It was a crazy moment that passed all too slowly. Perhaps the tension was making them all screwballs. He could see that Professor Bowyer had noticed something going on between them and was studiously trying to ignore it. It did not mean that he wasn't trying to listen.

Professor Bowyer said without moving his head. "Where did you find it?"

Jean and Ed Grann exchanged a startled glance. The professor went on. "I can guess. Give it to me. I'm the least likely to have it at my age. And I went nowhere near the bodies so they wouldn't suspect me."

"No."

The professor turned to give Grann a long, searching look. "Don't they teach you discipline at those American hospitals?"

"They do, sir, but you're not getting the gun."

Shaw started to walk back. Jean Sandingham said quickly. "Keep it until I give the word. Then I must have it quickly."

Shaw was edgy and kept looking down the ward towards McQueen, who seemed unaware of his scrutiny. Shaw's strength was that he had no previous record, had never before committed a crime. He did not want his advantage to disappear. He went to the empty room and, leaning forward across the corpses, put one hand on the windowsill to support his weight. The whole place had changed since their entry into the hospital almost three hours ago. The square was full of people and coppers and vehicles. By craning his neck he saw what he imagined to be the police mobile headquarters.

Shaw opened the window but stood well back with a hand over his face. A sea of people was already gazing up in his general direction. He wondered what rumours were floating around down there. How much truth had escaped? So far the crowd was loose and moving but it would thicken as time went on and the word spread. Already flashlights were exploding in the street like falling stars. They hurt his eyes, even so far away, and he closed the window.

He looked at the corpses again; they didn't disturb him as much as he'd expected. One of Barret's arms had slipped, the dead hand resting on the floor. It was a wonder his wig hadn't moved. The doctor had closed all their eyes and he was glad of that.

He went into the next room and gazed down at the emaciated figure of Lord Driver. With no one else there he no longer had to sit on his feelings. If ever he felt unsure he had only to come in here and his problems disappeared; he remembered what he was here for.

It hadn't been Lord Driver himself, of course, but the son: the Honourable Mark. The sleasy, cheating bastard. It was easy to be wise after the event, to understand why such a wealthy man should use such a small concern instead of one of the big contractors.

The reasons for breaking away and starting his own business had been Shaw's dream; he'd always wanted to do it to be independent and it was what Ruth wanted. He had qualified later than most and with little schooling behind him. But he'd always been improving himself and he'd worked long into the night to succeed.

When he finally started on his own he experienced the dignity of independence and was doubly pleased by the pride he put into Ruth. She was full of it; she loved to tell the neighbours how well he was doing. It had embarrassed him at times but he understood why she did it.

Ruth had come from a better family and her parents had objected to their marriage from the outset. But she had loved him, attracted by his looks, his vast determination to succeed and his obvious honesty. He was never devious with her. She believed in him, believed he would obtain from her parents the respect that he deserved. A delicate, sensitive girl, she had been deeply cut by the family rift but her feelings for Shaw were solid. One day he would triumph and the family would acknowledge their mistake and be proud of him.

He worked hard, much harder than when he'd been studying. Ruth gave him every encouragement and was self-sacrificing, and he bought her clothes they could not have afforded before. With her trim figure and long auburn hair she was very attractive. When she boasted to their friends it was her parents she wanted to get back at, but that was yet to come, when they were really well established.

Some of the money he should have ploughed back into the business went on Ruth as a reward for her faith in him and because he thought the world of her. How could anyone like him land someone like her? It often amazed him; he loved her the more.

And then he landed the big one. Through a friend of a friend he learned that Lord Driver's house, well, mansion really, needed completely rewiring and a new burglar alarm system installed. He made enquiries and discovered the name of the agent to the estate and went to see him. It was then he learned that the Hon. Mark Driver was responsible for contracting the work and that his father was ill. He was asked for an estimate, which meant going over the premises in detail. Vast. No wonder they wanted new burglar alarms, with the paintings and furniture they had. It was like stepping into a private museum.

It was a big job and if he landed it he'd have to employ extra labour. He went home and did his sums, cutting the price as fine as he dared. He knew he would have to pay for materials and labour in advance, but by being careful he could do it. And afterwards he'd have made the best profit ever and it would set him up for bigger things. He couldn't see a contractor giving a finer quotation and he was right.

He got the job; and the Hon. Mark Driver's signature was on the contract that the agent made with him. He put all his effort into the work, employing another man at high rates in order to attract him to work for a small, private contractor. He even asked Ruth to cut back on everything while he made the initial outlay.

She was wonderful about it. At a time when they had become used to better living she hid her disappointment but fully understood. Then one day halfway through the Driver's job he asked her to sell her fur coat. It was early spring and bitterly cold. He was tortured as her eyes misted and were pricked with tears.

"Yes, of course, darling."

But he could see how he'd hurt her. "Pawn it, then. Only for a while. I need the money to see the job through. I'll get it back or, better still, I'll get you another one." He held her by the shoulders while she lowered her head against his chest. It wasn't the coat that worried her but the fact that its absence would be noticed by her friends. Suddenly their dreams had received a jolt that all in their little world were going to see. Her parents were further away than ever.

He explained carefully, gently, and she understood. She did not argue but she couldn't keep the pain of her disappointment from showing. He knew how she felt. "Don't worry, Ruthy. When the job's finished we'll be well off."

She began to sleep badly but never once did she remonstrate with him. He went to the bank to try to raise a loan and was surprised when he didn't get one, considering the wealth of the Driver family. But he didn't look into the reason and the bank manager made no effort to give him one. In a way he was relieved, he much preferred to rely on his own resources. He deeply regretted, however, the effect on Ruth. He was learning the bitter lesson that the building of even a small business did not depend entirely on effort but needed capital.

When he sold the car Ruth became very withdrawn. She was pale and edgy and she didn't like being driven around in the tatty van he used for business. Then neighbours began to talk and for Ruth it was all her parents' predictions come true. She began taking pills to sleep, and he blamed himself for not having planned things better.

He had one big advantage over her. *He* could see the end of the tunnel. The job was going well. The Drivers' agent who examined it from time to time approved. Apart from a couple of servants whom he got to know, the house was virtually empty while the work was going on, although he twice saw Lady Driver and was struck by her beauty. Once he caught her glance, the soft, inward-looking eyes, and she bade him good morning very sweetly. But she was remote, from another planet.

By the time the job was finished he was more than feeling the strain. He was used to straightforward, honest-to-God issues and not the sort of crises he'd been enduring. He paid off his assistant, having stretched himself to the limit. He worked late into the night and sent off his account the following day. Even though he knew he probably wouldn't get his cheque for a month, he put on a cheerful face and told Ruth their fortunes were changing. She rallied a little but a lot of damage had already been done. Having shut herself off she found it difficult to face people again and had begun taking tranquillisers to ease her loneliness.

A month later, after sending out a second statement, he finally rang up the agent who told him he was waiting for Hon. Mark to approve the account.

"Approve the account? What are you talking about? The quotation was accepted; there are only a few extras."

"Nevertheless it has to be checked. He's a very busy man."

"So am I, mate. And I want my money."

"There's nothing abnormal in the procedure, Mr. Shaw. It's normal business practice. Five weeks is no time at all.

Many businesses are willing to wait three months, six months."

Three months! Six months! He wouldn't survive. He was already being pressed all round, he had precious little to live on. "Look," he pleaded desperately, "I'm not a big business. I'm a small man and I'm usually paid immediately after a job. Could you please do what you can to push it forward?"

"It sounds as though you're undercapitalised."

"I'm only asking for what's mine." He was sick of himself, begging for his own money.

"I'll do what I can, Mr. Shaw. I really will."

And he probably did. But Shaw received no money.

The final crunch came when he told Ruth that he would have to wind up the business. He was in debt; he couldn't pay his suppliers and the only way he could would be by selling their small home and getting a job.

He thought she was going to cry but she didn't. Trembling fingers touched her lips and she mutely implored him to reassure her. Then, almost inaudibly, "Bankrupt?"

"Voluntary liquidation, but it amounts to almost the same thing. I'm sorry, Ruth."

She sat down, pale and staring into space. He noticed how she'd lost weight over the last weeks.

"Oh, God! How can I face our friends?" But friends were only part of it. She dreaded her father saying "I told you so."

Bewildered, he didn't know what to do. He put an arm round her shoulders but she was like ice. It was like plunging a knife into his own guts. He'd been let down by Driver but in turn, he'd let Ruth down. He had done all he could and he had failed.

The next day she collected her frail resources, swallowed her pride and performed the hardest task of her life. To ask her father for the money was a feat she never really knew she could face. To suffer his refusal was the final humiliation. She suffered then as she'd never suffered; but Shaw knew none of this. Ruth was too ashamed to tell him she'd even been to see her family.

Over the next two days her obvious deterioration was his worst punishment. His resentment against Mark Driver began to fester. He found it strange that those with limited resources invariably paid their bills promptly, his at least, and those that wallowed in money hung on to it like grim death. He knew nothing of the mounting crisis within Mark Driver's banking world and if he had he would have seen it as no excuse. His bill was peanuts in the scheme of things.

The morning he woke up to find Ruth dead beside him was the day his world collapsed. At first he thought she was still sleeping but the coldness and stillness of her filled him with dread. He knelt over her, trying to get her to respond. He tried artificial respiration and then, flooded with despair, called the doctor. Long before the doctor arrived he knew it was all over.

In death she was spared the ignominy of the police visit, the examination of her drugs, the close questioning of Shaw, the temporary suspicion attached to him. And he bore it in a cold daze, barely aware of what was happening. She had by no means taken all her sleeping pills and it was doubtful if she had deliberately taken her own life. But the number she had taken, in her low state of health, had been enough to kill her. In any event the coroner gave her the benefit of the doubt. Accidental death. Shaw knew better. It was no accident; she had been reduced to it because a conniving aristocratic bastard hadn't paid his bill.

There were two days which he couldn't account for at all, when he'd had some form of black-out, as if the deadlines of truth had mercifully drugged him. But it was only a postponement. When clarity began to return definition took shape in a tremendous hatred for Mark Driver, a man he had never seen. He began to plan his dreadful revenge, at first unsure of direction but clear as to purpose.

When he discovered he had no hope of ruining Mark Driver it increased his frustration; his hate verged on madness. He developed cunning, something he had never used or known he possessed. He chatted up the servants he had befriended at Cleats Hall when he had been working there; and it was then that he discovered some facts about the Drivers that servants aren't supposed to know but cannot avoid learning when their employers' voices are raised.

He had sense enough to take himself in hand, to tidy himself, to start shaving again; over the course of time he learned enough to plan in detail. When he had his plan he needed money to finance it. He sold everything he had, including his van and house, and he left bills unpaid for the first time in his life. He no longer had a conscience about letting others down as he'd been let down. His thoughts were solely directed at extricating enough money from Mark Driver to ruin him through estate duties; if not to ruin, then to ensure that he never forgot.

As he watched Lord Driver's almost undetectable breathing he was tempted to turn off the machine. It was true that it was not the father but the son who had ruined him, who had lost him his wife, but it was the same family; what matter which part he hurt, provided the effect reached out to squeeze the life from one he hated most?

He went back to the Sister's office like a man in a trance. Professor Bowyer at once noticed the haggard lines, the strange light in his eyes. The man was still suffering trauma; he was right on the verge of a breakdown. Ed Grann noticed it, too. Whatever had happened to the stocky man it could not improve their position.

And then, with a tremendous effort of will, Shaw pulled himself round. This was what he had been waiting for, for so long; nothing must go wrong now.

Nurse O'Connor and Nurse Cummings had collected the tea things and had gone to wash them up. Observing Shaw's partial recovery, Professor Bowyer rose slowly and said, "I must attend to the patients, they've been neglected long enough."

"Sit down, prof. They'll survive a small delay."

"I don't call several hours a small delay. These are serious cases."

"Including old Stars and Stripes? Is he serious?"

"As we've had no time for a thorough examination it's difficult to say. But if he dies on us you'll walk out of here the poorer. Dr. Grann, will you prepare an anti-tetanus injection, please?"

"You're not injecting anyone, prof."

Professor Bowyer had turned towards Ed Grann, who was trying to read the older man's mind. An anti-tetanus injection? Who for?

Bowyer turned back to Shaw; his mood was one of quiet indifference. "One of my patients is your man by the door. The wound has been cauterised as well as possible in the circumstances but he must be immunised. There's no harm in it and he may be very sorry later if he doesn't have it."

"What did you inject him with at the time?"

"A very mild soporific to combat shock. If I'd wanted to drug him I could have done it then."

Shaw was uncertain.

The professor added, "How do you think it will help us if we put just one man out? Do you imagine we wouldn't expect you to do something to us? His muscles could lose their use if he's not injected."

Shaw looked at McQueen. They could be right, he reflected, and doctors might be difficult to come by for a while later on.

"All right. Any funny business and you've had it."

"I've no wish to die, young man. It must be understood that if I treat your man I must also attend the other patients."

As Shaw hesitated, the professor burst out angrily, "For heaven's sake, do you imagine I can give them boosters to cure their ills at the flick of a syringe? I treat all of them or none."

Shaw nodded. "One of us'll go with you."

Ed Grann understood the message and it worried him. The wounded man had already received a tetanus shot. The professor was buck-passing an enormous responsibility in the knowledge that Grann, at one time, had considered becoming an anaesthetist. He had finally found it unattractive but he was left with something more than basic knowledge. Two days ago, one of the research doctors working on the animals upstairs had been interrupted during a conference with Grann and had left three phials of a new drug he was working with. He had locked them in the drugs cabinet where they were still awaiting collection.

All these drugs were variations of the kind of muscle paralysers used to knock down wild animals. The usage, though, required specialist knowledge. It was important to gauge the weight of the animal, too much could stop the heart and respiratory muscles; too little would be ineffective.

Ed Grann opened the drugs cabinet. The gun under his surgical coat was a constant and uncomfortable reminder of the tight-rope they were all walking. He thought of Jean, scared like all of them but riding it with so much dignity that it gave her a false impression of aloofness. His concern for her came as no surprise, only its depth made him thoughtful. If he made a mess of this he'd be placing them all in danger, as if they weren't in enough already. With unsteady fingers he located the three bottles placed quite separately from the rest. Curare. Scoline, Flaxedil. They all did similar jobs but their timings were different. Flaxedil was the slowest. He was sweating as he took down the bottle and reached for a syringe. He prayed to God that he got the dosage right.

10

THE PRIME MINISTER looked across his desk at Harvey Reeve, the Home Secretary, with no expression at all. His cold blue eyes in the puffed florid face did not waver, nor did his hands, both on the desk, move at all. "I don't like it." It was the understatement of the year but Harvey Reeve knew his man well enough to know that the icily uttered complaint covered much more ground that it ostensibly implied. It meant that he didn't like any part of it; the way it had happened: the initial, and perhaps the present handling of it; the delay in it reaching him and that it should dare happen at all during his reign. His immediate concern was not for the safety of those involved but for the political repercussions. He now had the unenviable task of informing the

President that the identity of the Secretary of State had become known to the gunmen and that they had made their demands. He picked up the hot line to Washington, giving his Home Secretary a cool nod of dismissal.

Harvey Reeve left feeling more ruffled than he had for a long time. He went next door to telephone the Commissioner of Police, and was redirected to the mobile network. He gave instructions that the armed men were to be told that the Swiss were being contacted by telephone and that the money would be transferred. He also gave instructions that only the most senior of police officers were to be told the identity of the V.I.P. in the private wing and then only if the knowledge had some bearing on their action. Secrecy was paramount. He reconfirmed that the press could have the Driver story and hoped it would be smokescreen enough for the major problem. He made a solicitous enquiry into the condition of the two wounded police officers and insisted on being kept constantly in touch.

One of his main abilities was to know when not to interfere with the running of any project by competent professionals. He had nothing to offer them except any extra assistance that might need his authority; like the army. Also, at this stage, there was absolutely no political advantage in being publicly linked with the proceedings. He had full confidence in the police but he was also a realist. It was a very, very dangerous situation from which, at the moment, only the gunmen could gain. If the Secretary of State was harmed, or worse, he had no doubt that God at No. 10 would play musical chairs with his cabinet and he would be the one to be left standing.

*   *   *

Commander Gifford was satisfied that, short of using the army, he had as many men as he could reasonably hope to get. He knew that the answer was not in numbers alone; the gunmen would have anticipated all this. In fact the more men there were, the more difficult the control was, and the wider spread the range of authority the more open to error they became. But he could imagine what would be said if he didn't use them. The very show of strength imparted confidence to the American Ambassador and his small, troubled entourage. All the same, a good deal of what he'd done was showmanship he could have done without.

At the moment, much to the disgust of the police officers manning the telephones who had been pushed farther down the benches, Gifford had the hospital plans spread over the narrow table. With him was an architect. The two men poured over the detail in an effort to sort out any possible blocked-off old exits, or their proximity to tunnels. Opposite them was a man accustomed to being squeezed on a van bench; he was a main drainage inspector who had no plans of his own with him but knew every sewer in the area better than he knew his own back garden. And next to him was an electrical engineer who possessed similar knowledge about cable tunnels.

The call from the Home Secretary to the Commissioner came through while they were examining the plans. A constable went out for the Commissioner and Jack Gifford cursed the lack of space in the mobile. The Commissioner came in, kept the phone close to his ear and, apart from filling in on the state of the wounded men, confined himself politely to murmured yes, sirs, and no, sirs. He went outside after the call and a moment later the A.C. asked Gifford to come out. He left his experts to continue their paper search.

When he had been briefed Jack Gifford went to the Secretary's office to contact Ginger Shaw. The arrangement of using the extension wasn't the happiest method of communication but if that's what the villains wanted then he was stuck with it. And it did provide privacy.

When Gifford got through to Shaw, he said: "You're getting your three million. The Swiss will ring you as soon as the details are settled. As the call will be routed through the switchboard, which is constantly busy, the telephone exchange will be instructed to break in on calls to establish quick contact."

"Right. What about the other million?"

"It's still on its way. You should be feeling satisfied."

"Much more than that, copper. Much more."

"We'll see if you're around to enjoy it." Gifford disengaged quickly. When he got back to the mobile he received a message that a deserter named Beatty had the marksmanship ability of the man in the generator room. How many more of them were there?

The helicopter landed in the small central green of the square and caused a sensation. Speculation buzzed round the thickening crowd, who were being pushed back against the railings round the green. Gifford ran from the mobile, through a crowd of reporters and cameramen, through the iron gate which was immediately locked behind them, over to the machine. The whirlwind of air current eddied about them. As soon as he was strapped in, the gnat-shaped machine took off and tilted forward.

They kept low and resigned themselves to the inevitable complaints.

As they circled Gifford picked out the armed police strategically placed on the hospital roof. He decided that there should be more men on the adjoining roof just in case the gunmen tried to slip over that way. If they ever managed to filter into the crowd they'd never find them, not in the rush hour. And the underground station at Holborn was just below. He had the feeling that somehow they intended to reach the street. Gifford hated helicopters, not only because of their noise but because the air was not his element. It was like being carried in a flimsy balloon, floating up and down, leaving his stomach all over the place. But they had their uses. He concentrated on the problems. The men were bound to be wearing some easily detachable form of disguise. In the case of McQueen it was a wig. At least Gifford had an accurate description of that one.

They coasted across the top of the hospital, noting the bumps and bruises of outhouses and the varicose veins of the pipe networks. Gifford tried to attract the pilot but the machine drowned his voice. He tapped him on the arm. "Driver, do you think you could land there?"

Driver! The pilot gave him a look of disgust, noted the space on the hospital roof and gave a thumbs up. He took her down in a sweeping arc to get his own back on Gifford and then suddenly hovered. Gifford was stiff, his feet hard against the deck.

The pilot steadied, then lowered her gently on to the roof. Gifford climbed out a little shakily ducked away from the rotors, and stood looking around him. Even now his close mass of hair withstood the wind current. "Well, that answers that," he said to himself. He turned to the pilot. "You push off. I want to look around up here. I'll take the stairs."

As the helicopter lifted off to return to the green Gifford sought the stairs, making sure he avoided those that went either end of the private wing. He felt more like a copper back on earth.

When he located the wooden door leading to the stairs Gifford went down them thoughtfully. He knew that the operating theatres were just below the private wing but what was immediately above it? Ostensibly it could make no difference, the villains couldn't sprout wings, but on the way down he thought he'd check. He ran into a barrier of security that surprised him. What he found were the experimental laboratories containing animals. He didn't like what he saw, but it ended up all the same in his analytical memory.

By the time he reached the street the television boys were there poking 16-mm cameras into his face and asking him to explain the situation. He stuck to the time-honoured routine of "no comment" and referred them to Fred Jessel. In the mobile there was no further word from the Hon. Mark Driver and there were just less than two hours to deadline.

* * *

Professor Bowyer approached McQueen. Had the dosage been right? If Grann had been heavy-handed McQueen could die.

Nurse O'Connor gently rolled up the sleeve of McQueen's uninjured arm, noting the thick muscles under the mat of hair, feeling the combined suspicion and lechery from the ever-watchful eyes. McQueen stopped her and handed his Sterling to Allbright who stood just behind the professor.

Professor Bowyer took the syringe from the tray Nurse O'Connor had brought and cleared the needle of air. The nurse was qualified to make the injection but the professor had no intention of letting her take the responsibility. If there were repercussions they could fall on his head and Grann's. He inserted the needle, pressed the plunger and somehow closed his mind to the consequences of what he was doing. It was too late for second thoughts now. How long the drug took and its subsequent effect would depend on Grann's dosage. It was a bad time to have doubts.

At the other end of the ward Ginger Shaw had taken over so that Allbright could accompany the professor on his rounds and make a check on outside activity at the same time. For the moment some pressure was taken off those in the office.

Before the professor began his round Jean Sandingham checked her index in order to prepare the various injections, medicines and pills for the patients. Nurse O'Connor could only carry the requirements of one patient at a time, for safety reasons, and kept returning to the office. During this time it had been relatively easy for Jean to take out a roll of Elastoplast and leave it on the desk.

The crux of her plan to hide the gun depended on the height of the drugs cabinet, below which was a working top. While she was at the back of the office neither Shaw nor McQueen could see her but she knew that if she stayed there too long one of them was almost certain to investigate. Periodically she allowed herself to be seen, checking a medical chart and generally pottering around the desk. Nurse Cummings too, remained on view. The additional risk was Allbright, who, when he'd been previously popping in and out of rooms, had never failed to examine the office activity at each reappearance.

The professor selected the room with the three ladies first, after injecting McQueen. None were his patients, and that meant that he would have to take longer with them in order to know what he was talking about and to win their confidence under such extraordinary harrowing conditions. And if Allbright stayed with him it would tie up one gunman for a few minutes. He'd given Grann a heavy wink before he left the office and he'd expected his houseman to understand.

At first Grann was puzzled, but as the professor led the

way to the farthest room from the office, he realised what the older man had in mind. He waited until Jean was at the desk and then fiddled at the drugs cabinet, once he was sure that the professor had taken his escort into the far room. He pulled out the gun clumsily, afraid to look round, relying on Jean to give him some sort of warning if he was being watched. It hadn't felt so heavy when he had pocketed it. He laid the gun down on the work top, shielding it from view with his body. Jean had whispered for him to leave it there but he realised that he couldn't, not in full view. He was annoyed now that he hadn't asked her what she meant to do with it.

He picked it up again and held it down his side as he stepped back towards the desk. Nurse Cummings saw what was in his hand and was horrified. Jean Sandingham, seeing the nurse's look of shock, stepped between her and Shaw's line of vision and shot her a quick look of warning. Nurse Cummings recovered quickly but it was a nasty moment.

Allbright stepped from the end room, the Sterling under his arm, and looked straight towards the office. Grann didn't make the mistake of moving his arm, but he was unsure how much of the Beretta was visible. If Allbright raised the Sterling he'd know all right, for Allbright would shoot and that would mean the three of them, they were so close together. Nurse Cummings gulped and became frantically busy about the desk. Grann warmed to her, knowing she was trying to screen him from Allbright.

Jean Sandingham turned away from the desk in what Grann recognised as her professional pose, and went towards the drugs cabinet. She grasped the gun as she went past him and because she could not hesitate as she moved on, he thought she was going to drop it. He went cold, ignoring the pain when one of her nails bit deep into the back of his hand as she quickly shifted her grip. It was enough that this was happening at all, but to control his expression under Allbright's watchful eye was almost too much. Allbright was a man who literally looked for trouble, yet he must have seen no sign of it in the office for he went back into the room.

Both Grann and Nurse Cummings were still on view to Shaw and McQueen and there would be no let-up because

Allbright had gone. To act normally was the most difficult task of all.

At the back Jean Sandingham worked fast. She cut off strips of Elastoplast, with the gun laid down in front of her. Deftly she started to tape it under the drugs cabinet. It was awkward; she dared not bend to see what she was doing and the loaded gun was heavier than she had imagined. She had hardly begun when she dropped it on to the work top.

It was so quiet in the ward that the crash was heard by everyone. Nurse Cummings involuntarily screwed up a medical report, her short nails talonning through the paper into the palm of her hand, her gaze fixed. Allbright emerged again and Shaw and McQueen craned to see what had happened.

Grann knew he had to do something quickly but he was so afraid for Jean he could hardly move. His back was to her and he managed to turn slowly as if movement was something new, his muscles unused. Incredibly he heard her say, "I'm sorry if I scared you; I never could manage this damned bottle." She held a huge jar of Panadein and promptly put it down again, trying to remove the lid as if nothing had happened.

"There's a smaller bottle in the cabinet." Grann somehow managed to get the suggestion of a rebuke into his tone before he went to help her. They had played it just right. When he reached her she was counting out pills, to satisfy Allbright's curiosity; he had stepped farther down the ward to see what had happened. The gun lay in front of her, its muzzle pointing at her as if in warning. She was trembling, the pills rattling in her hand. Grann took the jar from her. "Let me help you," he said, and he thought she was going to burst into tears. Allbright disappeared again and Grann whispered, "Honey, you were terrific. Go back to the desk." She went because she was in no state to continue fastening the gun. Seeing what she had been trying to do was easy, with one strip still adhering to the gun and the others laid out ready. He finished taping the gun with the butt slightly angled towards him so that it would be easier to tear it away if the need arose.

He was glad he no longer had to carry it; the weight and

the bulk had been a constant worry. He went back to the desk with a tray full of drugs. Jean was pale but she'd stopped shaking. Nurse Cummings was trying to iron out the screwed-up report.

* * *

The Professor left two of the private rooms until last; Lord Driver's condition demanded no immediate treatment and the American V.I.P. was his own patient. He took the American first. He felt his pulse and was satisfied. Lifting each eyelid in turn he examined the pupils. His opinion hadn't changed from the first examination he had given him. The fellow needed rest, had missed so much sleep that he had found it impossible to sleep at all; a side effect of over-work and over-stress. The drug-induced sleep would help, followed by a period of rest. But did they ever take heed?

He went next door to Lord Driver and almost immediately he realised that the patient was dead. He made a rapid and thorough examination, and then warned Nurse O'Connor not to utter a word to anyone, that it could cost her her life. He was not exaggerating. The million-pound ransom depended on Lord Driver's survival.

Professor Bowyer straightened, aware that Nurse O'Connor was eyeing him speculatively. What should he do? If he told them they might react violently; but if he didn't there was always the danger of them finding out. The big man was sharp, the sort of man to recognise death when he saw it.

The machine was still humming. Professor Bowyer stood by the bed, glad that the eyelids were already closed and satisfied that any emergency action he himself took would be futile. There could be no reviving him this time. Lord Driver dead. My God. He put a hand heavily on Nurse O'Connor's shoulder. "Not a word, my child. Not a word."

"Don't worry, sir."

"I can't help it; for the others, for all of us." He gave her a fatherly smile. "Good girl. Let's keep this between us." They went back to the office.

11

ALLBRIGHT GAVE THE "duchess" a cold wink that made her snort angrily and turned to the girl. "What do they call you?"

She sank against the pillows, unsure and afraid of him still. "Pip Goldini."

"Pip?" He leaned against the wall, hitching his gun up under one arm and gazing down at her. "So if I squeeze you you'll fly away." He saw her fear. Her features were so delicate that she portrayed every emotion she felt, almost every thought. Yet he was unable to reassure her, knowing that if it came to the crunch she would be treated no differently from the rest. But she and the "duchess" had guts.

"When're you getting out of here?"

Her big luminous eyes looked up and he wasn't sure how much of him she could see.

"I don't know." She replied so softly that he had to lean forward to catch her words. "Perhaps never."

"Never's a long time. You can't tell what's round the corner. Look at our business. New locks, new safes like new diseases. We have to find new ways of treating them. They might come up with something for you."

It was the strangest reassurance she had ever received. She could see most of him but the sclerotomy removed pieces from his shape so that he was incomplete. His face was fuzzed at the edges; his voice was rough and uncompromising. Because she had been deprived of so much, people interested her more. Voices had new meaning and she had learned to interpret almost every inflection. There was little she had learned from this man except his unrelenting application. "Why do you do it?" She saw him harden and wondered if she'd gone too far.

"Stealing?"

"And killing?" Her pulse quickened as she realised the risk she was taking.

"You mean those out there?" He pointed back along the ward.

"If they are the only ones."

He had never heard a voice so pure. It fascinated him. "Well, this lot set about us first. We didn't expect them. You can't believe we'd stand by and let them shoot us?"

"What were armed men doing here?"

He told her. It didn't matter to him who knew.

"And how do you expect to get money?"

He told her that too, curious to see how far she would go.

"You'd kill the man if you don't get the money?"

"He's almost dead now. We'd only be helping him along a bit; probably be doing him a favour. You see, love, in my game you can't afford to issue empty threats. Once you fall down on one they know your weakness."

"Are we included in your threats?"

He hesitated. "Yes. All of you."

"So you'd kill us?" She had expected her voice to tremble as her hands fluttered involuntarily on the sheets, yet it sounded steady and she was pleased.

"If it is necessary."

"It doesn't worry you to kill innocent people?"

"I've never met an innocent person." Allbright scratched his head. He should stop this right now. This girl hadn't a clue how the other half lived, in spite of her problems. "Most coppers are bent, most judges too old and biased, and most juries stupid. Business men are as bent as I am and they destroy more people than we do." He hooked his thumb. "Don't tell me his lordship in there hasn't trampled on a few people in his time. No, miss. I don't think I've met an innocent person."

"I don't think *I've* ever harmed anyone to my knowledge."

"That doesn't make you innocent." He grinned awkwardly. "But it won't stop you getting knocked off if it comes to the point."

"Savage!" The "duchess" condensed a wealth of feeling into the word.

Allbright casually turned his head. Without rancour but with considerable iciness he said, "Bear it in mind, duchess."

"When did you start stealing?"

Allbright turned back to Pip Goldini in surprise. This girl never gave up. Maybe she had little to live for. Maybe they'd be doing her a favour. "I've been screwing around all my life. Started with scrumping; well, all kids do that. Then I went on to Woolworth's; I could hardly reach the counter." He was grinning reminiscently. "I can still see my little fingers reaching up to grab anything that was there and half the time not knowing what. After that I graduated to nicking tool kits from bikes outside cycle shops. I've never known anything different."

"You must have been to prison."

"Borstal, Scrubs, Dartmoor, Pentonville and Hull maximum security. I've seen most of them. But I'm not going back again, not this time."

"So you don't believe in justice?"

He scowled and she felt the danger.

"Justice? That's a strange old word. Never been sure what it means. There's not much about, I can tell you that. If I've been nicked for something I've done I've never complained. But it doesn't start or end there. It's a big subject and I'm too dead ignorant to discuss it. But tell me this; was it justice that I copped more than a child murderer? Was it justice that the leeches who lived off my stolen money for holing me up while the police were searching for me are still free while I did time for the money they blackmailed from me? Was it justice that they wouldn't let me out to my own wife's funeral because they said I was a top security risk? I've never broken out of nick in my life."

"They should have let you go to the funeral."

"They knew I wouldn't escape. They were too busy falling backwards over the bloody hardliners. It was politics, not justice." Allbright's voice had risen and suddenly he shook his head as if to remove memories. "You'd better drop it there, miss. You've been humoured enough."

The unfortunate mention of his wife had obviously upset him considerably. It would be easy to say he should not have turned to crime in the first place. Much too easy; he had not known any other way of life. He hadn't turned to it but had been born into it.

"I'm sorry."

He didn't answer but straightened and glared aggressively around the ward. It had filled in a little time. He went outside without another word.

As Allbright continued his inspection he saw the helicopter sweep down from the direction of the hospital roof and land on the green in the centre of the square, the air current rustling the tops of the trees. It was no more than he expected. All serious villains knew about Commander Gifford. He wasn't bent, which was a change. If everything they said about him was true then he'd have submarines down the bloody sewers. It made no difference. And he reckoned Gifford knew it.

When he looked through the window Allbright noticed how everything had increased; crowds, coppers, movement. The press would be down there making up what they couldn't find out. The police were obviously not going to try anything from the front of the hospital and time was now running against them. He thought they might have tried something up a turn-table ladder but he was glad they hadn't.

He took another look at their passport to millions. Just like his photographs really. Greying hair like frozen Cape rollers. Looked younger like this. Sleeping like a babe. One of the most important men in the world. He went next door to see Lord Driver. Looked dead already. But he'd better not be. The machine was still humming away.

* * *

In the Sister's office Professor Bowyer took a risk and sought out Ed Grann while Allbright was still doing his rounds. He made certain they were out of sight at the back of the office before he touched Grann on the arm. Jean Sandingham and the two nurses moved up front to put themselves on view. It was an undiscussed system they had fallen into whenever it was clear that one of them wanted to voice something.

"Driver's dead."

"Oh, no. That's all we needed, I guess."

"They mustn't find out. If they do they'll be walking a

nervous tightrope. The stocky fellow is already on the border line."

"I've noticed. I've been figuring how we might get information out. It would be useful to the police to know what's going on, how many are here."

"They'd kill us if we got anywhere near the doors."

"Maybe a note through one of the windows?"

They broke off with a sign, showing themselves to Shaw and McQueen before sidling back.

"Not so easy to write under close scrutiny. And I've just missed the opportunity. We won't be allowed back in the patient's rooms before they go."

"The telephone, then?"

The two doctors looked at each other almost shyly as if the idea had been there between them all the time and they had baulked at mentioning it.

"A terribly dangerous thing to do, Grann."

"I know. We *should* try something."

"He would see it."

"He might not. We could use it for a limited time."

"It would endanger us all."

They were talking in very low whispers, so low that they sometimes had to repeat themselves. And because Allbright made constant checks, they had to make it appear that they were reading and discussing reports from the index.

"I'm willing to take the blame if it's discovered."

"Be very, very careful. Good doctors are short."

"Thank you, sir." Grann smiled. "Will you ask the girls if they have any thread?"

With unspoken agreement the professor went back to the desk so that all but Grann were on view. The American took the Elastoplast from the cupboard and cut off a strip, folding it over and over until it formed a wedge. He left one end free. Jean Sandingham passed behind him and he suddenly found a reel of cotton by his side on the work top. Cutting a length he attached its end to the exposed sticky flap and folded it over to complete the wedge. He heard Allbright come from one of the rooms but his back was to him and he kept working. He palmed the wedge and returned to one of the chairs behind the desk.

The telephone was the type that had two buttons sticking up from its cradle. Grann bent down to gauge the gap between the receiver and the cradle. Judging his wedge to be too thick he compressed it between his fingers. He hoped he hadn't overdone it; he reckoned he'd only get one chance. It had to be done before Shaw was back.

Professor Bowyer was the only one to know what Grann wanted. Even though they hadn't discussed the actual method it was self-evident. The professor rose from his chair and clumsily knocked the desk as he reached for the indexes. He went round the side of the desk to straighten things out, thus blocking Shaw's view of the phone. Both he and Grann willed McQueen to make one of his frequent visits to the peephole but the old pug failed to pick up their message. At least he wasn't looking directly at them.

The professor, aware that he was overdoing fiddling about the desk, straightened, still blocking Shaw's view. Allbright came out of the V.I.P. room and disappeared into Lord Driver's. It was now or never. Jean Sandingham produced a mirror and started to straighten her cap, tucking loose fronds of hair back under it. She didn't know what exactly was happening but she was picking up signals from the professor. She moved to the other side of the desk to block off McQueen. They were all getting used to communicating with barely-seen signs and expressions. Blocking off the gunmen's view was becoming standard practice.

Grann leaned across the desk and pushed the wedge of Elastoplast under the receiver. It still seemed too big; the receiver was unevenly balanced. He pressed the receiver down, afraid that he might push too hard, and there was the faintest tinkle of the bell. Grann had to make a split-second decision whether to withdraw the wedge instantly or leave it. He left it, deftly running the cotton down under the dial and across the desk, letting its end dangle down the front where they had been sitting. He quickly covered it with some reports.

He was sweating when he sat down. Jean Sandingham lowered her mirror and casually moved back; the professor stayed where he was just a little longer. As neither Shaw nor McQueen had moved the tinkle of the bell could not have reached the far ends of the ward. Ed Grann picked up a pencil and began to tap it on the desk in a crude, unpractised Morse.

*   *   *

The tapping through the phone in the Secretary's office went at first unnoticed. The police constable standing constantly by the desk heard what he thought was an erratic crackle and ignored it. Then he realised there was a kind of elementary consistency to it and lowered his head to listen. It wasn't all that loud but it was regular. As the agreed signal was a flashing which was very audible he was inclined to discount it. Yet as it went on he became restless and finally picked up the receiver from the desk. The tapping was more distinct now and the phone was clearly off the hook unless the operator had inadvertently plugged into another line. He did not know the Morse Code but recognised some sort of signal; an amateur. Very quietly he said, "Hello."

When nothing happened he thought the phone may have been accidently knocked, the receiver dislodged. He said, "Hello," a little louder and waited a reasonable time without response. He raised his voice, frustrated by now. "*Hello.*" He could not know that the five people in the office heard him and were wondering how to smother his voice. Ed Grann was in despair, praying that the three gunmen could not hear.

The constable said "Hello," again, this time with more annoyance and he heard a sudden fit of coughing then a sibilant whisper in an American accent saying, "Shut up, you fool." It took him three seconds more to realise that the urgent plea had been addressed to him and not to the person coughing. He went cold as he guessed what had happened. "Christ!" He laid the phone down on the desk as if it was a stick of dynamite, kept his hand over the mouthpiece and turned to his colleague. "Get Commander Gifford quick. Tell him someone's tapping Morse through the phone." He raised the phone again and continued to listen.

As soon as Gifford received the message he was on his feet at once. "Find me someone who knows Morse." Gifford ran to the Secretary's office, took the phone from the constable as if it was a letter bomb and put his ear to it. The tapping was there but it was not Morse, it was too spaced, far too irregular.

He pulled out his handkerchief, stuffed the mouthpiece with it and turned to the constable.

"Is that the same as it was?"

The constable listened. "No, sir. It's changed."

It occurred to Jack Gifford that whoever was tapping out was taking a hell of a risk; they couldn't tap Morse for long, even a child would recognise its pattern. But they were still signalling nevertheless. How could he let them know that he understood what was happening? It had to be a noise to merge with the one they were making. Removing the handkerchief he took out a ballpoint, waited, timed it as best he could and interspersed three loud taps with those on the phone. He hoped that they heard. When the tapping stopped he knew that they had but had the villains also? There was no firing. He picked up the receiver and rammed it against his ear with the handkerchief in place and one big hand over the mouthpiece.

Someone near the phone had a fit of coughing and he heard a girl's voice, sympathetic; he caught the word water and it sounded as if the girl was telling someone else to fetch some. But he could only catch odd words and those very faintly. Then he stiffened as another voice reached him, clearer but still faint; American! When the Secretary had listed the staff up there he hadn't mentioned nationalities.

"Three men. One wounded in arm. Like a boxer. One shortish. Stocky. Called Ginger. One big . . ." The voice stopped abruptly and Gifford's heart beat faster and louder. He could only hang on. His concern was immediately for the speaker. He couldn't hear a damned thing except that the cougher was spluttering a little. Something was put down fairly heavily near the telephone. It was almost uncanny, like waiting to hear from the grave—the analogy could so easily turn out to be right.

There was a tap on the door and one of Jock McDonald's

men came in. His jacket swung open to reveal his gun as he wheeled and closed the door. Gifford pierced him with a look and signalled him to do up his jacket.

"Morse, sir. You wanted . . ."

"Sit over there. May not need you now." Gifford was straining to pick up any sound. God, it was quiet, as if they were waiting for him to speak. If they were then it would be the wrong party and he wasn't falling for that one. Then, at last, so faint he almost missed it. "Lord Driver is dead."

Driver dead! Christ, had they killed him? He wanted to ask the question but stood, stony-faced, giving nothing away to the others in the room. He waited, worried and anxious for these people who were risking so much to give him information. The silence became almost unbearable. There should be movement; something.

Gifford continued to hold on, increasingly afraid, knowing there was nothing he could do to help, not even if firing broke out. He heard receding footsteps which brought back a measure of normality and then approaching ones that suggested a new danger as they grew nearer the phone. There was another bout of coughing but much milder than before. While he waited he raced over what he had so far. Three gunmen in the ward and one in the generator room. Fewer than he thought. There must have been one more and he was dead. Four stiffs, Inspector Erskin had reported; three of ours and one of theirs unless a patient or one of the staff had been killed. McQueen wounded. Well, he already knew that. But Lord Driver dead. Jesus! How should he play that when the Hon. Mark pitched up with his million? He signalled Jock McDonald's man to come close.

"Get back to the mobile. Tell them to check for a shortish stocky man who answers to the name of Ginger. See if it ties in with the checks being made about McQueen's associates. And tell them to check with Cleats Hall; anyone of that description and nickname ever employed there. I want it now. Drop everything."

A long minute later Gifford relaxed enough to sit on the edge of the desk. He couldn't leave the phone while the other end was still so obviously off the hook in some way.

Then the heard a new voice, flat, concise but some distance from the phone; he had to strain to hear what was said.

*   *   *

When Allbright had finished his rounds he went past the Sister's office slowly on his return to the end of the ward. He took a look through the spy hole, and, satisfied, took over guard from Shaw who returned slowly to the office. Time was running out and the tension was building up again to the proportions of their first arrival. It was likely that everything would happen during the last hour. A million in ready cash and another three million to be picked up later. Even Shaw now thought in these overall terms.

Ed Grann watched Shaw's approach, the Sterling held tight under his arm, and wondered what to do. He was caught between deep fear, not solely for himself, and concern for the unsighted policemen who needed all the information they could get.

He was reluctant to pull the wedge away now that he'd established that someone was listening at the other end. He didn't know how much they had heard; it might all have been a dangerous waste of time but he understood that they wouldn't acknowledge again. When, belatedly, he realised that he was risking too much it was too late. Shaw's gaze was riveted on the phone as if he was hypnotised by it and Grann knew that his chance had gone.

Shaw stopped at his usual place outside the office, still fascinated by the instrument that would bring him good news or bad, news that would govern what happened to those inside the ward. The five behind the desk didn't know what to do; if they tried to distract him he might get suspicious, the man was on edge. Yet they all realised that their very silence could be a sign of guilt. Any move could be the wrong one.

Ed Grann, sitting directly behind the desk, stretched out his fingers without moving his arm. He couldn't find the cotton and he didn't dare lower his gaze to locate it. Suddenly Shaw looked away and started to walk up and down just in front of the office. He was feeling tense, more than at any time. Suddenly he stopped and turned to the professor.

"You'll be glad when it's over. You'd better hope you'll still be around." It was a statement.

"Yes." Professor Bowyer had surreptitiously been watching the changing expressions, had noticed the spasm of mental anguish. He raised his voice slightly for the benefit of the telephone. "You're not used to this, are you? This is something new to you."

Shaw shrugged angrily. Honesty seemed a long way off, so far that it might never have existed. His life had started in this ward. "I warned you before, prof."

"Yes, you did. I'm sorry. As a professional man I'm naturally interested in what makes a man as basically honest as you do such a thing as this. You must have strong reasons for your hatred of Lord Driver."

"It's not so much him . . ." Shaw growled. "For the last time cut it out, prof. Treat me as a specimen once more and I'll let you have it. I mean it. I'm beyond caring what happens to any of you."

And that was the truth. They all knew it. Shaw would hold on and would hold out because he was strong. But reason played no more part in what he was doing, if ever it had. He had been forced beyond his moral limits and there was no way back. As if to confirm his indifference Shaw turned his back on them. Professor Bowyer, knowing he had pushed the man as far as he dared, leaned back in his chair and turned his head towards Grann. He gave a brief, almost imperceptible nod. There was no point in further risk; they had done what they could; the wedge should be removed.

Ed Grann got the message. The old buzzard had done well, he'd given the cops a line to work on. Now if this half-deranged sonofabitch would keep his back turned, he'd whip the wedge out. He was covered on his left by the position of the professor and on his right by Jean Sandingham. He risked a look down, located the thread, grasped it between thumb and forefinger and gently pulled.

Nothing happened. He pulled again, a little more desperately, but the wedge would not move. He intercepted an anxious glance from Jean. Shaw half turned as he pulled once more. The receiver rocked but the wedge stayed where it was and he realised that a lip of adhesive had stuck to the cradle. He moved his hand forward across the desk as Shaw turned completely round to reach for the phone. He looked Grann in the eye and grabbed the receiver.

12

Commander Gifford almost dropped the phone as Shaw flashed. For a moment he was caught unawares. He had sent the second police officer chasing after the first with a follow-up message to concentrate solely on recent associates and staff of the Driver family. He wanted every local C.I.D. officer digging out quick facts from Cleats Hall. Whoever had guided the conversation with the man he took to be "Ginger" was brilliant. It had been made clear that Ginger was unlikely to be an old lag, a regular villain. The pointer was to a grudge.

Jack Gifford held the phone at arm's length and poked his ear with a finger. Recovering quickly he pulled the handkerchief from the mouthpiece, altered the tone of his voice and said gruffly, "Yes?"

"What's happened to the call from Switzerland?"

"I'll get the Commander."

"Hold it. Don't waste my time, copper. You don't even know what I'm talking about. You tell Commander bloody Gifford that the call from Switzerland is overdue and I'm getting edgy. You tell him."

"I'll tell him." Jack Gifford heard the phone being lowered the other end and realised that the line was still open. What was going on up there?

* * *

Ed Grann almost gave himself away when Shaw lifted the receiver. He froze in his chair and somehow met Shaw's gaze without sounding the alarm. The exercise paid off; Shaw didn't notice the wedge of Elastoplast. How his fingers missed it as he flashed was a minor miracle.

When Shaw spoke into the phone he half-turned away from his hostages, as if he was too conscious of his show of impatience. For Grann it was now or never. The professor was in the best position to create a diversion and he realised it. He climbed awkwardly to his feet, knocking the desk, and lifted the tumbler of water. He attracted Shaw's attention and Grann reached out for the wedge while Jean Sandingham blocked McQueen's view. Before Grann could grasp the wedge Shaw slammed the phone down, his eye still on the professor.

Grann released a long breath. Shaw hadn't noticed, but the wedge was still there. The same luck could not hold twice. He stood up restlessly; Shaw noticed but made no comment. The two nurses, interpreting the unspoken innuendos correctly, started to chatter quietly, nervously. Shaw, already tense, missed some of the build-up amongst the others. He started to pace again and as soon as his back was turned Grann lifted the receiver and ripped out the wedge. The tinkle of the receiver being lowered made Shaw wheel round, his gun raised.

Ed Grann used every nerve he had to continue what he was doing. He kept his fingers lightly on the receiver, pushing it a little so that it tinkled again, feeling Shaw's burning eyes and well aware that it would take practically nothing at this stage to make the man fire. "It still wasn't on properly," he said mildly. Shaw stared hard at the phone and then at Grann, who started fiddling with the stethoscope in his coat pocket. Shaw moved over to the phone, picked it up suspiciously, examined it and the cradle, then put it down again.

Ed Grann smiled nervously at him. "This type often slips.

We replaced them years ago in the States." He could feel his fingers trembling round the wedge still in his hand and he wondered if it had all been worth it.

* * *

The Hon. Mark Driver had told his available fellow directors about the ransom. He'd had to, in order to draw a million in twenty-pound-notes. They had to shop around for the money. They told the truth to get it; it was, after all, merely the transfer of a quantity of a particular denomination of bank notes from certain banks to another. Fifty thousand twenties. Their main difficulty was in the late realisation that, in their chase around the City of London for the money, they had almost overlooked the necessity of four cases in which to pack it. They sent a bank messenger armed with fivers to buy four large identical cases. At such short notice it wasn't easy. While tellers counted off the notes the messenger scoured the City. Twelve thousand five hundred notes per case. Net weight somewhere around one hundredweight, say a hundred and thirty pounds with wrappers. Thirty-three pounds per case, plus the weight of the suitcases. Roughly the tourist class allowance on an aircraft. A fairly heavy but distinctly manageable amount per case.

* * *

At Cleats Hall Lady Moira Driver received her daughter Annabel and explained the situation as best she could without really understanding the many complex side-issues. A tall, slender girl, Annabel had the pale, drawn looks of her brother Mark. But whereas his weakness showed about the mouth and superciliousness shone often in his pale eyes, Annabel possessed a petulant pout and a soft sensuousness in eyes that were moist brown. With her small breasts she had the figure of a model; there was a time when she had carried herself like one.
As she helped herself to a large brandy Lady Driver despaired yet again of ever finding something of herself in any

of her children. They were almost strangers to her. How was it that someone with so much love to offer could have passed none of this on? And then she recognised that in Annabel she had; but that too much of it had made her mature the wrong way. She was well aware of her daughter's near nymphomania and of the long suffering her husband still endured. She knew the agony of it only too well.

"It would have been merciful if they had turned the machine off; better for your father."

Annabel's long, beautiful fingers clutched the brandy glass as she stood with her back to the window, staring at her mother with disdain. One leg pushed out below the flat belly against the pencil-slim check skirt. "And we'd all be bloody broke, if Mark is right, and he usually is. My God, mother, there are times when I think you are not of this world."

"If money matters to you more than your father's welfare, I'm glad it doesn't to me."

Annabel laughed, her carefully pencilled brows rising to meet the widow's peak of her hairline. "Mother, you're deluding yourself. You don't want that machine switched off for father's sake. *You want him out of the way.* You've never forgiven him for whoring around. And you know it."

Lady Driver felt the blood leave her face and she sank on to the nearest chair. There seemed no end to her children's insults. Did they hold her in complete contempt? They were hard, practical realists but must they always sneer at her romanticism? Yet as she sat there, staring at nothing, one hand creeping up to her temple, a deep coldness filled the pit of her stomach. She moved her arm across to warm herself. Had she just heard the truth? She raised her head.

Annabel still stood in that loose pose of hers. There was a certain elegance in the way she raised her glass, then peered over it, expression masked but for a trace of satisfaction.

"Mother, the death duties could cripple us, those and the pile of debts Mark seems to think are floating around. Do you really want to be destitute? Do you know what would happen to us, what we would have to do?"

Lady Driver rose slowly, colourless and unsure of herself

except in one respect. She really did not care about the money. She did not understand it, she had always had it and could not conceive being without it. At least this was true. Greed was foreign to her. She clung to her certainties and faced her daughter, noting the faint sneer that accused her of being too unintelligent to grasp anything. But there was one thing she understood very well. For the first time in her life she made no effort to protect another's feelings. She drew herself upright and looked her daughter coolly in the eye, satisfied to see doubt erase the disdain there. "If we lose our inheritance, if it's as bad as you say, then I know what *you'll* have to do, my dear. You'll have to start *charging* for lying on your back."

The sudden deathly white of her daughter's face gave her no satisfaction. At last she had been reduced to her level. The taste was bitter. With what dignity she could muster, she left the room.

* * *

Back in the mobile Gifford stared down at the long list of staff, tradesmen, known commercial callers, and people who had supplied or done work for Cleats Hall over the last few months. He decided that the quickest approach was to speak directly to the estate agent. He interrupted the sergeant and asked him to get the agent's telephone number from the Panbury police. Armed with it he took over one of the phones and dialled. It was answered almost at once, the man at the other end tense and breathless.

"I'm Commander Gifford of Scotland Yard, sir. Are you Mr. Norman Truddle?"

"I've only just finished with the local police. God, I've spent hours with them."

"And we're most grateful, sir. You've been a tremendous help. This will only take a minute. Amongst the many staff names you've given us would one fit a description of a shortish, stocky man with ginger hair?"

"Good Lord! How far back do you want me to go?"

"As far as your memory takes you, sir. Ginger hair; short; stocky."

There was a long silence and then Truddle said, "I can recall no one of that description."

There was something about the way it was said that ruffled Gifford. "Look, sir, I think you should know that some very brave people have risked their lives getting that little bit of information to me. Could you please give it a little more thought? Go over your own records; I'll hold on."

"I don't like your tone, Commander. It suggests I'm not trying to help?"

It was then that Gifford knew that Truddle was holding back; he had heard that half baked, slightly aggressive self assertion too often before, it was a cover-up. "If you think that, you're entitled to make a complaint against me, sir. I suggest you write to the Commissioner direct. But before you do bear this in mind. If any of the men threatening your employer get away with it because vital information is withheld, I'll turn every stone to prove it. And that's a very serious criminal offence. You have records, you have met people. I cannot prove that you can remember them but I will eventually prove whether or not you have personally met them and, in a court of law, your loss of memory would then look suspect." In a milder voice, Gifford added, "I know you've been harassed, sir, it's a trying time. But do please give it a little more thought."

"It's difficult to think at all under this kind of pressure." The tone was more guarded.

Jack Gifford smiled grimly to himself. "I know, sir. I know. Please take your time."

At last Truddle came back on, speaking very carefully. His words might have been rehearsed. "I have a vague recollection of a man who might fit that description, but it was months ago. My impression might be wrong."

"His name, sir?"

"I'm trying to think. He was an electrical contractor—did some rewiring up at the Hall . . . he called in, very distraught, once . . ."

Gifford ran a finger down the list the sergeant had given him. "Shaw, sir? Shaw Electricals?"

"That's the man. I'm certain of it."

"Why was he distraught, sir?"

"I beg your pardon?"

"You said he was distraught when he called on you."

"I don't know. I can't remember a thing like that."

"Yet you remember his state. Why did he call, sir?"

"You're asking too much of me, Commander, this was some time ago."

"But his condition obviously left an impression on you. Was it before, during or after he had finished working at Cleats Hall?"

"That's impossible to answer. Nor can I remember why he called. I simply seem to remember that he was upset about something."

"Then it couldn't have been to do with you. I mean, if he had been upset about something you'd done you would remember that."

"Perhaps he'd had a row with his wife."

"Oh, he's married, sir? That's helpful. Do you know his wife?"

"I don't *know* that he's married. Are you trying to trap me, Commander?"

"God forbid, sir! What could you have to hide?"

"I *think* he was married. I believe I heard something."

"Had he any reason for a grudge against the Drivers?"

"I can't imagine one. He did the job and that was that."

"Was his account queried at all? Maybe that upset him."

"Not that I'm aware. His quotation was accepted, and the final account was little different."

Gifford picked up the nuance. Truddle was feeling his way, conveniently remembering what suited him.

"When was the bill paid, sir? Did he have to wait a long time for it?" The silence told Gifford something but not enough.

"You'll have to ask the Hon. Mark that."

"Come, sir. You're the managing agent. You would know."

"Not necessarily. Some accounts Mark Driver attends to himself."

"So you don't know when it was paid?"

"No."

"You won't mind if I arrange for the local C.I.D. to examine your books?"

"I find that insulting."

"You shouldn't, sir. If it helps substantiate what you say you should be pleased. Nothing personal. We just have to explore every possible angle. I'm sure you understand." Silence. Then Gifford followed up quietly, "I think you ought to determine whether you should defend Lord Driver's son or the law, sir. I'll ask one more question. *Was the account paid at all?*"

The silence this time was too prolonged as Truddle battled with his loyalties. Finally, he lied, as Gifford had guessed that he would.

"I'm afraid I can't answer that."

"I reckon you just have, sir. Good day to you." Gifford was ablaze when he put down the phone. It may have been a long call but it had been worth every second. He looked across the table at one of his inspectors. "Get on to the Panbury Police and tell them to examine all transactions in relation to Shaw Electricals and Cleats Hall, particularly accounts and payments. They'll have to fight for a court order with the power that bloody family wields."

Gifford didn't know Shaw's qualifications but if he ran an electrical outfit he presumably knew something about it. So had the man who had wrecked the main switch room. Was he also an explosives expert? Or had the job been split? One expert advising another? Criminal records were already chasing a list of "bombers". Now, at least, Gifford had a sparks man and possibly one with a grudge against the Drivers. He set an enquiry going into Shaw's background and left the mobile.

In the Secretary's office Gifford paced the room under the scrutiny of the two constables. It was unlike him to be indecisive but one wrong move and he could put the hostages in jeopardy. Yet he wanted to be sure about Shaw. If he could do that he had virtually identified three of the four villains. That might not prevent the crime but it would make rounding them up later a lot easier. If they got away from here. And Jack Gifford was nothing if not a realist.

He looked at the phone, knowing the Commissioner

would never approve. But the Commissioner was out pacifying the Americans. He grabbed the receiver and rattled the studs. The same voice answered but it was huskier, strained.

"This is Commander Gifford. I understand you're worried about the call from Switzerland. It takes time to sort out three million but it's all being done."

"There's not that much time left. You know what happens if it's balled up."

"We all know. But you knew that the delivery would be near your deadline or you wouldn't have set one." Gifford was being as amiable as he dared.

"So why are you ringing?"

"I'm worried about your hostages. Are they all right?"

"So far. Anything else to say?"

"Why? Are you in a hurry to ring off? We're all walking a tightrope; you *and* us. This is one way of passing the time. You're nearing your last chance of backing down."

The phone clicked and Gifford knew that the sixth floor receiver had been hung up. It had been a wasted exercise because he'd been afraid of giving the game away. The only thing he had learned from it was negative; no real villain would have been so polite. Even the phone had been replaced quietly. Anyone like McQueen would have voiced a flow of invective and then have slammed it down.

* * *

Beatty took his tie right off, rolled it round his fingers and put it in his pocket. It was not only hot in the generator room but virtually airless, the smell of oil contaminating the fresh air creeping through the slats. The automatic pistol in his hand had become slippery with sweat until he had rammed it back in his hip pocket and wiped his hand on his shirt. He would have been happier if they'd tried something stupid again so he could let off at somebody like he had when he was shooting the lanky copper in the guts. He idly wondered if the man had died. Either way he'd have suffered, which was what Beatty had intended.

Sweat trickled down the hollow of his throat and he wiped his eyes with the back of his hand. He wondered how they were getting on in the private wing. It was some time since he'd heard from Shaw. No news was good news. All he wanted to hear was that the money had arrived. Then they'd get to hell out of it.

Beyond the opening of the dead end still blocked by the two police cars he could see the fuzz holding back several rows of onlookers. Several times the coppers had tried to create a gap in the crowd, but it hadn't worked.

The press photographers, stupid bastards that they were, kept taking long-range shots of the generator housing as if they could see him. That was the sort of crap they fed their readers; pictures of bricks, mortar and concrete with a dramatic story wrapped round it. They'd get some pictures soon enough, my God, they would. He'd give them something to remember for the rest of their lives.

* * *

Pip Goldini eased her wasted body under the sheets. She had carried on a low-toned, intermittent discussion with the fuzzed outline of the woman Allbright knew as the duchess. Neither of them knew the terms or the hour of the deadline. Yet a sense of the approaching climax reached into the ward like unseen clamps squeezing at her frailty. Perhaps being ill and helpless made one receptive to other, unknown channels. But she could feel her increased heartbeat and the stiffening of her clutching fingers against the sheets.

Pip was not so afraid for herself; her condition had long since erased most earlier fears. But she prayed that nothing would happen to those around her; not only the other patients she had come to know but the hospital staff. They had been wonderful. More than anyone, she was worried for them.

* * *

Pain was at last reaching the stolid McQueen. His shoulder was on fire. It didn't worry him unduly; he could accept pain, he'd been on the receiving end of it one way or the other all his life. But his muscles were turning to jelly. Like the others, he knew that the last hour was going to be the toughest. The gelt hadn't arrived yet and none of them would be really happy until it had. Then there was the three million to Switzerland. Christ! It was going to be close. They'd known that. But until the money arrived it was going to make them all increasingly edgy.

Picking up the Sterling he stomped awkwardly about the chair for a few seconds and looked round the ward. Allbright was lounging on his chair. He was no mug; he didn't miss a trick. Shaw was roaming the front of the office like a captive; he was showing too many nerves. Bloody amateur.

McQueen couldn't see too much of the people in the office. That cool bitch the Ward Sister was always leaning forward, fiddling with papers and an index file. Given a chance he'd take the ice out of her. He crossed heavily to the double doors he had bolted and peered through the peep hole. Empty landing and stairs. No lurking shadows. He shuddered as he remembered the dog; that had *really* upset him. But the dog was safe; they'd had the sense to get it out the way.

The tool bag containing the weapons the bodyguards had used lay beside the chair where Shaw had put it. McQueen went back to his chair slowly, disgusted at himself for being unable to move faster, sat down, put the Sterling across his knees and opened the bag. He rummaged around, annoyed at the difficulty of movement, but curious about the guns the Americans had used and surpised by the shortness of the barrels. He opened the cylinders one at a time and closed them again.

Eventually he had three guns out beside the chair. As all were unloaded there was no risk in leaving them on view for the time being. He groped around the bag amongst some of the tools and frowned as he pulled the bag on to his knees, making certain not to dislodge the Sterling. He made a thorough search and called down the ward to Shaw.

"Where's Charlie's gun?"

Shaw turned, held up the Sterling. "Here."

"Not the typewriter. His lucky gun. The Beretta. It's not here."

Shaw looked confused. Allbright and McQueen rose at the same time. McQueen was half crouched, finding difficulty in straightening. He glared towards the office. "Which of you bastards has got it?"

13

SHAW QUICKLY REALISED the danger of dissent in front of the hostages. He went up the ward to McQueen and growled. "Keep your bloody voice down. You've already used a name."

"Christ, there are plenty of Charlies and this one's stiff. We can't take him with us. They'll find out about him anyway."

"You don't have to save them time."

The remonstrance scored over the slower-thinking McQueen and he looked flustered.

"What's this about a gun?"

"He always carried a Beretta. Thought it was lucky. Didn't do the poor bugger much good."

"We had our own arms. Why should he carry another?"

"He never used the thing. It was a mascot."

"Why didn't someone tell me? Allbright must've known when we collected the guns. Anyway, if he had it, it must still be on him." Shaw went into the empty room and felt glad that Barret was top of the heap. He searched the pockets. How could one tell if Barret had carried the gun? He ran his hands round the waistband of the trousers and the body sighed as if it was still alive. Unsettled by the unexpected escape of air Shaw continued with distaste. It was one thing viewing a stiff, quite another handling one. He found the squat holster clipped to the back of the waistband.

He undid the clip and removed the empty holster; it had a compartment for a spare magazine which was also empty. He sat back on his heels. Barret would hardly have carried an empty holster. So near to success he suddenly felt danger. One gun wouldn't be much use against three machineguns; what were they doing with it? What else were the five in the office up to? What other little surprises was he going to find at this late hour?

Shaw felt a tick in his eye.

He rose slowly from Barret's corpse, the holster in his hand, went to the door, looked across to the office and saw a roomful of enemies. He held up the holster.

"Which of you took the gun?" He didn't expect a reply. Five white blobs of faces stared back at him with not a movement amongst them. Three women, two men. If it was a woman it would almost certainly be that proud bitch of a Sister who was looking at him so coolly with those steady clear eyes of hers. Almost certainly it was one of the men. And it could be either of them. "You two. Out in front here."

The professor and Ed Grann came slowly from the office.

"Get your hands up high and wide and walk up to the end of the ward." Shaw herded them to Allbright who took a quick look through the spyhole before separating the two men and making them stand with their legs apart and their hands against the wall.

Allbright kept the Sterling in his right hand, fingers on the trigger, and carefully searched Ed Grann with his left. He did it thoroughly and crudely, making the American wince, while Shaw kept his gun levelled at the professor. He then searched the professor who protested angrily. "What on earth do you imagine we can do with one gun? None of us would know how to fire it."

It was convincing because it was true. None realised the truth of it more than Grann, who wondered why he'd ever been so foolish as to take it.

"Come down here a bit," Shaw said, "where I can keep my eye on you."

The two doctors came a few yards towards Shaw and stood near the door of the toilets.

"Now you three; out you come."

The three nurses came round the counter, close together as if contact with each other made them safer.

"Take your clothes off."

"*No.* For Pete's sake leave them some dignity." Ed Grann stepped forward and pulled up sharply as Shaw swung round. There were changes taking place in the stocky guy which he didn't care for. It was the closest he'd come to dying; he didn't like the sensation.

Cold-eyed, Shaw said, "They can either strip or have my hand up their clouts, I'm not fussy."

"It's all right, doctor. It's no worse than a medical." Jean Sandingham smiled in a devastating way. She could see how close Shaw was to firing and she was already unbuttoning her uniform.

Shaw caught sight of something he hadn't seen in her before; a flashing glimpse of warmth, of a personality carefully hidden behind formality, or perhaps fear. He knew she was acting; no one could feel like smiling at such a time, but it was a good performance. His trigger eased before his next thought, more bitter, entered his mind. But the moment of danger had passed.

"Come on, girls." Jean stepped out of her uniform, her long legs encased in black tights. "We've asked the patient to do it often enough."

Professionally, nudity meant nothing to any of the staff, a naked body being simply a subject for critical examination. But beyond the bounds of professionalism doctors and nurses suffered the same carnal reactions as everyone else. This was not a professional occasion; there was too much fear and anxiety and tension for it to become a crude strip show. Except to McQueen, and, to a lesser degree, Allbright.

McQueen climbed to his feet and shuffled forward as the three girls undressed, dropping their clothes at their feet. He stood, grinning. "Let's put it to music. You can leave your little caps on." Allbright hid his interest behind a rigid mask.

When they reached the bra and pantie stage McQueen lowered his gun, his eyes bright. The professor observed quietly. "Surely that's enough. We can all see they're hiding nothing that's not their own."

Shaw, who was unmoved by the whole procedure, nodded acquiescence. All he wanted to do was to find the gun. McQueen quelled his disappointment and Allbright went round each girl slowly, his experienced eyes taking their time, seeking bulges that were no part of nature. For a moment or two he adopted the same professionalism as the doctors near him. This was no time for diversion. Like Shaw, he was worried about the gun. Only when he was satisfied that it was not on their persons did he again absorb the fullness of figure, the firm roundness of youth. He picked up their clothes and searched them article by article. When he had finished he gave a signal for the girls to dress and a disgruntled McQueen returned to his post.

The girls joined the men and Allbright returned to his post but covered the five from where he stood by his chair. Shaw went into the office and started searching. He tipped out the desk drawers and emptied the contents on to the floor. It was a savage, disorganised search that showed nothing of his earlier control. If they tried anything he'd kill the lot of them. He would not be robbed of satisfaction at this late stage. He had suffered, planned, waited, far too long. The strain had been tremendous but never like it was now. The internal pressures he had so far controlled felt ready to burst.

His search grew more frantic as he failed to produce the gun. The office rapidly became a shambles as he ripped out the drawers of index cards and upended them on to the heap that was already there. He circled the office like a scavenger, discarding, destroying, panicking. When he reached the drugs cabinet he opened the doors and indiscriminately swept everything on to the floor with wild sweeps of a hand. The sound of breaking glass, escaping liquid, and the rattle of rolling pills were the only sounds in the ward. In sudden frustration he tried to rip the cabinet from the wall. Had he succeeded he would almost certainly have found the gun; had he been calmer it might, too, have produced results.

He glared round, crushing glass and drugs underfoot, barely aware of the mixture of smells arising from the chaos. And still he hadn't found the gun. At the end of the ward Allbright changed his position so that he could better see what Shaw was up to. It sounded as though he was going berserk.

By now Shaw attacked anything out of hand; instead of stepping on to bottles and containers he deliberately ground them into the floor. The waste bin had been left until last because it was too obvious, and in any event it had been emptied before. He grabbed it and upturned it on to the desk.

At first the plug of Elastoplast did not attract him, then the cotton wound round it caught his eye and intrigued him. He picked up the Elastoplast and held it in the palm of his hand. It was like a balm. In it he recognised some form of danger without knowing what it was. It had the effect of making him think and thinking returned him to near normal. He unwound the cotton and dangled the wedge at the end of it.

The little gadget fascinated him. He went to the front of the office and held it up like a spider on the end of a strand of web.

"What was this used for?" He was much calmer now.

No one answered. Shaw said softly. "First you pinch a gun and hide it. Now no one knows what this was used for."

"From here it looks like a piece of Elastoplast. It could've been used for anything. We get through miles of the stuff."

"Then there should be more in the bin. I don't know what you're plotting, but I'll kill the lot of you if you try fouling me up now."

He held the wedge higher, spinning it between his fingers. "You don't think it's queer that this piece has got a tail?"

"If it's cotton it could've stuck to the Elastoplast in the trash can."

"It could've." Shaw slowly unfolded the wedge; the cotton was stuck well in. "But it didn't. What d'you use cotton for? Sewing up operations?"

"There are all sorts of uses for it." Jean Sandingham tried to keep her voice steady. "The nurses sew on buttons and things for the patients. You must have found needles and thread while you searched."

Shaw grinned. It was lopsided and nervous. He felt the whole job was being undermined. He jerked the thread and caught the wedge as it shot up. He held it in one closed hand and stared across at the five. "I'm not going to get the truth without killing or torturing some of you." For some seconds he did not move. He thought of the missing gun. To find it now could mean turning out all the rooms. He didn't put it past the professor to have hidden it while doing his rounds, but that would take a great deal of time. There was an easier method. He moved towards the five then stopped, caught by an idea. Going back to the office he went in behind the desk so that he could still see his captives. He lifted the phone and ran a finger over the cradle, feeling a tackiness near the front. He went cold.

He turned his back because he knew his face was a complete giveaway just then; it was screwed up and savage with rage. Fear, too; the fear of being prevented from achieving what he'd set out to do. What happened to him personally had never been of much consequence. How much had they heard the other end? It didn't alter the scheme at all; but ust how much had they learned downstairs?

He sat down behind the desk and looked thoughtfully at the telephone. The professor had done the odd bit of questioning. Crafty old devil. And so had the American, who was the most likely to have nicked the gun. No names had been mentioned, he was sure of that. The American had been sitting near the phone and he could now see the smokescreen of movement and noise the others had put up. So the young doctor had passed on information. But what the hell could he pass on that would really help the police?

Suddenly Shaw realised with disgust that he had virtually thanked the American for putting the receiver on properly; the bastard had been removing the wedge which had probably stuck. It was this that hurt him most. He was an amateur and had acted like one, among hardened professionals. That hit his pride. He could make an issue of it but if he did that he would lose face with Allbright and McQueen. Now, he'd re-established his position he didn't want to lose it again. But there was still the gun.

He looked round the office, suddenly surprised at the mess he had created. It was as if his mind was operating in two channels. Okay, he was under strain, but it was all right for the other three; they were hardened bastards well used to violence and crime. It was time to show he could be as tough.

* * *

The girls had dressed and joined the two doctors by the wall under Allbright's close scrutiny. Now that the last hour was being squeezed out vigilance was increasing; not that it had ever relaxed. Every so often Allbright would signal McQueen which meant the latter was now responsible for the group while Allbright checked his spyhole. Then McQueen would do the same. They were all closing in on the final stages and it was all just as open as when they had arrived except that if any of them were to die it would happen within the hour.

Jean Sandingham sought Ed Grann and her hand crept into his. Whatever form their relationship might take, whether it developed or died, right then she desperately needed his comfort. He squeezed her hand tightly. "Thanks, Jean. The strip was timely. That guy was just about to pop off at me."

"I know. He's vacillating dreadfully."

When Shaw approached the group, still dangling the Elastoplast, they all, in their different ways, noticed a change in him.

As he came nearer he was all-seeing, his eyes bright. Too bright. They were surprised when he didn't pursue the matter of the wedge and relieved when he went back to the office after his brief questioning. When he touched the phone cradle they realised he had deduced the truth. As he sat behind the desk it was not too difficult to guess something of his dilemma. When he approached them again it was clear he could not afford to take a soft line.

He stood in front of them, powerful, broad-shouldered, his earlier image difficult to trace as if it had been fragmented, the pieces re-assembled in a different way. His Sterling was under his left arm. He took the automatic Colt ·45 from his hip pocket and held it forward, almost as if he was offering it to them.

"If one of you don't tell me where you've hidden the gun I'm going to kill the first patient now." He spoke clearly, ensuring that Allbright and McQueen heard him.

At the back of the group Jean Sandingham dug her short nails into the palm of Ed Grann's hand as a warning for him to be quiet. She wasn't worried about the discovery of the gun, but she felt sick at the thought of a reprisal against him.

Grann didn't think Shaw was bluffing but he wasn't entirely sure. He decided to hold out as long as he dared. There was no sign of the others weakening and it was clear that they were leaving it to his own judgment. It was a mute sign of loyalty that moved him. When it came down to it he hardly knew these people.

"All right. All of you into the women's room."

Shaw herded them in. When they entered it was difficult to judge whether Pip Goldini and the "duchess" had heard. They were both sitting upright in bed, the "duchess" as defiant as ever and Pip clutching hard at the bedclothes. They were scared, trying to hold on to themselves.

"How long has she got to live?" Shaw indicated Pip who remained quite still. It was a brutal question with the girl there.

Professor Bowyer refused to be drawn in front of her. He couldn't judge what would make it difficult for Shaw. "As long as any young person of her age might expect."

Shaw grimaced. "Then I've news for you. She's dying. She's just a few seconds to live." He moved forward and placed the Colt against the side of Pip's pale forehead.

Pip couldn't move now; she was stiff with fright and although none of the figures about her were clear the cold steel circle of the muzzle against her temple was the most realistic thing she had experienced. She couldn't see it but she understood its every detail. And she was terrified. Suddenly the uncertainty of what she had to face in life was sweet. *She wanted to live.* "Please don't shoot." Her plea was barely audible.

The "duchess" made a strange gurgled cry and fell sideways on her pillow. Nurse O'Conner moved instinctively towards her and was rebuked by the professor. "Leave her, nurse. Her head is down. She'll revive." He spoke so matter of factly that it almost worked, like a snap of the fingers might rouse a man under hypnosis. For a moment he had shown that he was not in awe of the situation but as Shaw hesitated the seconds passed and the professor's bluff, splendid that it was, collapsed against the mind of the man who had to prove himself.

Shaw shook his head sharply as if he had been punched, steadied the gun and said, "Ten seconds."

Immediately Grann said, "Okay, you can take the gun away . . ." But before he could continue there was a loud shout from Allbright. Nurse Cummings, who was nearest the door, relayed, "He said the telephone is ringing."

Shaw's head shot up, his hesitation fractional. "All out. Back to the office. But don't think we've finished."

They waded through the mess he'd created and started to clean it up but Shaw stopped them, finding it difficult to hear. He suddenly grinned widely. It was perhaps the first completely natural thing that he had done since arriving. Immediately it showed an open, even boyish face, unmarked by worry, almost too innocent to be true.

It was clear that the call was from Switzerland. It was equally clear that Shaw's earlier reluctance to cash in on the American Secretary of State had gone by the board. His values had changed during the few hours he had been here. His glee was unbounded. As he listened he signalled Nurse Cummings to produce a ballpoint and paper. She scrummaged through the mess, while he impatiently asked the caller to hang on, and eventually found what he wanted.

"Give me the number again and the address." He frantically scribbled on the piece of crumpled paper and thrust it in his pocket. "Name?" He thought about that then glanced towards the room where the cause of their new fortune lay, slowly rising from layers of deep sleep. "Singer.

Keith Ian. I'll send you a specimen signature in due course." He straightened out a couple of details and hung up, then shouted disbelievingly. "We're millionaires."

A loud cheer went up from Allbright and McQueen. They were overwhelmed by the fantastic bonus of three million pounds. None of them suggested opting out now. The money was in Switzerland; it had to be collected. Meanwhile the million from Mark Driver would be ready cash, usable, invaluable, an immediate commodity.

Underneath the elation Shaw was well aware that the police would have tapped the phone call, but it didn't matter. The Government had probably made a deal with the Swiss bank. The police would probably be waiting for anyone who tried to draw on the account. But Shaw had given it some thought and considered that he had a way round it; one or two possible ways. He pulled out his radio, flicked up the aerial and called Beatty, not using his name.

"We're in the money. Three million in Switzerland. I'll buzz you when the last million arrives here."

In the generator room Beatty wiped the sweat from his eyes and gave a yell of triumph that the police heard and wondered about at the entrance to the dead end. The blood raced through his veins; he had to celebrate!

Wiping his eyes again he rubbed the palm of his right hand down his trousers and took out the Browning. He was grinning wickedly when he peered through the slats to the mouth of the dead end. There they were, the useless stupid bastards. Onlookers. Jostling the fuzz to get a cheap thrill out of someone else's mischief. Couldn't do it themselves. They'd go home and tell their families all about it, it'd make their day. Well, he'd give 'em something to talk about. And he'd do the job the fuzz couldn't do for themselves. He'd clear the crowd from the entrance. Just watch the stupid sods move. Three million. Jesus. He raised his gun and fired.

The blue flasher on the right-hand police car shattered. At first nobody seemed to know how it had happened. Then Beatty fired twice more and punctured a front tyre in each of the cars that blocked the entrance. The crowd suddenly surged either side, breaking away, pushing, fighting, anything to move from the line of fire. The police had to fight to hold a so far placid audience that was now being swollen by those trying to escape. A couple of helmets went flying as the cordon broke and Beatty could hear the scuffling and frantic voices.

He lowered his gun hand, leaned against the side wall and laughed until the tears rolled down his cheeks. Oh, boy! *That* was a little celebration. Even as he laughed he removed the depleted clip from the Browning and replaced it with the full one.

* * *

Shaw temporarily forgot his worries. He hadn't quite forgotten the gun, but its importance diminished in the light of the fantastic news he'd just received. They couldn't stage a one-man gun battle against the Sterlings and the three million had raised him unassailably high in the eyes of his companions. He was so pleased that he allowed the medical staff to start clearing up the mess he'd made in the office.

It would be difficult now to lose spirit. There was so little time left to hang on. But why hadn't Mark Driver's money turned up? What had happened? The thought steadied him but he was reluctant to reach for the phone again. At five o'clock Lord Driver died if there was no money, and the police knew it. So what had gone wrong?

His mind reached for its anchor and his eyes strayed to Lord Driver's room. He crossed to it to reassure himself. Standing by the bed he gazed down at Lord Driver. The machine was humming away. Surely he couldn't last much longer anyway? He would make certain that the patient would die after they'd got their million. That would teach Mark Driver. My God, it would. Lord Driver looked dead already. He'd thought so at the outset. He put out a hand to touch the face, to reassure himself. He hadn't expected it to be very warm but it felt cold to him. Startled, he cautiously raised one of the wafer-thin lids. What he saw frightened him. The pale eye was unseeing, he was sure of it. He had no idea how an eye should appear in a coma, but this one made him go cold.

As he held the lid back Shaw's fingers started to tremble and he released the delicate fold of skin but he was startled to see it stay where it was, the eye staring up at him without expression. The trembling crept from his fingers up his arms and through his whole body, reaching his legs. He moved behind the door so that the others couldn't see him. Was this the Drivers' last sick joke on him?

He leaned against the wall and tried to reason it out. But the emotion he believed he had beaten down took a deep hold and he couldn't stop shaking. It wasn't supposed to go like this. This was the *real* reason for being here. He was certain that Lord Driver was dead. Did it make a difference? It could make all the difference, if anyone outside found out.

There was a whimper and, surprised, he realised that it came from his own throat. He was to be cheated. Right at the eleventh hour he was to be denied his right. It was suddenly cold and he was rattling inside his clothes. Just when he had things as he wanted them he was being deprived of the only thing that mattered. In a confused way he was partially aware of not reasoning properly. The top of his head was dulled; his brain felt as if it had been flooded. God, he had to think straight. *He had to be sure*. Somehow he made the door, leaned against the jamb, the gun under his arm, pressed close to his body, hands clutched deep in his trouser pockets as he tried to steady them; shoulders hunched, head thrust forward like a bird of prey.

The group in the office seemed to have merged and were miles away, in another dimension. Trying to stop his teeth from chattering Shaw couldn't understand how he had reached this state without warning. The warnings had been there but he'd been too involved to notice. "Hey! You two. You two bloody quacks. Come over here. *Fast.*"

14

Professor Bowyer thought: this is it, the moment I've dreaded. He's gone over the edge. He would be unpredictable from now on. The two doctors crossed the width of the corridor eyeing Shaw cautiously, the shaking becoming apparent as they neared.

The professor said, "You've had a shock of some sort. We can do something for it."

Shaw sneered. "You know what bloody shock I've had. I wouldn't touch your poison."

"I don't understand."

"Cut the crap, prof." Shaw jerked his head back. "Is he dead?"

They stepped past Shaw and approached the bed, one either side of it, avoiding glancing at each other. As the professor carried out an examination, Grann thought: now, which way is he going to jump?

"Yes, he's dead." Professor Bowyer moved over to the machine and was about to turn it off when Shaw yelled, "Don't do that. Whaddyer think you're doing? Revive him. Give him the kiss of life or something."

The professor stood quite still by the machine, afraid to humour Shaw.

He said flatly, "It won't help. He was too far gone."

"Do it, damn you." Shaw's eyes were wild.

The professor stood his ground. "It won't help. This was likely to happen at any time. It was a constant source of surprise to me that it didn't happen before."

Shaw raised the Sterling. "You bloody well give him the kiss of life."

The professor shrugged. "All right. But what difference does it make to you? It doesn't affect anything."

"You do it pronto and then I might tell you what it affects."

Grann said, "I'll breathe into him, sir, if you'll resuscitate."

The professor did not argue. Breathing into a dead mouth

is not pleasant no matter how long one had been in medicine. Grann cupped his lips over the prematurely wrinkled mouth and tried to shut his mind to what he was doing while the professor pushed with both hands on the sunken chest. They were humouring a near madman.

When they stopped the professor confirmed that it had made no difference. Shaw walked round the bed, his eyes on the corpse.

"How long has he been dead?"

"It's impossible to say exactly, but he's not been dead long."

"You knew he was dead when you examined the patients."

"That's ridiculous. It's my job to record deaths."

"You bloody well kept it from me."

"Why should he do that?" Grann, recognising the signs, did his best to pacify Shaw. The man was demented. The whole symbol of his revenge lay uselessly in front of him. They realised then that Shaw had intended to kill Driver before he left; a last outlet for his hatred.

"I'll tell you why, you Yankee bastard." Shaw was hunched, his body tense with new belief. "You've told the coppers over the phone that he's dead. *That million's never coming.*"

In the silence that followed Shaw's half-screamed assertion, the respirator sounded like a factory at full stretch. The noise invaded the room, thrumming, partially hypnotic, as the two doctors clung to its sound as the one thing they could understand. Both were almost afraid to speak.

Finally Grann said, "They can't possibly know; we've only just found out ourselves. But supposing they did know? Just supposing. What difference? They'll still pay up."

Shaw looked at Grann pityingly, his head cocked at an angle.

"You poor bastard. You don't know what we're up against, do you? If you've told them downstairs that he's dead, Mark Driver will never pay up. Do you think he cares about you lot? The patients? He doesn't even care about his old man except to hope that he holds out for a few days."

He peered up at Grann, trying to extract the truth from him by the sheer power of his stare, unaware of the traces of madness in it. He licked his lips. "If that million doesn't arrive you're going to join him." Shaw inclined his head towards the corpse. "All of you. Make no mistake about that. And I'll do it personally."

"You've already made three million pounds. That's an awful lot of money."

Shaw smiled grimly. "That sounded like a confession, doc. It's the *one* million that interests me. You'd better pray like the clappers that your little message wasn't heard. Five o'clock's the deadline. For the money and for all of you." The doctors stood still, then, with a half shrug of resignation, the professor, the Sterling pointing at him all the way, rounded the bed and switched off the machine. It was so quiet then that it was as if he had switched off for all of them.

Just as the doctors had kept the truth of Lord Driver's death from Shaw, he, too, now kept it from his colleagues. They were riding high and he was supreme. He wanted to do nothing that might change the position. To that degree his appraisal was sane. But his whole purpose had been removed from under his nose. He felt as a deep sea diver might feel if he suddenly, unexplicably, lost his weighted boots.

Hiding his feelings as best he could, he went into the room where the American Secretary of State lay peacefully. The two doctors followed him with considerable trepidation. Neither liked the way Shaw was eyeing him. A form of transference was operating as they watched. Shaw was convincing himself that he'd found a substitute for Lord Driver.

He wasn't really aware that the doctors had followed him in until Grann spoke. "Don't you think he's served his purpose?"

Shaw swung round. His reflexes sharpened; his finger immediately on the trigger. Grann knotted his stomach muscles as a hopeless barrier to the bullets that might come. It would be like this all the time now; they'd never know how they stood from moment to moment. Shaw looked down at the sleeping figure again. "No, he hasn't," he replied savagely. "He hasn't started to play his part. He's the main feature."

"What do you intend to do to him?"

"Be your age, doc. There are several things we might do to him. It just depends, doesn't it? The first question is whether that million turns up or not."

Grann bitterly regretted passing on the news of Driver's death. Had it been picked up? And if it had, would Mark Driver get to know? He supposed Driver would have to be told.

Shaw looked at his watch, clutching at his sleeve with shaking fingers. "Well, doc, there's not much more than half an hour before the deadline. If the money doesn't pitch up that represents the rest of your lifespan. You and the rest."

They left the room. The two doctors were ordered back to the office and Shaw took up his usual position in front of it, walking up and down jerkily.

Allbright, disturbed at the sudden change in Shaw, felt nervous. He called out. "What's goin' on? Has the old geezer snuffed it?"

Shaw would normally have gone up to speak to Allbright but he called back instead: "No. He's still ticking over. Everything's okay."

Allbright wasn't satisfied. It seemed to him that Shaw was cracking up. He'd have to keep an eye on him.

At the other end of the ward McQueen was feeling increasingly weak. His head was clear so he knew it wasn't a fever but the difficulty of movement worried him and he had little control over his muscles. He would cope all right, but it annoyed him. Because of his preoccupation with himself just then he missed much of Shaw's outward change and the concern in Allbright's questioning. Three million, though. He couldn't believe it. He'd stay on his feet with a bellyful of lead for that much.

* * *

Commander Gifford was showing signs of strain. The Commissioner and Assistant Commissioner Roberts were now with him all the time. The American Ambassador had returned but had been persuaded to go back to his Embassy in Grosvenor Square as he would almost certainly be recognised by the crowds. Recognition would inevitably mean the kind of speculation that would do none of them any good. The press had already recognised him and had rushed off reports which would be sat on by their editors under a D notice. Some had already guessed fairly accurately. All were convinced that there was something much bigger going on than the Driver ransom.

Gifford suggested telling some reporters that the American police officers were there to study British police methods. The press didn't believe it but at least it was something to print.

Meanwhile Gifford was deeply worried about the approach of the deadline, and what would happen if the money didn't come. The Honourable Mark bloody Driver hadn't yet turned up with the million. Gifford had put in a call to the bank but Driver had left some time ago with the money. Gifford had obtained from Mark Driver's secretary the make of car and the registration number. He'd raised traffic control from inside the mobile and asked them to come up with some likely routes from the bank to the hospital and to send a patrol car or two to extricate Mark Driver from any traffic jam he might have landed himself in. The rush hour was already in full swing.

He was annoyed with himself for not insisting on a police escort. When he'd first contacted Mark Driver he had told him he would arrange for outriders and send a car to bring Driver in with the money. Driver had thrown a tantrum and screamed that he didn't want policemen near the place, nor even one in sight. He would bring the money himself in his own car. Whatever his reasons he had expressed them vehemently enough and Gifford had reluctantly conceded. If the bloody man had left in good time there would have been no problem. So what was delaying him? Mark Driver had failed to inform the police of the hold-up with the suitcases but he *had* told them that the money had been raised long before the traffic build up.

It was another precious ten minutes before a patrolman finally found him almost trapped in a jam in Fleet Street.

* * *

Commander Gifford transferred himself to the Secretary's office. From now on he wouldn't move from there. He'd done everything he could. Enquiries were still being made into the background of Ginger Shaw, Mark Driver's affairs, Stan Beatty's activities and McQueen's recent contacts. But that was the long term. He had with him a Detective Superintendent and a Detective Sergeant, both of his own Serious Crime Squad.

Every few seconds now they would look at their watches, the action of one prompting another, until there was almost a comic sequence to it.

Jack Gifford had allowed as much time to lapse as he dared. They were far too close to the deadline and the money still hadn't arrived. He flashed the phone and the speed with which it was picked up warned him that the nerves of the man he thought to be Shaw were as frayed as his own.

"Is the money there?" Shaw spoke before Gifford opened his mouth. There was a desperate wildness about the question and Gifford was wary; this man was near the end of his tether; his voice had changed considerably.

"It's on its way. He's been caught up in a king-sized traffic jam. You know how it is." Gifford was casual, he didn't want this character doing his nut. If he was right about him he was unused to crime, let alone one of this magnitude. Could he take the strain? The silence that met his news was uncomfortable, the sharp intake of breath a giveaway. Still keeping his voice neutral Gifford added; "Give us another half hour. That should more than do it."

"No." It was vehement. Then, with less steam, "No. Five o'clock we start killing."

"Be reasonable. The man can't help getting snarled up. We're helping him in."

"He's had plenty of time. We *have* been reasonable. Five o'clock."

"They had trouble getting the money together. He was late leaving. Fifteen minutes then. It's little to ask."

"No. There can be no compromise."

Gifford thought the voice was strange. It was difficult to

analyse the tone and he wondered what had happened to the man since he had last spoken to him. There was a suggestion of hysteria in his words, as if Shaw was having difficulty holding himself back. Gifford could understand some of it. Shaw had two other colleagues up there, one, probably both, hardened criminals; he wouldn't want to appear weak in front of them. "Look," he said quietly, "why throw away a million? We're not trying to trap you. This isn't a ploy, I give you my word."

"The word of a copper? I don't take anybody's word. Not anybody's." Shaw hung up.

Gifford flashed the phone again as the Commissioner and A.C. Roberts came into the office. Shaw came on again at once and Gifford got in quickly. "Don't hang up. Speak to the Commissioner. Maybe you'll take *his* word."

Over the open phone Gifford filled the Commissioner in. He did it deliberately so that Shaw would hear every word and realise they weren't trying to pull a fast one.

The Commissioner took the phone, introduced himself and said persuasively, "Surely fifteen minutes can make no difference one way or the other?"

The others watching him saw his jaw tighten, as he slowly laid the phone on the desk. "Well, that's it, gentlemen. He's hung up. Five o'clock. He said he *can't* extend the deadline. By the sound of him he'd crack up if he did and that might not be funny. It was the *way* he said it, though, as if the time has a special significance; that the deadline can't be extended for some very definite reason."

15

The Commissioner looked at Gifford. "Does it mean anything to you?"

"The light starts to go after five. Darkness might be important to them."

There was a commotion at the door, which opened to reveal a police officer trying to restrain a determined Art Caplan and the other American security man. In the background Chief Superintendent Taffy Evans was murmuring polite words of protest.

Jack Gifford quickly accepted that they'd caught up with him at last. He might as well get it over.

"All right, let them in." Before the Americans could speak the Commissioner instructed, "Everybody out except the Commander, the A.C. and our American friends. Taff, you'd better come in."

The door was closed and only those who were aware that the American Secretary of State was upstairs remained in the room.

Art Caplan took his hat off and laid it on the desk. He looked tougher with it on. The thin strands of hair suddenly aged him. He gave a nod and said, "We're sorry to bust in like this, Commissioner, but you understand our feelings. We'd like to be updated on the state of affairs up there." He thumbed towards the ceiling.

"Fill them in, Commander."

Gifford gave it to them straight and finished by telling them that the Driver ransom hadn't yet arrived.

Caplan thrust his raincoat back and pushed his hands into his trouser pockets. His head cocked like a sparrow's, he eyed Gifford shrewdly. "With respect, Commander, we don't give a goddam about the Driver guy. We're worried about our own man. He's an international figure. And we dunno whether he's alive or dead. I understand that your Prime Minister has been on to the President and that the ransom has been promised."

"The ransom's been paid into a Swiss Bank account. Your Ambassador's been informed, Mr. Caplan."

Caplan suddenly grinned; it was sidemouthed but immediately friendly, the dark brown eyes crinkled with reluctant humour. "I guessed you knew my name. You been trying to keep us out of your hair, Commander, and I appreciate that. I don't envy you your job. But I don't think we'll have one to go back to unless we get a few answers."

"Like whether he's dead or alive?"

"Right. Jack, isn't it? They call me Art."

Taffy Evans, on the fringe of the small group, couldn't resist a smile. He had worked with Caplan often before, knew how he could break down barriers with that deceptively lazy manner of his. Two shrewd foxes faced each other. Neither deceived the other.

But Gifford had a problem. He was about to delve into politics and he'd never done that before. He wasn't sure which way to jump. Art Caplan was entitled to know as much as there was to know and Gifford was sitting on information. His reasons were selfless but if it went wrong he'd crucify himself. He was aware that they were all watching him, highly experienced men judging his reaction, and he reasoned that they'd decide he was holding something back. He turned to gaze out of the window, at the crowd which had thickened as far as the narrow square would allow, at the uniformed row of police.

An ambulance pulled up while he watched, to remind him that this was, after all, a hospital. At times it was impossible to believe. Yet upstairs were two wounded police officers, one of them on the blink, from the latest information he'd received. Three dead security men, one dead villain, one wounded. He tried to dispel the sickness in the pit of his guts that persistently suggested the carnage was not over. He glanced at his watch. He had to make up his mind now.

"All right." He turned to face them. He matched Caplan and tucked his own hands away. "My strong belief is that your man is alive."

"Just how positive are you?"

"It's a well-founded guess. Not long ago messages were relayed through that phone by someone up there who had propped up the receiver in some way. I was given the number of villains; there are three of them, apart from the one in the generator room. All have sub-machineguns. If your man had been harmed I'm sure that would have been the first thing they would have relayed." The Commissioner looked puzzled and a little annoyed.

"That there are three men is important. Why keep it to yourself? Everyone needs to know that."

"I intended to tell you, sir. Anyway, we're all pretty certain of their escape method, if not in detail ay least in essence. If we're right the information wouldn't have helped." Even now Gifford was reluctant to put into words what he expected to happen. He might be wrong. "The reason I held back, and the main reason why I think the Secretary is at present safe, is because I was told that Lord Driver is dead. It was knowledge I would have preferred to keep to myself."

The penny dropped accurately in each slot around the room. The deep silence was a vote of sympathy for Gifford. No one wanted to be the first to speak and finally the Commissioner accepted his responsibility. "You feel that by keeping it to yourself you could have denied all knowledge; that nobody could prove what you heard?"

"Yes, sir. The constable outside was here but he couldn't know what was said and how much I heard. It wasn't easy listening."

"Presumably those upstairs don't know whether you heard or not?"

"They can only guess. It was a very brave act."

"Indeed."

The silence fell again. Caplan took his hands from his pockets and at first it looked as if he was about to ring them. Then he blurted out, "Hell, I'm sorry, Jack. I had no idea. I didn't mean to squeeze *that* outa you."

Gifford shrugged. "You probably did me a favour, Art. It was bound to come out sooner or later."

Nobody wanted to add anything. They all understood the grave implications. The Commissioner suddenly grimaced bitterly at Gifford. "Mark Driver is entitled to know his father is dead."

"Yes, sir."

"You can't put yourself in the position of misleading him."

"No, sir."

"We'd never never get away with it."

"I know. Maybe it's all academic. The money's not here, anyway. At five the generator goes off."

Knowing what was in his mind the Commissioner observed shrewdly: "You can't expect a man to put up a million of his own money to save people he doesn't know, has never seen."

"No, sir."

"You'd have lied to him? Told him his father was still alive?"

"No, sir. I wouldn't. Not like that."

The Commissioner moved to the door, spoke more formally, "Commander, you've lost us time. I've now the impossible task of trying to persuade the Home Secretary to put up an extra million, this time in cash. Even if he's willing, and I suppose he'll have to be, it cannot be done in the time."

"You can have my resignation as soon as this is over, sir."

The Commander gave Gifford a blistering glare and slammed out of the office.

When he'd gone Art Caplan held up his hands in supplication.

"Jesus, I'm *so* sorry. So *sorry*. You should've sat on it."

"With you lot on to me? You all knew I had *something*. Anyway, it'll make no difference. If my enquiries lead me to where I expect them to, chummy upstairs won't accept government money for Lord Driver. I believe we're on to a personal grudge. The money *has* to come from the Drivers."

"His cronies might not stand for *that*." A.C. Roberts put in his pennyworth. He was upset over Gifford. He would have backed him to do the correct thing, which didn't necessarily mean the right thing.

There was a rap on the door and they all turned to face the young, pink face of a police constable. "Message from Able 23, sir. They've picked up the Hon. Mark Driver with four suitcases of money. Should be here in about five minutes." His grin made him look too young to wear uniform. "Last message was that he was travelling upstream up

Fetter Lane at a fair rate of knots. Once they reach Bream's Buildings they'll be in the right flow."

They all understood the message except Caplan, who didn't know the one-way traffic system in London. It was the first light relief that day. Without exception, they looked at their watches at the same time. *It could be done.* But how would Driver react to the fact that his father was dead?

*   *   *

Allbright liked Shaw's behaviour less and less. He wasn't slow to see or to hear the changes in the man. Shaw was going round the bend, but what the hell had triggered it? Ginger wasn't used to this sort of strain, but he wasn't soft. He had a blind spot somewhere about the Drivers. Anyone could see that, even McQueen, lolling there on his chair.

Allbright was too sensible and too experienced to rock the boat at this stage. The money hadn't come and that worried him. Not much time left. But he didn't think it was only the money that was gnawing at Ginger Shaw. Over the years he'd seen blokes crack up on a long job; it took them in all sorts of ways, most of them unpleasant. Yet this was different. Shaw's personality change was something he hadn't seen before. At the moment it worried Allbright more than the money. He didn't want a balls-up when they were escaping. It had started when Shaw had left his bloody lordship's room. Making a quick check through the spyhole he called to Shaw to man his post and ran, lightly for his size, straight to Lord Driver's room.

As soon as he entered he knew something was wrong; it was too quiet. And then he realised that the machine had been turned off. Driver would never be more dead.

He came out of the room, Sterling half-raised in readiness, a reflex action. "Why didn't you tell me he'd croaked?"

Shaw shrugged nervously. "What difference does it make?"

"It can make a bloody lot of difference if the word gets round." Allbright scanned each face in turn, suspicious and cautious and sensing something had happened that he didn't know about. He stared at the phone, the only line of communication outside the ward.

"Have they got word out?"

"How could they?"

"Through that bloody thing."

"We would've noticed." Shaw was now afraid to confess the worst to his colleague; and the staff were hardly likely to tell him.

Allbright wasn't satisfied. Something was up. He became less concerned about airing his dirty washing in front of the others.

"Some of us might've. Is that why the gelt's not here?"

"Whatever happens here we've still got three million in Switzerland."

"Right now that's a long way off. We need some here."

The two men glowered at one another and Allbright realised that Shaw was not in awe of him, nor of anybody. The tick in Shaw's face wasn't from fear, not the kind he knew anyway. Something had happened to the man that Allbright didn't understand, except that it was somehow tied up with what had motivated him in the first place. And then he noticed something else. The two doctors and the three nurses had formed a gap so that none of them were directly behind Shaw in his line of vision. At first it puzzled him. Then he saw why. They were trying to get out of a possible line of fire. As he was a long way from firing himself they must be expecting Shaw to start it. When he looked again he saw that they were right. Shaw was on the brink. The bloody fool.

Shaw said, "Get back to the doors."

Allbright didn't argue. He went not out of submission but because it was sensible. He could wait. What was most important, much more important than Shaw and his present tantrum was the money. What the hell had happened to that? By the time he'd reached the doors the first of Commander Gifford's calls came through. Well, at least Shaw handled that all right, although he sounded dodgy, too highly strung. He didn't agree to a time extension; they couldn't risk it and he didn't trust the police, anyway.

After the second call Shaw threw out an olive branch,

including McQueen in it as he turned his head to each in turn. "That was the Commissioner of Police himself. What do you think of that? The top copper in person. Driver's held up in a traffic jam but the money's with him and they're out looking for him. It'll be here in time." When he added the last sentence Shaw was not convinced of its truth. He didn't really believe it but somehow he had to keep the peace. He was well aware how close he'd been to firing at Allbright, who'd done nothing wrong. He was frightened by the way his mind had closed in, by the urge to squeeze the trigger merely to blot out further complications, to shut off criticism. It scared him because he used to be so placid. He prayed fervently that the money did come in time.

Behind the desk they breathed a soundless sigh of relief. There had been a moment when they were convinced they were about to be caught in a gun battle. From now on the pattern with Shaw would remain the same; rational one moment, totally irrational the next.

Ed Grann no longer hid his feelings. He didn't care whether it was the thing to do over here or not. Maybe the old fox would frown on him but he couldn't help it. He couldn't keep his eyes off Jean; there were moments when he hoped she was feeling the same as he was. It was sometimes difficult to decide whether she needed his protection or his love.

In the four hours or so that they'd been prisoners in their own ward they had passed through a lifetime of emotional experience. Sandwiched between these drastic events he had managed a lot of heart searching. There was a good deal to be straightened out; who knows, perhaps for both of them. The unexpected dangers were forcing out thoughts and emotions at an unusual pace. They were both aware of the fact that they could lose what was only just beginning. They both looked at the clock. Fifteen minutes to go.

* * *

Able 12 entered the square in a semi-controlled skid that gave the expectant onlookers a preview of the action. With the blue light still rotating the patrolman double parked and switched off his siren. He was halfway out of the car while his finger was still on the switch.

Mark Driver moved even faster. The journey up here had been nerve-racking; wasn't he suffering enough? He had the door open before the car had stopped and was heaving the first case out of the back while the patrolman was racing round to the boot. All at once there were too many helping hands. The four cases disappeared under Driver's eyes. Startled to see a million pounds vanishing so quickly he almost panicked again, and then ran after the policemen.

Cameras flashed and reporters shouted at him questions they knew would not be answered. The crowd craned forward. They had long since known of the ransom demand; some of them had even read about it from the rushed editions of the *News* and *Standard* sold by enterprising vendors up and down their ranks. A million quid. They'd never see the like again. A rustle went through them. After the long wait things were perking up.

Four policemen rushed into the Secretary's office, stacked the suitcases on to the floor and left. Mark Driver followed them in, winded after the short run. Jack Gifford introduced himself and then the A.C. and the Commissioner as they came in. The two Americans backed off to the corner and wondered if the slim, thin-faced, unfit youngster with the truculent mouth was representative of British aristocracy. Art Caplan, with his wider experience, guessed he was not; it took all sorts.

Jack Gifford, determined not to be deprived of the case, decided to continue. If the Commissioner wanted him off it he could say so in front of the others. But he guessed it wouldn't happen and he was right.

"All the money there, sir? Equally divided?"

Driver nodded, still struggling for breath. "It's been the very devil getting here. You should have sent an escort."

Gifford bit back a retort. The young bastard. "With your permission I'll ring through and tell them, sir. This phone has direct access."

Mark Driver held up a restraining hand. He appeared lost amongst the stern-faced police officers. "We have a little time in hand, I want to be sure first that my father is still alive."

"Of course, sir. However, may I ask if it will make a difference? The threat is to switch off the generator in addition to your father's machine if the money isn't delivered by five. Other people in the private wing will also be in considerable danger."

"That's not how I understood it, Commander. When you spoke to me earlier the threat was to my father alone."

"That's true, sir, but the conditions have since changed."

Mark Driver was immediately suspicious. He stared round at the blank faces and found no comfort. The Commissioner said, "It's true, I'm afraid. The additional threat came late but I spoke to the man myself not long ago."

Jack Gifford was sweating, wondering if the Commissioner would sabotage him and grateful when he didn't. The Commissioner was obviously willing for him to hang himself, and if he didn't handle it right he would have to step in with the truth. But it was a useful concession. He realised that the Commissioner could be putting his own head on the block.

Fourteen minutes to go but Gifford was determined to hang on as long as possible.

Driver, finding no friendly reaction, no damned sympathy from any of them, blurted out, "Are you seriously suggesting that I'm responsible for the whole hospital? Good Lord, that's government responsibility."

"No, sir. We can't expect you to be responsible. It is, as you say, government responsibility. I was on to the Home Secretary only minutes ago; the Treasury are frantically trying to raise the money in time but the new threat came too late. All you'd really be doing would be loaning the money until the other arrived."

Mark Driver knew all about loans, government or otherwise. He preferred agreements on paper. It was all right for the Police Commissioner to talk like that but the Treasury would have the last word. And then he went very cold, his legs weak.

"You're talking as if my father is dead."

The Commissioner glanced at Gifford without a flicker

and the Commander accepted the pass; he could not complain.

"We're merely giving you the position, sir. This way there's a chance you may get your money back."

"You mean you *know* my father's dead? Or do you mean you're not sure?" Mark Driver had difficulty with his words, stuttering over them. He was filled with dread.

"The only people who really know whether your father is dead or alive are in the private wing."

"I'm not clear about what you're saying, Commander. Am I to understand that by handing the money over without information on my father, I get the money back? Oh, no. I'm not taking that on. Not without guarantees. What *is* important to me is the welfare of my father. If he's dead, I'm not handing over." Driver was very pale now, his skin like new plaster not yet dried out. His long fingers were trembling as he gestured. If the old man was dead, please God no, he'd never get the million back; once his affairs were uncovered they'd sit on it with the rest of his assets. Assets? That was a joke. The only asset he had was six floors up; if he was still breathing. And he was beginning to believe that the old man wasn't.

Gifford had reached crisis point, not only because of the time factor but because what he said next would decide the whole issue one way or the other. He set out to save lives, possibly at his own expense. "Right, sir. Then I think the only thing for you to do is to ring through to the ward and satisfy yourself."

The Commissioner shot Gifford a shrewd look. A.C. Roberts, to relieve his tension, turned to Art Caplan and his colleague who had been silent spectators. Caplan, unsighted by Driver, blew out a silent whistle. This limey cop was a crafty bastard. But would it work?

Gifford picked up the phone and handed it over. Mark Driver took it, his mouth dry, afraid to ask the question he knew could decide his fate. Gifford flashed the phone for him, his expression masked.

Shaw came on. Mark Driver licked his lips, his gaze flickering round the room but avoiding everyone. "This is Driver. I have the money here. Is my father still alive?"

The phone shifted against his ear in a hand he couldn't keep steady.

In the private wing Shaw almost dropped the phone in his excitement. Ten minutes to go and the money had arrived. He could hardly believe it. After all the worry and the heartache. It was so brain-bending he could barely think anymore. The others disappeared before his eyes; he was alone in splendid triumph. He wiped his lips. And just as suddenly he was aware of the complete silence; that he was the centre of attention. Christ, he'd better sober up. "Look," he wavered, "get Commander Giff—get him on."

"I'm not paying a cent until I know about my father."

Mark Driver's cold tones went through Shaw's head with sharp clarity. The whole story came back to him in a bitterly sane moment. He almost choked. "Listen, you twisting bastard, this is one bill you'll pay even if it's the last one. Now get the copper on the phone."

"I'm not paying until I'm sure my father is alive."

Shaw floundered. It wasn't supposed to be like this. Then he recalled his own earlier appreciation of Mark Driver; of course, the Honourable wouldn't give a monkey's for the rest of them. He stared across the counter with a wild-eyed challenge, then spoke into the phone, "Of course he's alive. That's what it's all about."

In the office, a badly shaken Mark Driver placed his hand over the mouthpiece and turned to Gifford. "What's the name of the chief medic up there?"

"Professor Bowyer."

Driver removed his hand, "I don't trust you. Put Professor Bowyer on."

Shaw snarled down the line. "I'm not a bloody swindling thief like you. Any more of that and I'll switch the machine off." It took him a second or two to remember that the machine was already off. God, what was happening? Clarity again. Necessity. He raised his gun, took up the slack on the trigger and very deliberately pointed the barrel at the professor's chest. "He wants to speak to you." He handed over the phone. He said no more, there was no need.

"Professor Bowyer."

"This is Mark Driver, professor. I want to know if my father is alive."

Art Caplan called out, "Ask him how the Secretary is." But Driver ignored him.

The professor answered calmly. "He was the last time I examined him."

"Are you being threatened, professor?"

"My dear fellow, we have all been threatened all day. But it has not influenced my reply. Do you want me to send Dr. Grann for a final check? I can see no reason for a change in his condition."

"No. Thanks. I'll get the Commander." Mark Driver was almost sick with relief. He well knew the professor was being intimidated but there had been no hesitation, no fear in the authoritative voice. And he had heard what he wanted to believe.

Professor Bowyer wearily handed back the phone to Shaw and sat down. He felt a hand on his shoulder and turned to see Grann. He was grateful for the unmistakable gesture of complicity. There had been *some* truth in what he'd said. He would have lied under the threat of the gun in any event, but it would have been less convincing. Gifford had been able to circumvent the direct lie; he had not. He searched the faces of the three women and saw only young friendship, youthful understanding and he knew that he need have no fear of the truth escaping from any of them.

Shaw smiled; there was something to be said for a gun. He was smiling more often now but it wasn't because he was amused. "Commander? Right! This is what you do. I want one suitcase taken to the generator room and left outside. Any attempt to get at our man and we'll shoot the American big wig and turn off Lord Driver's machine." He was back to believing the machine was on again.

Gifford didn't argue the morality of the threat. There was no point in saying that the three million in ransom had already been paid for the American. In his present state the man Shaw was beyond reasoning. It was better to keep his mouth shut; he didn't want to give Art Caplan a heart attack.

Shaw continued, "Keep the other three cases in the

office until you hear from me, but stay put, remain on the phone."

Then Shaw put the receiver down and raised Beatty on the radio.

*   *   *

The police officer who took the suitcase was the one who'd been manning the Secretary's phone for most of the time. He had found it boring, wishing at times for a more active role outside. Now he'd got it he wished he was back by the phone.

The square was deathly quiet as he stepped out with the case. It wasn't hard to guess what was going on. The suitcase, cheap and new, attracted more concentrated attention than the Chancellor of the Exchequer's budget box ever had. A quarter of a million pounds passed before their eyes in the grip of a solitary, upright policeman. His tread was quite audible; he found it unnerving. The cameras flashed again. He enjoyed all the attention until he turned the corner.

The generator room looked a long way off. As he passed the two police cars blocking the dead end he noticed their slight cant and looked down to see the evidence of the gunman's marksmanship in the two burst tyres; he couldn't miss the shattered flasher, the fragments in the street and on the car roof. The constable started to feel as Inspector Erskin had felt. His nape pricked and his legs lost strength. Anyone who shot a copper so deliberately and unnecessarily was crazy.

As he neared the housing he noticed movement behind the slats but it was impossible to make out any shapes. All he knew was that he was being covered all the way. The thump of the generating plant reached him and then a voice said, "Hello, sonny boy. Taking them under age, are they? Put it down, nice and steady."

The constable placed the case to the side of the door. It was uncanny; he could feel the man next to him only inches away. He could see the disseminated patches behind the slats, could even hear his breathing. Yet he could do nothing. The initiative lay entirely against him.

"Now trot off, sonny, or I'll give you one up the arse."

The constable walked away, determined not to run and never having felt more like doing so. There was movement behind the crowd. Then he saw that television crews were erecting lights and cameras at vantage points. They were probably television blokes. When he concentrated on their activity he found it easier to walk back with dignity. The nearest part of the crowd clapped their hands when he reached the corner and the sound followed him as he entered the square again. He grinned, boyishly; for him, at least, it was over.

In the generator room Beatty sized it all up, noticing the cameras. He knew it would make no ultimate difference. When he was satisfied, he opened the door and pulled in the case. Laying it flat on the floor he flipped the catches and pulled back the lid. He sat back on his haunches and stared. Ten thousand twenty-pound-notes. He still didn't know that Barret was dead, that in fact there were twelve thousand five hundred. Unwrapped, they had been jogged into one huge untidy bundle. He riffled through just to make sure that they were all notes and he checked for bugging devices. He kept shaking his head from side to side, too dumb-struck to express his elation.

Beatty closed the lid and kept his hands on it. *They had done it.* That was all he could think, over and over again. It was the quietest few seconds he had known; Stan Beatty, speechless. He pulled out a mirror and checked his wig, put on dark glasses. He had already tidied everything up; his stuff was in the grip, which he would leave. There were no prints; he had worn gloves all day, as they all had. The powder on his eyebrows still held but they weren't visible anyway above the rims of the glasses. He was sorry to leave the Sterling; even though he hadn't used it. It wouldn't be traced, the number had been ground off long since. He was taking the Browning with him instead; and he made sure it was in his hip pocket. Most of the rest of the stuff had been stolen, even the vacuum flask and the grip. There was nothing that would lead back to him. He was completely satisfied when he pressed the switch on the radio; that would come with him, his safeguard.

With a strange sense of nostalgia he gazed around the generator room, sniffing at the fumes, no longer irritated by them. Whatever it was, however uncomfortable, it had been a haven. He sighed, then spoke into the radio.

"Okay. Get me out of here."

16

SHAW CALLED GIFFORD again. "My man's coming out. I want no following, no hindering, nothing. We'll be in constant radio touch. The first panic call he makes, or the first radio silence we get we blow off the head of the American. You understand?"

"I understand." Gifford had expected nothing else. He covered the phone and turned to A.C. Roberts. "Plan one, sir." He had already arranged for a team to follow Beatty at a safe distance but only on foot. A.C. Roberts bustled from the room to get them operative. It would be a delicate game, hampered by the crowds and yet covered by them. And there was nothing any of them could do until Beatty was out of radio range.

In the generator room Beatty took a last look round his self-imposed prison. He pulled the tie from his pocket and put it on. He looked at the switches, very tempted to turn them off before he left, but he realised it might give him extra problems. He opened the door and stepped out, the suitcase in one hand, the radio in the other.

"I'm leaving now. Keep the channel wide open, boyo, and let the pigs listen in so they don't make any mistakes."

The suitcase was manageable but it was awkward keeping the radio up all the time. He walked towards the lame cars, whose wheels the coppers hadn't dared to change, and towards a crowd from which he could have heard a pin drop. Suddenly there was blinding light in his face and he almost called into the receiver, expecting a trap. When he realised it was from the arc lamps of the television crew he grinned. A bloody film star couldn't have more attention than he had now. They were all fascinated by him, and quite right too. He was carrying a few hours earnings that were worth more than they would see all their miserable lives.

The press cameras flashed, the crowd stared and the police stood uselessly around as Beatty advanced towards them. It was his finest hour. He wasn't concerned that he would be seen on television screens up and down the country, he'd look quite different with a few simple adjustments. He was actually delighted at the prospect of the publicity; he hoped he'd be settled at home in time to switch on. Tomorrow he'd buy all the newspapers.

"I've reached the corner. Turning left into Powis Place." Those in the square facing the entrance to Powis Place could now see him and were frustrated when he walked away from them. From their safer distance someone booed, a solitary sound breaking the silence. Then came a second boo that caught echoes through the crowd. The crescendo caught on, spread through the square and finally flooded down Powis Place until Beatty wanted to cover his ears.

What had happened to their idolatry? The sound was deafening, right in his ears. The bloody snivelling bastards! They dared to judge him? The weak-kneed shower. He stopped in the middle of the street, at bay and livid. He snarled back at the crowd, cursed them. If only he had the Sterling with him now. He had the Browning but it wasn't enough, they might lynch him before he could empty it into them. The Sterling would have been different.

* * *

With the gun at the head of the Secretary of State Shaw heard the crescendo through his radio. He could hear the crowd from down below in the street. Unless Beatty switched to receive he had no idea of what was really happening. He rushed to the window and noticed that it was largely the crowd section to his left, facing Powis Place, that was shouting. Even at a football match he'd never seen a crowd so angry. Ordinary people like himself gone berserk because they were sick at what was happening. Like himself? He shook the radio in his hand as if by his action it could transmit to Beatty. Like himself? Just how far had he come from them? It could never be the same, ever. Whatever happened to him now, however rich he became, he would not be the man people once liked. He had become a different person and that's how he would stay. For ever.

Beatty's voice broke his bitter reverie. "It's all right. I thought for a moment they were going to have a go at me. They haven't the guts. It's just yelling." But Beatty sounded breathless, shaken. "It's okay," he repeated. "But hang about."

* * *

Beatty had reached the car. The meter had been fed from time to time but even if he'd collected a ticket it wouldn't have mattered. And if they'd towed it away, which was unlikely, he'd have demanded a police car. Anyway, it wasn't his, and the number plates were false. He unlocked it and climbed in.

The tinted windows were useful; they made it almost impossible for anyone trying to look in, far away as they'd have to be anyway. "Okay, I'm in." The car shut out the noise. He felt safer in the car. He had heaved the suitcase on to the back seat; now he leaned round the head rest and opened it. From the floor beside him he pulled up a grip and placed it on the front passenger seat. With mounting excitement he crammed the money into the grip and closed the suitcase. He switched on the ignition and let her run for a minute or two while he ripped off his overalls.

Beatty had no fear of being followed. He had assumed that police would be in the crowd to foot-follow him, but they wouldn't dare do it by car with the risk of him spotting them. An all station call would go out for patrol cars to survey and report but Beatty wasn't going far. He spoke into the radio again. "I'm pulling out. At the first sign of the fuzz following I'll give a yell so you can start knocking off the patients. Keep her open, matey."

He pulled out and drove off. Behind him the crowd broke the cordon and surged across the road. Police stationed at strategic points noted number, car, colour and direction and reported by radio on a pre-arranged wave length.

He sweated out the jam, putting in frequent calls to keep Shaw in touch and to let the police know that they'd better not try anything. He turned left into Holborn, the traffic snailing along. His direction was towards the City. At the first set of traffic lights that held him up he was positioned in the outside lane a few cars back from the lights. "I'm in the main stream." It was his last signal. He tore off his wig and gloves and dropped them on the floor. His dark glasses were already in his pocket and he'd been rubbing out the powder from his eyebrows as he drove, behind the safety of the tinted windows. He climbed across to the passenger seat, opened the door with a handkerchief, climbed out with his grip, slammed the door and waved as if the driver was still there. "Thanks, Charlie." Then he was skipping through the traffic to the other side of the road.

He cut back the way he'd been travelling. There were uniformed police about, many more than usual; he could see them keeping their eyes skinned. They weren't looking for the man he looked like now. In fact he was wrong; they had both descriptions, the real one having been passed on by the army. But there *were* differences—no suitcase, no boiler suit—and the police's task in the evening rush hour was impossible.

Beatty knew that the main Holborn underground station was almost bound to have police in its concourse, but as the crowds now pushed through the entrances it seemed a good place to disappear. Yet he'd thought it all out before; he didn't like the idea of being confined to a train, even with the protection the sheer number of people would give him. And he reckoned the fuzz would be extra vigilant down there, they might expect him to do it. He continued past the station and turned down Kingsway, walking towards the Strand. He simply walked away from the scene a quarter of a million pounds richer, glad to be rid of the wig and the gloves and the radio, and missing only the Sterling. Later, he would meet up with Shaw.

He was already too far away to hear the commotion at the lights when his car, the engine still running, caused another jam. By the time the police had rushed to the scene the other lanes had moved off and the only man to have any recollection of Beatty at all was in the car immediately behind. And he was so angry at being stopped when he was already late that his description had been of little use. He did seem to recall that Beatty had somehow kept his head averted because he really couldn't remember seeing the face. But dark hair, that was it, dark hair. Clothes? "I dunno what clothes. Christ, I wasn't interested." It would take the police some time to calm him down enough to get a useful description.

* * *

Jack Gifford sat on the edge of the desk, cradling the phone in his lap. He was depressed but his nerves were racing. He wasn't particularly worried about Beatty at the moment. An all-stations call had gone out, ports, railway stations, airports and an army photograph was being rushed through which he hoped to have in time to process for the late television news. A police mugshot of McQueen was already available but that chapter was yet to start. At this stage Beatty didn't matter; the generator threat had been lifted and a weight was off their shoulders. A section of the Serious Crime Squad was already in the generator room, cleaning up and dusting and rushing items off to the lab.

The main problem still faced them: nine patients and five hospital staff held by three gunmen as desperate as they'd ever be—especially now that one of their trump cards had been removed. Gifford wasn't optimistic. Nor was anyone else, including the Americans. The Commissioner was talking quietly to them; it was all he could do. He had persuaded Mark Driver to go home.

* * *

Ginger Shaw received Beatty's last call, waited for five minutes and then called Gifford. "Okay, Commander, this is my last call to you so you'd better get it right. Don't forget a single thing. I want all your men removed from the roofs at once. The chopper is to stay grounded. The three suitcases of money are to be sent up in the east lift which we'll send down. If anyone comes up in the lift, or if anyone approaches the doors, if the chopper so much as lifts off and if one single man is left on the roof, we will shoot the American we are taking with us as hostage."

Downstairs Gifford swallowed. He could have predicted all this but that didn't make it any better. His strong features relaxed for just a second, his hard stare glazed over, and then it was gone. He had to try. "Will you speak to the Commissioner first?" The Commissioner moved forward to take the phone but Gifford shook his head as Shaw spoke again.

"It'll do no good talking to him. I prefer to deal with you. I think we understand one another."

Well, that was a fact, reflected Gifford bitterly. He put his hand over the mouthpiece and said to the Commissioner, "He refuses to speak to you, sir."

It occurred to the Commissioner that Gifford was getting too much power. There was really nothing he could do about it at the moment.

Gifford, more than anything, was worried about Shaw. He had stated his demands rationally but there was a very noticeable quiver in his voice that was getting worse. He said, "Okay. But why take the American? Why not someone else? That must have been your original plan."

"Right. But the American is better insurance. He'll make you more careful."

"You've already promised his safety. You've been paid for him."

"We still promise his safety; if you're sensible." Shaw's voice rose, displaying his own guilt and uncertainty. "No more waffle, Commander. The lift's on its way."

Gifford hesitated fractionally, unsure whether to test Shaw's identity. But it was too risky; the man was on a tightrope, he could fall either way. In any event Shaw had hung up.

From the corner of the room Art Caplan said, "So they're taking the Secretary of State?"

Gifford looked across at him apologetically. "I'm afraid so. I'm sorry."

"It figures. There'll be hell to pay over this. Do you think they'll kill him?"

"I don't know. I don't think the man's a natural killer, like some of your torpedoes, but he's on the verge of a breakdown, or so it seems to me. And *that* is the danger. It's no use kidding you."

The Commissioner said, "I gather they want the money sent up."

"Yes, sir."

"Then you'd better get it round."

"Yes, sir."

"They're flying out?"

"It looks like it. For the Secretary's sake I think we'd better meet all their demands."

"Once the Secretary's gone there'll be no holding the press, D notice or not. It'll be round the world in seconds. I'd better report to the Home Secretary. It's best that the President is notified by the Prime Minister."

Gifford had called in two policemen to take the cases round to the lift and the Commissioner turned to him as they were both leaving the room, his voice more friendly. "What are the chances, Jack?"

"Of the Secretary's safety? I'd be happier if we were dealing with a professional."

"You don't think the others might stop him?"

"I doubt they'll be able to. McQueen wouldn't, he couldn't think that far. And I don't know who the other man is. Anyway, they've already killed three blokes; what have they got to lose?"

From behind them Art Caplan said, "I'd better call the Ambassador."

The Commissioner turned round quickly. "There's no need. The Home Office will inform him as soon as my call's through." He paused. "We'd all have given anything for this not to have happened. If you prefer to stay with Commander Gifford I'm sure he'll have no objection."

It was a directive to Gifford but he didn't mind. He raised a twisted smile. "At the moment I'd be glad to hold anyone's hand."

Caplan knew how he felt.

Meanwhile A.C. Roberts had departed to find Jock McDonald to call down his firearms squad from the roofs and to have instructions sent to the helicopter pilot to stay grounded in the Square.

The cases were put in the lift and the button pressed. The temptation to put men in with them was strong but the lift would probably have become their coffin.

Gifford, with Caplan, rushed back to the mobile and sent out an all-stations call to track a helicopter from the ground on his further signal. The Commissioner was just winding up his call to the Home Secretary; the radios had gone strangely quiet as if re-energising for the final rush.

Gifford took Caplan outside. The light was just beginning to deteriorate. The space that had been created for Mark Driver's Rolls-Royce had been filled again by another police car. The crowd was becoming restless.

"Art, there's one more thing we can do but I need your agreement. There are two army snipers over there and others on standby; we can take them up to the adjoining roof, and, given a clear range of fire, they can let off."

"They'd have to be given very strict instructions. Youngsters are apt to take chances. We can't cut corners on this."

"We can go up with them." Gifford gave Caplan a nudge. "As they're army they don't come under Jock McDonald. The light might get too bad and the range too long for pistols. Let's talk to their officer." Gifford left full instructions at the mobile and took a two-way radio with him.

* * *

When Shaw put down the phone he signalled McQueen to send down the lift. McQueen got off his chair with the greatest difficulty. His head was clear but his muscles simply didn't want to move. The lift was right next to him yet it took all his effort to reach it. He had to put his Sterling on the chair before he could reach in and press the button for the ground floor. The simple act of kicking the wedge from between the doors was like trying to move a tree trunk. This was more than reaction from the bullet wound; those bloody quacks must've fixed him with that last injection. Right. Before he left he'd fix them, that was for sure. The lift doors slowly closed and he heard it descend.

The atmosphere in the ward was one of complete uncertainty. When there should have been jubilation amongst the gunmen there was only an extreme nervous wariness. The confused need to survive had kept Shaw lucid as he talked with Commander Gifford; that, together with the importance to him to remain in charge; self-respect still dangled by a thread. But his head was aching, his thoughts slow and overlapping.

Most of this was evident to Allbright. He was ready to step in, if it came to it. He had the sense to realise that it was best not to, not now. Shaw had managed okay with the fuzz. His voice had been queer but the right words had come out. There wasn't long to go. And the money was on the way. They should all be crazy with delight at the mere thought of it. Instead, McQueen was moving like a paralytic, Shaw acting like a nutter and he was worried about the pair of them.

In the office the staff were afraid to speak; they felt they were sitting on a high explosive with the fuse already ignited.

When the lift doors opened the three gunmen had their Sterlings pointed at it but all that was revealed were the three cases in the otherwise empty cavity. McQueen had so much difficulty trying to lift the first one that he had to call out for help. Shaw rushed up and pulled the cases out himself, leaving them near the lift. McQueen leaned against the wall, breathing shallowly. Even that was difficult. He glared hatefully towards the office. They'd pay for this.

Shaw laid the cases flat and released the catches. One by one he opened the lids. At the sight of three quarters of a million pounds McQueen regained some equanimity.

From the other end of the ward Allbright couldn't make it out. McQueen was behaving like he was in a drunken stupor and Shaw was squatting on his haunches, just staring

vacantly into the cases; no expression from either of them.
"Is it there?"

The shout roused Shaw, who looked up, dived his hand in and held up a number of notes for Allbright to see. Allbright grinned widely, the only one. Brother, had they struck it rich.

Shaw, still squatting, wondered what the money was doing there. It swam before his eyes. It *should* be there, he knew that, but what had happened. Then his defence against the others prodded him, he had to maintain his ascendancy. There was something he had to do, something important. Self-preservation again; he raised the aerial of his radio and tried to remember the words. "Come in and collect your prize money." It wasn't quite as arranged but it was near enough. A voice said, "Okay," so it was all right.

There was something else. God, but his head hurt, right across the eyes. Something else. He stood up, staring at the money and all it meant to him was coloured paper. This wasn't revenge; this was not what he *really* wanted. But that wasn't it. Striving for clarity he stepped forward and accidently tripped against one of the cases. The hostage. He went down the ward, leaving McQueen to close the cases; McQueen, who could hardly move, but was going to do it, even if he had to use his teeth.

The ward had stretched, it was longer. And to Shaw he was approaching a set of figures in the far distance. He reached the office. There they sat, the five dummies like a porcelain group, all white gloss and silence. "Get the American out of the room." He'd got that right.

"He's still unconscious." Grann stood up.

"What's that got to do with it? Get him out." He was better when they challenged him; it made him concentrate, assert himself.

"Take me instead. He's not fit. If he wakes up in some strange place, or in an aircraft, the shock might kill him after the sedation he's been under." Grann looked to the professor for backing and received it in a resigned nod of agreement.

"Then give him another shot to see him through. If everyone behaves themselves he'll wake up back here. If he doesn't wake up he's nothing to worry about."

"I'd rather go——"

"Look, doc, get him bloody well out here or I'll blow your bloody head off. *Now get him out*." Shaw, red in the face, was heaving with temper. He'd had enough. From them all.

Ed Grann didn't argue further; he was scared and seething at the same time. The professor, knowing his problem, left it to him; it was something Grann had to sort out for himself. Nurse O'Connor was sent to the storeroom for a collapsible wheelchair and she and Grann trundled it to the V.I.P.'s room.

In spite of the movement in the ward it had become very quiet. The staff had been reduced to a numbed defeat and the gunmen seemed to be listening for something. In their rooms, those patients who were conscious were silently willing the gunmen to go away. Perhaps six minutes passed, while Ed Grann injected the Secretary of State and then, with Nurse O'Connor's help, got a dressing gown on him and lifted him into the wheelchair. He was deceptively heavy.

The thudding of the chopper was at first faint, like the sound of a distant pump, but as it got nearer Allbright grinned. When the noise filled the ward he looked up at the ceiling. Shaw seemed unaware of the sound, even when it faded above their heads. When it finally stopped he gazed rapidly at his radio, as if expecting something to happen. Something did. A voice came through the receiver: "I'm squatting on your heads."

Shaw didn't respond until Allbright shouted at him and then he lifted his radio and acknowledged. Shaw was aware of something wrong within himself; he shouldn't feel as empty of purpose as he did. In an indefinable way he'd been cheated. He went into Lord Driver's room, to where the object of his hate lay dead. He had no right to die; it should have happened at *his* hand. This was the moment when he should have turned off the switch as a final reprisal against Mark Driver. And he'd been deprived of doing it. Cheated. To hell with the money. Where was his satisfaction? An indescribable swelling sensation filled his head. Almost in tears he raised the Sterling and fired at the figure in the bed, keeping his finger on the trigger.

The sheets jerked as if fingers plucked at them; the body moved sideways under the blast and rocked away from Shaw. But there was no reaction from the corpse; the face, impassive in death, enraged Shaw the more.

The shattering, unexpected thunder of the machinegun after such a sustained period of comparative silence brought everyone to their feet.

Allbright, stunned for a couple of seconds, charged down the ward like a bull. When he reached Lord Driver's room Shaw was just about emptying his magazine. Allbright didn't change pace; he kicked Shaw in the back and sent him flying on to the bed to join the butchered corpse. Following up, he punched hard at the base of Shaw's head, knocking it down between the emaciated, useless legs under the sheets. Then he grabbed the Sterling and flung it across the room. Still with the same hand he grabbed Shaw's collar and pulled him towards the door, finally flinging him through it, rage giving him extra strength.

"You stupid mad bastard. You'll have the police flooding up here." He ran to each set of doors and put a burst through them, not knowing whether the police had reached them or not. He didn't have to be a genius to know that they'd certainly be on the floor below. Anyway, that would put them off for a bit. But even in his anger he'd controlled the bursts; he had to keep some rounds in hand.

He returned to Shaw who lay on his back, stirring, slowly reaching back to rub the nape of his neck. Allbright stood over him, the gun pointing down, his mood murderous. The idiot had almost ballsed up the whole business. Shooting a dead man; he must be raving. He was hovering between compassion and murder when a weak cry came from down the ward.

"For God's sake stop it. Please!"

Pip Goldini stood in the doorway of her room, supported by the matronly "duchess". "Haven't you done enough damage? Can't you just go and leave us alone?"

Allbright almost shot her then. When he stared into those luminous, half-sightless eyes, he felt the depth of her accusation and he didn't like it. "Get back to bed while you can."

"Please go and leave us alone. You have your money."

He aimed at her as the "duchess" forced her round into the room. He eased the pressure on the trigger and kicked out at Shaw, as an alternative to shooting the girl. Tension had to be released in some way. "Get up, you stupid bastard."

Shaw scrambled up, holding his head.

"Get those cases back in the lift and wedge the doors again."

Shaw shuffled off at Allbright's command, his last battle over; self-respect finally lost in the shadows of a clouded mind.

Allbright crossed to the phone and flashed. He didn't know whose voice it was at the other end and he didn't care. "Have those areas been cleared?" He received an affirmative from Assistant Commissioner Roberts who hastily queried the firing. "Don't worry," assured Allbright. "One of our blokes got his finger stuck. No one hurt. But there will be if you try any tricks." He hung up.

*　　*　　*

Ed Grann had missed his chance. He was in the wrong place at the wrong time. There would never be another opportunity like that and he was on the wrong side of the ward for the gun. The firing had unnerved him, yet once Allbright rushed past he realised that to reach the office he'd have to cross McQueen's sights. And even a slowed-down McQueen could give some form of warning and still manage to shoot. However inaccurate he was, the wild firing might hurt the others. He was never sure whether he was simply being rational or whether it was fear that governed these quick decisions.

The Secretary of State was in the wheelchair, his head falling forward. Nurse O'Connor had been putting thick surgical socks on his feet when the firing had first started; now she finished the job with unsteady hands. They had all been badly shaken. Grann slipped the horn-rimmed spectacles into the dressing-gown pocket. He couldn't imagine the man without them.

Now that it was safe enough they wheeled the unconscious figure out. One way or the other the Secretary was destined for the longest sleep of his life. They wheeled the chair out and Allbright signalled Grann and Nurse O'Connor back to the office.

Allbright pulled the chair towards the lift so that he could keep an eye on the office. Grann watched the unceremonious way the great man was dragged back. Of all men this one had probably put more time and energy into finding world peace than any other. Yet he was being handled like a sack of trash by men who deserved to be nowhere near him. Grann felt sick with anguish and turned his back as Allbright reached the lift.

Facing the drugs cabinet reminded him again of the gun. Jean Sandingham noticed the direction of his glance and gave him a pleading, warning look. But he had to do something; or try to at least. He went to the cabinet and peeled off the strips of adhesive while Jean tried to pull him away.

"You'll attract their attention." He gave her a side-mouthed warning.

"Please don't."

"I'm only removing the gun. Just in case." He didn't believe it, nor did she.

"They'll kill you." She repeated her earlier warning.

"I can't sit on my arse. There's more to it than a life or two."

"Oh, God."

"Don't worry. I don't intend to commit suicide." He quickly worked out the operation of the safety catch and shoved the gun in his pocket, locating the trigger and easing his finger through. He turned back to the desk.

Allbright and a demoralised Shaw were backing the wheelchair into the lift. There was plenty of room, the lift was designed to take surgical trolleys. When it was in Shaw hung back in the lift as if he was afraid to show his face again. Allbright was about to step in when McQueen said awkwardly, "I've a last job to do." He had the greatest difficulty in speaking.

Allbright said, "I can guess what it is. Forget it. Let's get out."

"You forget it. I can't. They've fixed me." The words were slow and forced. He sounded like a man who'd just been to the dentist. He started to amble up the ward, trying to raise his gun. Allbright put out a hand and grabbed his jacket to pull him back.

Grann stepped out, gun in hand. He'd missed the last opportunity and this one would not be repeated.

17

BOTH GUNMEN HAD their Sterlings lowered as Grann raised the Beretta. He wasn't sure whether he was holding it correctly or of what to say. "Stay where you are. Keep your guns down."

Allbright, still holding the jacket, had McQueen partially between himself and Grann and McQueen hadn't the strength to get away.

"Drop your guns or I'll fire."

Allbright kept his grip on McQueen; after the first shock he found the situation amusing. He gave Grann a wide, easy grin. "I didn't think you were so dumb, doc. Don't forget to keep your gun in line with your forearm and your wrist straight. Keep the whole lot nice and parallel with the floor."

It took Grann all his time not to look at the gun; he wasn't even sure whether it was actually aiming at them; from Allbright's display of easiness he guessed that it wasn't.

It wasn't so easy to fire even when you were threatened. He knew that *he* was the one in danger, even though the Sterlings were pointed at the floor. He almost threw the gun down.

McQueen started to struggle ponderously but Allbright had no intention of releasing such a convenient shield. If McQueen's muscles had been functioning it might have been a fascinating contest.

Allbright was still grinning. "Take up the slack, doc; that's right. Now fire." He laughed outright. "What's the matter? Finding it difficult to kill? Don't worry, you have to hit us first."

With the helpless McQueen shielding Allbright, Grann hesitated. He couldn't shoot an already wounded man who was barely able to stand. He couldn't suddenly become a cold-blooded killer. The provocation he needed came as Allbright raised his Sterling left-handed, the magazine sticking out awkwardly.

Grann fired twice as Shaw came racing from the lift and momentarily distracted Allbright. Seeing a last opportunity to re-establish himself Shaw fired his Colt at Grann. Allbright released McQueen to get better purchase of his weapon.

Grann, realising he'd missed, heard the frightening shriek of a heavy slug fly past his head. With his ear still ringing he dropped to his knees, partly from shock and partly as an instinctive move to reduce his target area. He fired again, using both hands to steady the gun. One of the girls screamed but to him it was a far distant sound like a wheeling gull.

Shaw fired again at Grann, this time hitting him and spinning him round. As Grann fell his knees dragged along the floor, his body twisting at the waist from the impact. Shaw surged forward and raised his gun to finish the job. Grann sagged sideways on the floor like a dying mantis. Jean Sandingham grabbed a bottle and flung it wildly at Shaw, who raised his arm to protect himself just as he fired. The shot shattered one of the recessed ceiling lights.

In the office the staff searched frantically for anything that could be thrown but Shaw had already smashed many of the bottles during his earlier rampage. Before they could gather themselves Allbright confronted them with deadly reality.

"The next thing thrown and I'll spray the lot of you." Their pitiful attempt to save Grann was never launched. But their activity did, momentarily, distract Shaw.

Between Shaw and Grann, McQueen was standing loosely on legs scarcely his own. He couldn't raise his wounded arm to balance himself and the Sterling still hung down from his other hand. If he dropped the gun his whole body would go; it was a symbol he clung to. Somehow he stayed on his feet.

Shaw levelled his gun quite icily at Grann, who was trying to straighten up. He fired fractionally after McQueen reeled sideways in front of him. It was doubtful if he realised he had hit McQueen for he kept firing repeatedly and McQueen took the lot in the back. The Sterling slipped to the floor. McQueen, his muscles at last deprived of the enormous force that had motivated them, collapsed in a strange heap on top of Grann. He lay twitching spasmodically. The bottle that had hit Shaw rolled slowly across the floor.

Shaw was still firing but his gun was as empty as his mind. Grann had collapsed under the weight of McQueen. He made no movement. Jean Sandingham came from the office to try to help him.

"Stand back. All of you." Allbright was livid. The only reason he didn't fire at them was to save his ammunition; he might need it later. But it was touch and go; his big frame was tense, his eyes hard and narrowed. Even the act of the staff backing away from Grann was perilous.

"One more move from any of you and you're dead." His voice trembled with emotion but his features were stone hard. He addressed the professor. "Get on that phone quick and tell them that if any attempt's made to get in here we'll slaughter everybody, and that includes the American."

Professor Bowyer needed no prodding. He spoke rapidly into the phone, afraid for all of them.

Allbright advanced towards the two bodies where Shaw was retrieving McQueen's Sterling. He knelt down, his gaze sweeping towards the office, ready for the slightest move. He was already convinced but he had to be certain. He sought the thick wrist on the strangely humped body and found no trace of a pulse. McQueen was dead, shot by that bloody loony Shaw. Everything had been under control until Shaw had buggered it up again. The American doctor had hit no one, craters in the plaster near the lift testified to his bad aim. McQueen had deserved better, he'd stuck it out. Allbright completely overlooked the way he had used McQueen as cover.

Shaw seemed unaware of any of them except Allbright. His bright eyes were unfocused, his movements uncoordinated. "Come on," he said briskly under the illusion that he was once more in control. "Let's get going."

The only thing that stopped Allbright from killing him then was the fact that he needed him. First things first. And he was too disgusted to argue. They had started out as five and now there were three. Only Beatty had so far got away. They backed slowly towards the lift with Allbright wary all the way. Shaw seemed completely unaware of, and certainly unmoved by the killing of one of his own men. It was as if McQueen had never existed. They flanked the wheelchair, Sterlings still raised.

As the lift doors closed they had a narrowing view of all three nurses and the professor trying to remove McQueen's body from Grann. Jean Sandingham was slightly turned their way, her face deathly white. The silly bugger should never have tried a gun on them; he hadn't stood a chance.

* * *

As they pulled McQueen off him Grann struggled to get up. His upper left arm throbbed terribly but he knew from his condition that the bullet had missed the main artery. His left sleeve was blood-soaked and the nurses were pulling his surgical coat from him.

While the others were helping Grann the professor phoned down to tell the police that the gunmen had left with the Secretary of State. He then turned to Grann. "Let's get you into the office."

"There's no time." Grann bent down for his gun and almost fainted.

"You're not going after them?" It was almost a cry of anguish from Jean.

"I don't know what I'm going to do but I do know that they're not just walking off, with *that* hostage." He had straightened and was trying to clear his head.

"You've got a bullet in your arm and you're haemorrhaging."

"I can feel the bullet and the bleeding looks worse than it is. If you're worried, fix a transfusion for when I get back, you know my group."

"I'm ordering you to stay here, doctor."

"I'm sorry, sir. I really am. Jean, get a bandage."

Grann winced with pain as his jacket finally came off. Nurse O'Connor quickly cut away the bloodied shirt sleeve while Jean bandaged his arm. It was the quickest, least professional dressing they had ever performed but they saw Grann's uncompromising grimness and, anyway, if he could defy the professor he could defy anybody.

Professor Bowyer stood silently to one side, looking thoughtfully at his houseman. He was not annoyed by the insubordination; he understood it fully. But Grann was being rash. "You're not very good with that thing; do be careful you don't hit the wrong man. I still advise you not to go."

Grann gazed down at the gun he was holding. He grimaced and tucked it in his waistband. "I don't suppose I'll ever use it again. I know I can't beat them at their own game. But I do know that I have to go."

"Then be very careful. Last time you were lucky."

As Grann strode towards the second lift, jacketless and with one shirt sleeve missing, he felt slightly ludicrous. What *could* he do? Yet he continued, fighting pain and dizziness and suddenly aware that Jean was with him. Before he could speak she said, "Don't argue. My presence might calm you down a bit. What you did back there was stupid."

"I don't want you endangered, Jean. Please, honey."

"Nor I, you. Let's leave it at that."

When he next looked at her they were in the lift. He could no more dissuade her than she could him. He angrily kicked away the wooden block between the doors.

Neither spoke again. As Grann pressed the button the nurses were bringing in a stretcher to load the heavy McQueen on to. In a silence composed of many emotions Grann and Jean Sandingham felt the lift surge beneath them. They looked more like enemies than near-lovers.

* * *

Since Beatty's escape the crowd had become restless and alive. When they heard the long machinegun burst, followed a few minutes later by the rapid firing of a pistol, speculation burst out in a rapid exchange that spread round the square. The sound of shots reached those facing the hospital like distant range firing. But it was identifiable; there could be no mistake. What the hell was happening up there? And what were the police doing?

The Commissioner and his colleagues heard the shots from outside the mobile. Dreading the worst they knew there was nothing they could do until the men had left the private wing. Even if people had been killed, any precipitous action on their part could make things worse. They had to exercise their patience just a little longer.

Assistant Commissioner Roberts didn't hear the shots because he had returned to the hospital secretary's office. When he received the two phone calls, first from Allbright and then from the professor he knew something had gone wrong but he had no way of determining precisely what. The gunmen were still in the ward. He had to wait. When the professor rang a second time to tell him the ward was clear he immediately despatched a waiting team of armed detectives.

Jack Gifford and Art Caplan with the two army snipers also missed the firing. During the first burst they were already on an adjoining roof, having reached it from one of the other buildings. They were just in time to see the chopper land, and lucky to be some distance from it. They didn't think they had been seen. With extreme caution they started to look for a vantage point that would also give them solid cover.

* * *

Allbright and Shaw reached the top floor and stood behind the wheelchair with levelled guns as the doors opened. But nobody was going to try anything with the American there. They pushed the wheelchair on to the landing and Allbright stood guard while Shaw took the cases up the stone stairs to the door leading to the roof. Together they pulled the wheelchair backwards up the stairs. Both men were strong and Shaw's present instability gave him the added strength of near panic; he wanted it over.

The door opened out on to the roof. Before they went out they fixed one case across the thighs of the Secretary and fastened the dressing-gown belt through the handle to hold it steady. They took a case each. Shaw pushed the wheelchair one-handed with the Sterling under his arm while Allbright, also one-handed, kept his Sterling pointing at the Secretary's head. Both men kept as close to the wheelchair as possible and did their best to crouch. It was their most vulnerable moment.

As soon as they stepped on to the roof they heard the slow thump of the rotors. It was near dusk, the light failing fast. The operation had depended on sufficient light for the chopper to land safely on a small area. Taking off was a different matter. They trundled the wheelchair awkwardly across the uneven roof. There was a difficult moment when they had to ease it over a projection but they were able to crouch to do it and then pick up the cases again. For an operation originally planned for four men, two were finding problems. Nor had they expected the hostage to be unconscious; they'd not intended to take one of the doctors, but the extra protection he provided was worth the effort.

* * *

Seventy yards away Jack Gifford, Art Caplan and the two army snipers crouched hidden behind a huge chimney stack. It offered them fire cover and a reasonable field of view. The snipers considered the range was an insult to their prowess. The light was poor but good enough for the marksmen if there weren't too many restrictions.

There were times when it seemed possible to shoot Allbright who was nearest to them, but he was hunched low, always close to the chair and his gun was clearly directed at the man in the wheelchair. Of Shaw they saw little and this was the main problem. They would have to get both men simultaneously; shooting one would almost certainly provoke the other. Perhaps they were over-cautious but neither Gifford or Caplan were willing to take less than a ninety per cent chance in their favour, and even that was stretching it. There had been disastrous police shoot-ups before, particularly on the continent.

The two army boys, rifles ready, saw several chances which they themselves might possibly have taken. They considered the two civilians chicken. They didn't know who the man in the wheelchair was. All of them could see the rotor blades flapping round. The engine noise was harsh.

Gifford said, "Why only two of them?"

"Maybe they had trouble down there. We don't have much sight of them in this light, do we?"

Gifford nodded. "It doesn't look too good for a shot."

Caplan shook his head despondently. "No way," he moaned, "no way."

Their main consideration had to be to keep the Secretary alive; unless Shaw and Allbright separated from the chair they'd remain an elusive target. Maybe when they climbed into the helicopter . . .

Gifford had forbidden any radio calls to him with the risk of the buzzer being heard in the clearer air above the roofs. There was no way he could have known that the police were at that moment breaking into the private wing.

* * *

Ed Grann and Jean Sandingham reached the roof when Allbright and Shaw were halfway to the helicopter. They had regained some lost time while the two men were coping with their extra load. Taking advantage of the occasional problems caused by the wheelchair they crept from the door, crouched, headed towards the helicopter and positioned themselves behind a small outhouse. Both knew there would be no more reprieve; the men would shoot anyone who tried to stop them taking off.

Grann was nervous and afraid; unsure of what to do next. It didn't occur to him to go back. A good deal of his fear was for the girl beside him. Ahead, and below the level of the helicopter, there was a glass roof protrusion built to allow light into the room below it. The glass was frosted and it afforded reasonable cover. Jean might slow him down. He had to be brutal. He kept his voice to a whisper. "If you follow me this time you'll get us both killed. Stay here and don't argue." There was no affection in his tone; he hoped he'd be around later to explain. But he underestimated her. She nodded briefly, aware of what was in his mind. "Good girl." He squeezed her shoulder with the hand of his injured arm and the pain made him gasp. He had almost forgotten the wound.

Making sure that Allbright and Shaw weren't facing his way Grann crawled from behind the outhouse. Beyond its protective walls he felt exposed. The nape of his neck prickled. What the hell was he playing at? Yet out there, not far away now, was the Secretary of State; he simply had to keep going.

As he crawled the pain in his arm worsened to an excruciating state. The bleeding increased with the pressure. His main ally was the slow pumping noise of the chopper blades, for he knew that his own movements were far from silent. As he neared the glass Frame he realised how flimsy it was, how useless as any form of real protection. He tried to keep his head lower.

* * *

Art Caplan said quickly, "There's someone else over there."

Gifford had already broken his imposed radio silence; his lips were almost touching the small microphone when he snapped, "Who else is up here besides us? Who's disobeyed my orders?" He waited impatiently, his back to the chimney. Art Caplan said; "They've split. I swear there were two. One must've stayed behind that shack, the other's belly-crawling towards that glass hump. Vision's not too good; he's the far side of the gunmen."

Gifford snarled, "Whoever it is will be out of the force when I get at him. If he's seen we're in trouble."

"Right now he's okay. That glass thing's between him and the hoods." Art Caplan made no comment on the dangers; that was Jack Gifford's baby and Gifford was getting steamed up.

Gifford got his answer after a check had been made with the private wing. He turned worriedly to Caplan. "It's two of the hospital staff. Dr. Grann and a nurse. Christ! What the bloody hell do they think they can do?"

Art Caplan said softly, "The American doctor?"

Gifford nodded, too angry to speak.

"I can understand it. We're all more protective about our own on foreign soil. And he's been closely involved for the last five hours. What are we going to do?"

Grann disappeared behind the glass framework under the troubled gaze of Gifford and Caplan. They could only watch; there was no form of communication. Caplan said dryly, "If that guy's seen, all hell will break loose."

Gifford silently agreed. He would rather see the Secretary taken off than cause sudden panic from the two gunmen, particularly as one of them seemed to have gone off his head. That's what the police in the private wing were saying.

* * *

Allbright and Shaw reached the chopper without relaxing vigil for a second. Shaw, now motiveless, was almost unaware of the tears streaming down his face. He had only his imagined leadership to cling to. A good deal of his hate still rested on the Secretary; he was much more likely to kill him than was Allbright, who recognised that once they'd taken the extreme step there was no further protection. It was the threat that held the police at bay. His justification lost, Shaw felt the seeping realisation that it was Ruth he wanted, had always wanted, and that revenge was no substitute for a lost love.

The heavily moustached pilot leaned across to look down without putting his head out. "Where're the others?"

"They won't be coming, Sam. Which means you get a fat

bonus. It's all here." Allbright could afford to be generous—he didn't want the pilot worried.

The wheelchair was by the chopper. The wind blast rustled the hair of the wigs and feathered the hair of the unconscious Secretary of State. His head lolled over the case on his knees. Shaw said, "Let's get him in," and wiped his eyes.

"No." Allbright noticed Shaw's almost childish truculence. He tried to keep his voice gentle, as he would with a kid. Twice Shaw had almost blown it; he didn't want a third time. With shock he realised that it wasn't a weakness of eyes, nor the downdraught from the rotor blades that was causing Shaw's eyes to stream; the man was actually crying. "If he goes in first we're left exposed. One of us up quick as a flash then the other one with matey here. Okay, Ginger? You go first then you can help with old stars and stripes. I can't do it without you."

Shaw no longer knew what he wanted to do, certainly nothing suggested by Allbright. But he knew what he *wanted*. Suddenly his hands shot to his face and the Sterling clattered on the roof. He was holding his hands up, fingers spread, pressing hard as if to prevent his head from falling apart. Between his fingers he kept repeating, "Ruth, Ruth, Ruth," over and over again.

Allbright was startled but he thought coolly. Police marksmen would be somewhere; the police weren't fools; they'd be around waiting for half a chance. He kept his gun pointing at the Secretary's head and he kept very close to him. While he did that he was safe. He was in favour of leaving Shaw but he didn't want to leave him alive to babble his head off. If he directed his gun at Shaw a wide-awake marksman could have his chance. He called to the pilot, "Sam, slip out your side, crawl under the belly, pick up Shaw's gun and let him have it."

Sam was shaken as he looked down. "That's your part of it. I wouldn't know one end of a gun from the other."

"For Christ's sake, we can't leave him. He'll shop us both."

"I'm not shooting him. I'm being paid as pilot."

"Sod you, you yellow bastard. You've just talked your way out've that bonus."

Allbright surveyed the roof, detecting the points where the police might be hiding. There wouldn't be many of them. He registered various projections in the fading light, including the chimney stack behind which Gifford and Caplan were lying flat on the roof, their bodies pulsing with tension. He noticed the outhouse. He noticed the glass frame where Grann crouched in pain, but didn't rate it; as no professional would use it as cover and any fuzz up here would be one hundred per cent professional. While he looked around him his aim didn't vary, his finger was almost too tightly on the trigger. In spite of his present safety he knew he had his back to the wall.

Shaw was wandering around the roof with his hands to his head. At first Allbright wondered why he hadn't been picked off before he realised the police would need to get them both. With where his gun was pointing they daren't twitch a muscle. And then suddenly the thing was resolving itself. Allbright almost laughed. That crazy loon Shaw was mounting the parapet. Deliberately. He was silhouetted in the twilight, a stocky bent frame that suddenly straightened. The hands came away from his face and reached up to tear off his wig. He looked over towards Allbright, who could no longer see whether he was still crying or not. Then Shaw stepped into space with an agonised cry for Ruth that was maintained in a dreadful fading wail that suddenly ended in total silence; the only obituary was the still slowly thudding blades above Allbright's head.

* * *

Gifford and Caplan felt totally defeated. They had watched helplessly while Shaw roamed the roof and had been horrified at one stage that he might bump into the American doctor Grann hidden behind the glass frame. And then he had stepped off the roof and the echo of his pitiful wail still hung in the air. But the other villain knew his business well. He was close to the wheelchair at all times. They saw him take stock, guessed that he expected someone to be up here. When he raised the Secretary in a fireman's lift their dejection was complete and unspoken. There was nothing they could do now, not even when they thought they saw him put the gun down; the body draped over him was the best protection he could have.

When they saw movement from behind the glass frame they couldn't believe their eyes. Gifford and Caplan were at opposite ends of the chimney stack, each with a sniper. There was no time to compare reactions. Both were stupefied at the sight of the young doctor who was certainly committing suicide as he raced forward in a crouch towards the chopper. Unbelievably, from behind the distant outhouse the girl emerged, racing after him.

Gifford was stunned. His instinct was to run out to help them but at all times his consideration must be the safety of the hostage. He felt that the doctor and nurse were hurrying into the wrong end of a bullet. The doctor reached the chopper and leaned in for the Sterling as Gifford made up his mind. "Fan out and get over there. *Fast*."

They rushed from behind the stack, jumping over pipes and obstructions as if on an obstacle course. While they ran Gifford heard a shout from the pilot. The big man hurled the Secretary halfway into the chopper before he turned to grapple with Grann, getting one hand on the barrel of the Sterling. The doctor was game but Gifford could now see that he had an arm bandaged. The big man brought his fist down on the bandage with full force and the doctor's agonised shout reached the four racing figures clearly. God, it seemed a long way. One of the soldiers stumbled as Gifford tried desperately to close the gap.

Grann sagged backwards just as the body of the Secretary slid down from the chopper to form an unconscious heap almost beneath it. Grann was practically on his knees when the big man flipped the Sterling round as if it were a toy. The nurse cried out "No!" in a voice that carried across the roofs, stopped, whipped off a shoe and flung it. It did no damage but the big man stepped back, stumbling very slightly against the body of the Secretary as he fired a short burst. Grann bent double, clutching his stomach, collapsed and rolled over on his side. The girl ran towards him as the Sterling was aimed towards her.

One of the snipers fired from the hip as he ran. The round

smacked into the chopper near the big man, who swung round to meet the new danger. He wheeled, flinging the Sterling into the cabin. "Get her up. *Quick*."

Gifford heard the shout but knew that he was still too far away. Art Caplan was just behind him and the two snipers had flanked out to shoot the big fellow as soon as ordered. It was doubtful if Gifford had breath left to give the command. But shooting was a last resort. He raced on, trying to make extra speed and knowing he couldn't.

The big man hurled himself forward as the chopper lifted prematurely. The movement of the machine confused him but he managed to get his body in, his legs hanging down. The pilot, aware that he'd acted hastily, kept her suspended just above the roof to give his colleague a chance to pull himself in.

To Jack Gifford those few seconds made the difference. With throat and chest burning, breath rasping, jacket flapping he came pounding across the roof propelled by the momentum of pace and weight; he couldn't now stop if he wanted to. He flung both arms round Allbright's legs as they rose before him. Hanging on like grim death he pulled. Allbright began to slide back, and then, with horror, Gifford realised his own feet had left the roof. *They were airborne*. In a moment of near-panic Gifford almost let go. How high were they? He was aware of the movement of the machine then felt it slew round and he suddenly felt sick. Allbright's body was slowly slipping back. Gifford closed his eyes and now clung on for life hoping that he didn't pull Allbright down.

But Allbright couldn't hold on. He had failed to get proper purchase in the first place and he not only had to contend with a good deal of his own weight hanging loose but the full weight of Gifford. And that stupid bastard Sam did no more than gaze down helplessly at him instead of giving a hand. He tried to kick Gifford loose but the copper had such a frantic grip on his legs he could barely move them. He was going. Oh, Christ, he couldn't hold on, his fingers were giving way before his eyes. And then he was falling backwards.

When Gifford felt Allbright go a safety mechanism clicked

in and he partially blacked out. He was aware of falling, as if in a dream; the experience was no less frightening. When he hit the roof a terrible pain shot through his legs and something crushed his chest and smothered his face. Then darkness. He came to within seconds to hear a soldier telling him to keep still and felt him pushing a jacket under his head. The pain was in his legs; he sat up without moving them, guessing what had happened, grateful he was alive, his lungs still searing, his legs below his knees agonising. He looked round, searching for Allbright, villain-chasing to the end. He grinned painfully and the sweat broke out on his face. Art Caplan was standing easily, with the Sterling pointed at a squatting and empty faced Allbright. The second soldier had rushed off for medical help.

"How far did we drop?"

The soldier by Gifford grimaced. "Only about twenty feet, sir."

Only. Christ! "Both legs broken?"

"Looks like it, sir."

"It bloody well feels like it." He looked over to where Jean Sandingham was silently cradling Grann and wondered if the doctor was alive; they had guts, those two. Then he looked at the still hunched form of the Secretary of State. "He all right?"

Art Caplan said, "He's okay."

Gifford reached for his radio. It was still working. "Get that chopper in the gardens airborne. The other one's heading north. Only the pilot's aboard. The money's with him." He looked at the sullen Allbright and then turned to Caplan. "I suppose that bastard is in one piece after landing on me?"

Art Caplan smiled. "That's the way it goes. Anything I can do for you, Jack?"

Gifford considered it. "Yes there is, Art. Tomorrow you can buy me the biggest bone you can find for a dog called Banks."

* * *

Ed Grann could feel the slugs in his guts; he thought there were two. The burning sensation was spreading. He'd been lucky, if that was the right word. But for Jean's action he would have stopped the lot. He was barely conscious but aware of the silent comfort of her soothing hands. He rallied his reserves:

"Have you ever considered pitching for the New York Mets?" Then he collapsed against her.

* * *

The American Secretary of State was back in his hospital room without ever being aware of leaving it. The hot line between London and Washington worked overtime while the President and the Prime Minister decided on the best line of action. There were sound political reasons why the truth should be quashed, whatever the rumours already circulating. With a guile and experience they would have denied possessing government sources on both sides of the Atlantic put out a few distracting rumours of their own.

When the Secretary of State emerged from his enforced sleep he felt a different man. He was rather surprised by the excess of bodyguards around the ward; he would have been even more surprised at the number throughout the hospital endeavouring to merge with the staff. He was to leave the hospital the next morning after a rigorous examination and a plea to take things easier, which was endorsed by his own newly arrived physician and his wife. He thanked the doctors and nurses and shook hands with them all. Later, in private, he was told what had happened. He didn't believe it until he read the newspaper accounts of the police siege and saw a video-tape of the scenes. It was then that he humorously promised to take things easier on the grounds that he couldn't afford the risk of being in hospital.

While the Secretary of State was still unconscious Professor Bowyer, who had expected his kingdom back after the departure of the gunmen, found himself more a prisoner than before. On his own territory it was insufferable. He went about scowling with open distaste at the security men, who all but asked him to prove his identity every time he went near the great man. Finally he gave up and went to the next room but one where Ed Grann occupied the previously empty bed. He had been operated on and a blood drip was fastened to his arm. Jean Sandingham stood by the bed. Her tour of duty was long since over.

The professor looked at her shrewdly. "Why don't you leave it to the night staff?"

She turned, caught out in her expression. "I can't, sir."

"Come now, he'll be fine. Tough as old boots."

She smiled. But she'd heard doctor's reassurances too often.

"I mean it. He'll be up in a week. Speak to the surgeon. Go home. You need the rest. He won't wake for a few hours yet." He smiled and she couldn't recall him doing that before. "I can't afford to let him pop off; he's too good a doctor to lose."

He moved forward to take her arm to lead her from the room. She couldn't very well resist. "Mind you," he said thoughtfully, "I really thought these Westerners were much better shots."

She knew he was teasing her and she smiled; there were times when he could be very deliberately naïve. "He's from the Eastern seaboard. New York."

"Really! Is there a difference?"

Suddenly she felt better, knowing he wouldn't joke like this if there was danger; not the professor.

* * *

Inspector Erskin died of his wounds, but he did so with his wife and daughter at his bedside, each holding a hand. In the midst of the siege and the tension they had been routinely notified and smuggled almost unseen into the ward where he lay with screens around him. It had taken a tragedy to reunite the family.

And it was a tragic irony that in his death he had achieved the accolades he'd always yearned for yet known he would never obtain. The press made a hero of him—"*single-handed and unarmed*"—when he should have been severely censured for a reckless act. Later the police authorities saw some virtue in the romanticism of the press and a distinct propaganda advantage to themselves. Instead of finishing with a blemish on the closing chapter of his police record he was posthumously awarded the George Cross. He died a hero and public sympathy made one of its terrific surges towards the welfare of the police at a time when their popularity had been low. Inspector Erskin had served his purpose and the family that had despised him walked proud, his widow relating his life story to one of the Sunday newspapers.

* * *

The Hon. Mark Driver collapsed when he heard the news of his father's death. When he made his shaky recovery, his mother by his side, his fertile mind started seeking escapes. Meanwhile Norman Truddle, his agent, phoned to inform him of the police enquiries into unpaid bills, and particularly Shaw's. Good Lord, there were dozens of unpaid bills. People knew him. Their money was safe. The damned man had only to wait. Do you mean to say that this whole dreadful business arose because one piddling bill hadn't been settled promptly? He considered suing the hospital for false information and the recovery of his million, but he'd need more than that. Anyway, the cunning medics had put it out that his father had probably died just before that maniac shot him.

Adept at self-deception, he didn't try to shrink from the consequences now facing him. Within days the state of his affairs would hit the City. He didn't relish a life behind bars so he gathered what funds he could and left the country the next day, leaving his wife and mother to face problems they would never begin to understand.

* * *

Beatty had brought in a take-away Chinese meal. He sat with his jacket and shoes off, his feet propped up, the television flickering a few feet from him. While he waited for the news he considered the two passports he had ready; the one to take him on a cruise ship which he would leave at Nassau and the second on which he'd obtain a visa for his continuing journey to the United States. He was well organised; his money had already been split and distributed in safe places.

The news came on and the hospital caper was the first item. Wham! He sat back smirking. He was immediately satisfied; it had pushed the international crises right off the screen. There were crowds, the fuzz, the scene outside the hospital which he hadn't been able to see from the generator room, the damage to the police cars and a brief interview with the Commissioner. He wallowed in it.

Until it turned sour in a way he couldn't have anticipated. He was grinning when he saw the pictures of himself leaving the generator building; nobody could recognise him from them. Then it was replaced by a photograph as he really was. He shot up from his chair, his plate crashing to the floor, the *chow mein* creeping over the carpet. *How could they have got on to him so soon?* It was bloody impossible. It never occurred to him that he'd been betrayed by his own vanity, that if his shooting had been less proficient the police might still have been scratching. But that was only the first hammer blow.

Shaw had stepped off the roof; Sam the pilot had been caught as he landed in Bedfordshire; he had offered no resistance. Two men were shot dead, no mention of who, and another was helping police with their enquiries. He was the only one free. FREE? For Christ's sake, the thing was ripping apart.

Beatty stood gaping at the screen; faces came and went, voices rumbled on, but he was beyond hearing. Other news eventually came on and he switched off the set as a reflex action. He had to think objectively.

Two shot! And Sam caught! They hadn't even met so there was no risk there; he had never been involved with the helicopter escape. But Ginger stepping off the roof! What had happened? And who were they holding? It didn't matter. *The fuzz now knew who he was.*

The cruise would have to be cancelled. The passports might be bent but they bore *his* mug shot. He'd have to get out of his flat; too many knew he lived here. And he dared not show his face, not now. He crossed to the phone and dialled.

"Joe? I need a billet, quick."

"I know. That was a very good likeness on the tele."

"Can you fix me?"

"You're too hot, mate. You shot a copper."
"I've money. Plenty of it."
"You'll need plenty."
"How much?"
"Half. Take it or leave it."
"You twisting bastard."
"Please yourself."

When he put down the phone, a very pale Beatty had committed himself to falling into the hands of the leeches he had despised Allbright for using after the bullion job. His world had collapsed in the space of half an hour.

He was to be picked up six weeks later at London airport with a poorly forged passport, the most expensive he had ever bought. In a grip was just under twenty thousand pounds in twenties. He swore that he had no more hidden, that it had been used for protection. He was so demoralised that although he still carried the Browning he made no attempt to shoot it out. Eventually he joined Allbright in a top security prison. Through their common dislike of each other and their total failure they never discussed the crime. It was as though it had never happened, as though prison was a natural home.